VILE
STARS

ALSO BY SERA MILANO

This Can Never Not Be Real

'Told in a bold style, *This Can Never Not Be Real* is utterly gripping from the first page to the last. It's a heart-in-mouth, heavy breathing, oh my gosh what's just happened, compulsive read that you will be racing to get to the end of. In a word, stunning' – George Lester, author of *Boy Queen*

'Heart-rending and utterly gripping' – Kat Ellis, author of *Harrow Lake* and *Wicked Little Deeds*

'A much-needed novel for our times that shows that no matter what horrors we might have to endure, we will always come out stronger . . .' – Mel Darbon, author of *Rosie Loves Jack*

'Five urgent voices, five lives dangling by a thread. A heart-in-the-mouth story about fighting for survival, the fragility of life, and finding love in the darkest places' – Finbar Hawkins

VILE STARS

SERA MILANO

Content warning

Vile Stars is set in England during the early phases of the Covid-19 pandemic, which casts its shadow over the events of the book. Also casting a shadow is the recent loss of a parent. Content to be aware of in this book includes depictions of gaslighting, the threat of violence, implied suicidal ideation, loss, grief, description of transphobic and homophobic comments and negative body image.

Just before our love got lost you said
'I am as constant as a northern star'
And I said 'Constantly in the darkness
Where's that at?
If you want me, I'll be in the bar.'

Joni Mitchell, 'A Case of You'

First published in Great Britain in 2022
by Electric Monkey, part of Farshore
An imprint of HarperCollins*Publishers*
1 London Bridge Street, London SE1 9GF

farshore.co.uk

HarperCollinsPublishers
1st Floor, Watermarque Building, Ringsend Road Dublin 4, Ireland

Text copyright © 2022 Sera Milano

The moral rights of the author have been asserted
A CIP catalogue record of this title is available from the British Library

ISBN 978 0 7555 0074 1
Printed and bound in the UK using 100% renewable electricity at
CPI Group (UK) Ltd
1

Typeset by Avon DataSet Ltd, Alcester, Warwickshire

MIX
Paper from
responsible sources
FSC™ C007454

This book is produced from independently certified FSC™ paper
to ensure responsible forest management.

For more information visit: www.harpercollins.co.uk/green

To Talia, and Katy, and Rosina, and Nicola, and Madeleine, and Hannah, and Sarah.

The dead parent club isn't one anyone wants to be part of, but I can't complain about the company.

ONE

MY NAME IS LUKA: INTRO
'LIFE GOES ON'

ANITA REDMAN, ASSISTANT STATION MANAGER

Of course, the first priority's getting the mess off the tracks.

JAMES TABBETH, STATION MANAGER

The first priority's respectfully dealing with the removal of
the body. Transport Police handle it. Call the ambulances and
all that. We clear the station and wait. Sometimes they're not
quite dead at first. Sometimes families need to be called.
Then the wait's longer. We're always respectful.

ANITA

And once that's done, you need to get the mess off the tracks.
There's a schedule to keep to, and the public can't be let back
until it's all tidy again. Not sparkling – it's never *sparkling*
round here. But no mess. Then the trains have to get back

1

on track or there'll be problems right down the line, and passengers complaining like they do. Shouting and groaning about not getting where they need to. Nobody cares about someone's personal tragedy if they might be missing their dinner.

ROISIN KELLY, 18, FRIEND

All I really remember is the screaming.

ANITA

All I'm saying is, we have to get the mess off the tracks sharpish. That's first on the list with a fatality.

ROISIN

When I got Theo's call that day about finding Luka – he barely said a word, but I could hear everything I'd been afraid of in the tone of his voice. The way it shook. And this sound rose in my throat that I didn't recognise as being me. As being human. Before I even knew. Before I had any idea just what the reality of it was. Before he could tell me any of it, I remember screaming. And screaming.

ANITA

And then we can get back to normal. That's the priority with things like this.

Life goes on.

TWO

Dear Mom,

It's one year today, and just so you know, I haven't forgiven you. I haven't forgiven you for marrying William. I haven't forgiven you for up and dragging us all to this stupid country to live in his stupid house. I haven't forgiven you for trying to make us all fit in with his stupid life.

I want you to know that I still miss Arizona. I miss the strongman silhouettes of Saguaro cacti, and edible Mexican food. Mountains spiking the skyline and coyotes wailing like sirens in the dark. I miss dry heat and hot rain. I want you to know I haven't forgiven you for making me live somewhere there's wet heat and wet wet and nothing in between.

Mostly, I haven't forgiven you for dying. I know it's not supposed to be your fault but, since we're being honest here, I still feel like it was a really shitty move.

4

One year. One year I've been breathing and eating and sleeping and miserable pretty much every minute and you haven't been here for any of it. How many more years are you going to be missing? I'm barely eighteen. Way, way too many.

I just don't understand. I don't understand where you are now. Why you're not in the next room waiting for me. Why it still feels like you *should be* even when the rational part of my brain whispers *impossible* at the same time as the hopeful part holds its breath.

Where are you?

Do you know that I've googled 'how do you bring dead people back' enough times that it comes up as soon as I click into the search bar, and now I can't let anyone else use my laptop so they won't think I've flipped? Missing you makes me feel insane. I'm not insane. I don't *think* I'm insane, but I don't think I'm whole either. You were such a big part of my life that now you're gone it's like trying to get around with a missing limb. One that most people don't even notice isn't there.

But it's not there, and I'm off balance all the time.

I haven't forgiven you.

I haven't forgiven *me* for not being enough for you to stay for. Why couldn't you have stayed for me and Alec and Allegra? We needed you. I haven't forgiven cancer, obviously, but it still feels like we should have been able to save you. Loving us should have been enough to help you recover. We should have been able to do something more than watch.

Anything.

Anyway.

Since you're dead, and since perfectly well-intentioned people keep telling me you're watching over me, like that's supposed to fix the fact that you're not here, I figure I get to make some requests for this next year. Year Two of no you. If I have to survive it, I'd like a chance to feel like I'm living again, at least a little bit. So:

1. I want to not think about you every second of the day.

2. I want to not feel guilty for not thinking about you during the seconds when I don't.

3. I want William to stop asking me if I'm okay. In fact, if he could stop speaking to me at all ever, that would also be great.

4. I want to get through school. If I can get through school with the set of perfect grades I've been predicted, then that would be ideal, but for now survival's enough.

5. A boyfriend would be nice. Shallow, but it's like everyone in my year is suddenly turning up with one and I missed the memo, or the giveaway or something. I know, it's a dumb thing to care about. I'd just like to *have* someone, I think. I think it might help.

6. I want to be happy, Mom. I want to remember what that feels like.

That's it. If I have any more requests I'll be in touch, but it seems like enough to work on for now. There's some kind of star-gazing party tomorrow. If you can call it a party, since we're going with the school. Maybe I'll find a star to wish on too.

Anyway, unhappy anniversary, Mommy. I miss you.

I haven't forgiven you.

I love you so much.

Love,

Luka

THREE

**MY NAME IS LUKA: EPISODE 1
AUGUST 2020
'WHEREVER YOU THINK IT ALL BEGAN'**

ALEC BOOTH, 17, BROTHER

Okay, it's recording. You can go.

ROISIN

Where do you want me to start then? It's just that I've never been much good at telling stories. Just look at my English results. And it still feels wrong somehow, talking about Luka without her here.

ALEC

Right, but *not* talking about her, and what was happening with her, was always half the problem. We all kept our own parts of the story to ourselves. That's the whole point of doing this. I know none of us want to go through it all again, but I think maybe we need to. Maybe after we've gone through it all, put it on the record, we'll see what we missed. What we could have done.

THEO APFEL, 17, FRIEND

It might help some of us figure out that sometimes there *wasn't* anything we could have done.

ALEC

I guess that's also possible. And I'm doing it this way – recording it, turning it into a podcast – because it means we have to go through everything. We can't be gentle on ourselves, or on her. We can't skip parts, or the story won't make sense. And we've got her letters – her voice is going to be as much a part of it as anyone's. But mostly I'm recording it because maybe someone else who needs it will listen to the podcast and find *their* voice. I think that would be enough for me.

THEO

You can start where you want, Ro. Wherever you think it all began.

ROISIN

So that would be, I suppose, the night we went to that astrology thingy.

THEO

Astronomy.

ROISIN

Theo, really, if they *wanted* people to care about the difference, they'd have changed more than one letter. And anyway, you were there too. Both of you were sitting on the bed with us before we left. I was taking my time, as usual, and just then she hadn't any patience for it.

THEO

She kept asking what was taking so long. Everyone was ready, dressed, and waiting. And waiting.

ROISIN

I was doing my face still. 'You're *fine*, Ro,' she said, and I shook my head at my reflection in the little mirror she was holding up for me.

'And since when has *fine* been anybody's aim? No, give

10

me five more minutes. I want my eyebrows to be so strong they look like they could walk off my face and kick you in yours.'

ALEC

I remember that. I raised *my* eyebrows. 'She's right. None of us should be leaving the house without assault-brows. It's not about what's hot, it's a matter of self-defence. Pass the pencil – I need to power up my body hair.' I tried to grab for it, while Theo laughed and tackled me round the waist.

ROISIN

Luka groaned beside me and said we were *never* going to go out if you two got started. She was antsy, that night – it was almost like she was waiting for something. And she looked amazing despite a total lack of effort, the way she always bloody did and never believed was true. She was just in black jeans and a band shirt she'd cut the neckline out of, with that pendant hanging at her throat.

ALEC

Mom's locket. There's a little curl of her hair braided with Mom's clasped inside the two halves of the heart. She never took it off.

ROISIN

No makeup, even. It was so unfair. *That's* why she never got why I like to put enough paint on you could hang me in a gallery. It's just how I am. I feel better that way. And it takes time to achieve greatness, naturally, but she was over it by then, dropping the mirror in her lap. 'It's going to be dark, Rosh. No one's going to know whether your eyebrows are dancing the Cha-Cha Slide. If we've got to go to this shooting-star thing, can we just go?'

THEO

'Meteor shower,' I put in, from somewhere under Alec, and I felt everyone turn and look at me, which always makes me tense up somehow. 'The Orionids. They're not actual shooting stars. It's the falling sediment from a comet's tail.'

'Oh, well, that sounds much more romantic.' Rosh was busy tucking brushes and powders into a little bag. I didn't take the sniping personally.

ROISIN

Wait, hold on a minute. Are we supposed to be talking about each other like we're not all in the same room, now?

ALEC

Please? For the recording. We're trying to tell a story. If everyone just uses 'you' all the time it's going to be really confusing listening back. Just . . . treat it like you're telling a stranger how it went. That's exactly what this is, really.

ROISIN

This is *so* weird, Alec. Fine. So *Theo* cracked on with his scintillating description.

THEO

Hey –

ROISIN

Hush, I'm *telling a story to a stranger.*

'There's a comet in the sky right now too,' he said. 'I don't think it's visible to the naked eye, but we might be able to see it if we can get to one of the telescopes. Comet ASASSN.'

'Comet Assassin?' I said. 'Again, that sounds romantic.'

'Why are we expecting a party being put on by an observatory to be romantic exactly?' Alec chipped in. 'Pretty sure the school's only requiring attendance because they're expecting it to be fully chaste. The only people turned on by

13

comets are science nerds like Theo.'

Theo tackled him again. I waited for Luka to chime in with a fresh round of exasperation.

ALEC

'*Comets are vile stars*,' she said instead, reading something off her phone. 'According to this. According to some ancient Chinese astronomer. *Every time they appear . . . something happens to wipe out the old and establish the new.*'

THEO

She stood and picked up her bag.

ROISIN

'Well, I'm ready for that,' she said. 'Let's go.'

FOUR

ALEC

The Observatory courtyard was packed, despite how late it was. Mostly school groups like ours, from what I could tell, but the evening was open to the public too, so there was a nice mix of hipsters, first dates and kids out way past their bedtimes being shepherded by their grandparents.

ROISIN

The walk up the murderously steep hill in Greenwich Park to get there almost wiped me out, so I couldn't believe how many old people there were in attendance I don't know how anyone without the legs of a gazelle would survive.

Obviously, for any of us who go to school in the vicinity, Greenwich Royal Observatory's old news. If it's not the obligatory school trip, then your parents are taking you for 'educational fun' looking at a collection of old clocks. I couldn't tell you why something becomes educational just because it's old. If you've had an iPhone more than

15

five minutes it's old news, but a clock somebody made five hundred years ago is supposed to be fascinating.

All the stuff about the stars is better, though. Even I can admit it's a little more interesting than looking at someone's elderly Casio collection.

ALEC

We skipped past the gang of tourists getting their pictures taken straddling the prime meridian – which I always think of as the split at the centre of the world. Theo glanced around, and just as I turned my head to see what he was looking for, I felt him reach for my hand.

THEO

Just a quick arsehole check. Always necessary when you want to be affectionate with your boyfriend in public.

I'd been to loads of events at the Royal Observatory. As Rosh ably observes, I can be something of a cosmology nerd, and we live in a part of London that is, quite honestly, nerd heaven. There are regular evenings where they bring astronomers on-site to chat with the public and answer questions. They have the usual Planetarium shows, and if you're willing to wait, they'll let you look through the gigantic Victorian telescope housed under the observatory dome. I get shivers every time.

That night was madly busy, though, far more than usual.

ALEC

It wasn't quite my idea of a party, but then the parties I go to don't tend to hire a string quartet. They were set up on a little podium in the middle of the courtyard, playing something that was pretty, but sounded like a hymn.

THEO

'Jupiter' from *The Planets*. Around the base of the podium an elderly couple were twirling each other to the music, and a small gang of children had gathered to do the same.

Most of the people our age had migrated to the edges of the courtyard or gone back down on to the hill, ignoring the occasional announcement that a new talk or Planetarium session was starting inside to gossip in the dark.

Tiny string lights flecked the trees and climbed the railings at the edges of the courtyard, and there were staff on hand giving out hot drinks and little tubs of roast chestnuts, glistening with sugar. It was busy but beautiful.

ROISIN

Luka tipped her head back as we headed through the courtyard, frowning. 'Why don't they turn the lights off? I can't see a single falling star.'

ALEC

Theo, my patron saint of infinite patience, smiled at her. 'It's not peak time for the meteor shower yet. The event's not really about *seeing* anything, just learning about the stars. We can go down into the park afterwards to stargaze, or get in the queue for the telescope. That's probably the only way anyone's catching a glimpse of the comet.'

THEO

I have a bit of a love affair with the Great Equatorial Telescope. It's the largest in the UK, and sits in a room full of ladders and struts under the dome at the top of the observatory tower. From the outside it looks like somewhere Dr Frankenstein might raise his monster. Inside, it looks more like a storeroom. But there's a whole universe in it.

ALEC

Theo's taken me to look at it before. 'The universe'. The thing is, you don't realise how much of it there is. Look up at the night sky and the dark looks endless, nothing but black with a pinprick scatter of brighter spots.

But through the telescope it's more like someone's spilt sugar on a black tablecloth. There's so much light out there. So many stars, on and on forever in different colours, hazy or sharp, making patterns that your brain wants to solve.

After you see that, you can't really think of the sky as darkness any more. It's just a thin veil to all that hidden light.

'You *have* to try the telescope.' I gave Luka's shoulder a little shove. 'Go and get in line early. Theo wants to watch the Planetarium show for the billionth time.'

ROISIN

'Theo wants to snuggle up in the dark,' I put in. Naturally, I'd be staying with Luka. Nobody wants to be the third wheel to a collective nerdgasm.

THEO

'They bring in guest astronomers for these evenings! I want to hear from someone new!'

ALEC

Theo totally wanted to snuggle up in the dark.

ROISIN

We watched the boys walk off, getting more tangled in each other before they had to pull apart to get through the door. Luka had the smile on her face she keeps for when she thinks people aren't looking. 'You look like a proud –'

I almost said 'mother'. Of course I did – it's how the expression goes, but it caught against my teeth just as my brain cottoned on to the insensitivity of that one. By then, of course, the sudden silence had been as obvious as if I'd held up a neon sign and performed a Broadway tap dance number about it.

'Well, a proud sister. Like you are.'

I'm a bloody idiot, but there are so many words you have to watch when someone's mother's died. The 'your mum' jokes in our class vanished for a few weeks after Luka came back to school, but then started to creep in again, and you should see how much a tough lad can wilt when he realises what he's just said to someone without a mother to joke about.

I try to be more careful, even though Luka always said it was fine, that the word *mom* didn't stop existing just because she didn't have one. At any rate, that night she just smiled and forgave me with her eyes, then glossed straight over it as she replied, 'I know how much it took for them to get together. And now at least I think Alec's happy. That's all I want.'

She paused. And then the flinch that should have come earlier tugged at her mouth.

'Someone should be.'

ALEC

I can't help wishing we hadn't gone inside. When I replay
all this – when I'm looking for moments where I could have
changed things, it feels like the only spot where one different
decision would have altered the future without anyone
getting hurt.

ROISIN

We missed the telescope and its view of the infinite universe.
After weighing up the pros and cons of spending an hour
lining up to see something you can just download as a
background for your phone, the decision was made to get
drinks instead. They had hot cocoa and mulled apple juice,
like it was Christmas, and I had a little bottle of something
warmer, if you know what I mean . . .

I mean alcohol, of course. I'd brought some vodka.
It tasted mad mixed in with the chocolate. And we ducked
through the crowds towards the edge of the courtyard, trying
to balance our drinks and our phones.

ALEC

One different choice. I could have stayed. I could have got in
line with her for the telescope. I could have caught her phone.

ROISIN

Some heavy-handed dickhead shouldered into us, and Luka's phone went right over the railings.

THEO

You couldn't have known, Alec. None of us could have known.

ROISIN

We looked down after it. And there was this boy, looking up.

ALEC

And that was it.

FIVE

LETTER FROM LUKA
23 OCTOBER 2019

Dear Mom,

His name is Cosmo.

ROISIN

'His name's *Cosmo*!' Luka called up to me, laughing. I was still picking my way down towards them, trying not to break a heel, but I could see her with her phone in her hands, turning it over to check for new cracks to the screen and then smiling up at him. 'I don't believe you. Cosmo like "cosmic"? Like the *cosmos*?'

LETTER FROM LUKA

I'm *still* not sure I believe him. It was too coincidental. Like I went to see a meteor shower and a boy dropped right out of the heavens just to catch my phone. Cosmo.

ROISIN

'Like a . . . *cosmet*?' I tried, catching them up. I know –
terrible, but she'd been through all the good ones. His eyes
flickered briefly over me, then back to Luka, as if I was just an
object in orbit around her bright sun. Not flattering but still, it
gave me a minute to look him over. And I have to say for the
record: he wasn't bad to look at. Close cropped hair, dark eyes
you couldn't quite tell the colour of in the night. Tall, broad.
Skin pale save for a flecking of stubble. He had a bit of a nose
on him, but it worked well with the hard angles of his face.

LETTER FROM LUKA

He smiled (it was a great smile, Mom) and said, 'Like Cosmo.
It's just a name. Are you American?'

And I grinned like he'd just guessed my birthday or
pulled my chosen card from a pack. As if my accent is hard to
pick up on. I've kept it stubbornly for the seven years I've been
here, refusing to soften it to something transatlantic like Alec's
and getting frustrated with Allegra for never developing one at
all. I've always considered it one of the only interesting things
about me. And something that connected me to you.

ROISIN

Obviously she was American. It was one of the things we
connected over when we first met. When I first started at

the school everyone made a fuss over my accent, because Londoners don't count any of the dozen or so they hear every day as being difficult to understand at all but Irish? Somehow incomprehensible. Anyway there she was: American, everyone thinking she was so cool. And there I was: Irish, being asked to repeat every second word I said.

A couple of days after we first met, after a long, long day of being asked to say 'thirty-three and a third' by numerous overgrown infants from our year, she leaned over to me and said, 'Never lose it. Who wants to sound like them?'

So yes, she was *clearly* American. As she pushed a hand back through her hair and replied 'Sure. Arizona transplant,' I discreetly rolled my eyes.

'That's cool,' he said. He was much taller than the both of us, though I've a few inches on Luka, especially in heels. He craned his head in to speak to her, his attention a spotlight that left me out of its focus entirely.

'I know a lot of people find American accents really annoying, but yours sounds good to me.'

Bit of a weird compliment, but she seemed to take it as flattering. Ah, I don't know, maybe his cheekbones were doing the real talking.

I have to admit, the bone structure was on point.

LETTER FROM LUKA

We couldn't chat too much with Roisin standing right there. I love her but she's less a gooseberry than a whole fruit pie sometimes. She was hovering around like a hired chaperone. But you know when you meet someone and there's just an electric connection between you? Like they're a power socket and you're a metal fork? Well, I never knew what that was like before, but I do now.

Talking to him, I felt electrified.

ROISIN

It wasn't anything special. The usual boring small talk you'd get from anyone who came up to you on a night out. *What's your name? What school do you go to?* and all that.

He didn't go to school. He was nineteen, he said, and taking a year out before starting university to decide if three years unfettered drinking would be worth all the debt. He said he didn't think he'd bother going, really.

Now, the thing is, Luka's had plans to take History at Bristol for basically ever. I held her hand through all the form filling when she applied. She's always had this plan to do History, then a master's in International Relations, and then work for a charity or go into politics. One way or another she'd change the world.

So when she laughed and looked down and said, 'No, I don't know if I'll bother, either' that's when I had to walk away for a minute.

LETTER FROM LUKA

But when we finally had a few moments we had so much in common. We've seen the same bands. We were even both at Adamantium festival last year. Isn't that crazy? Three days in the same big field and it takes a year to for us circle round and run in to each other. Maybe the timing hadn't been right back then. We needed to wait until the stars aligned.

He asked if I was there to see the meteors, and I told him my brother's boyfriend wouldn't let us leave until we had. Then I got bold enough to ask if he wanted to come down the hill with us. And he said –

ROISIN

He said, 'How am I supposed to see any meteors when you're outshining everything round here?'

I'd stepped away, but it didn't mean I wasn't listening. And a line like that tends to silence everything around it. I fully expected her to reply the way I would: *And I heard the moon was made of cheese, but it turns out that's just you.*

But I looked round, and he had a hand on her arm, while she had a blush going like a beacon in the dark.

He may have just called her human light pollution but, despite myself, at the sight of that I couldn't help smiling too.

LETTER FROM LUKA

Then he asked for my number and I put it in his phone.
He put his in mine, too, but I scrolled through later and
couldn't find it under C.

I ran down the list and, finally, it was there. He'd entered
his name as *Like Cosmic*.

Mom, I think this boy's going to be a problem.

ROISIN

The Planetarium must have finally kicked out its romantic
little show, because up in the courtyard I could hear Alec
hollering both our names, like a cow that had got bored of
the same old lines. 'Loooooooka? Rooooooooosh?'

'That's us,' I said, inserting myself into Luka's line
of sight to see if I could break the romantic trance. It was
Cosmo who looked at me first, snapping his head round,
a little line of irritation threaded between his eyebrows. I
smiled sweetly. 'With a few less vowels, more consonants.
This is Luka.' I gestured at her, then at myself. 'I'm Roisin.'

I let the *not that you've asked* sit on the end of my
tongue, but I think he heard it.

'Sorry, yeah. Nice to meet you too, Roisin.'

He butchered my name, which takes talent given I'd
just said it. But 'Russian' instead of 'Ro-sheen' isn't the worst
attempt I've heard. I get called 'Raisin' all the time. It really
makes you feel for the Caoimhes and Saiorses of this world.

Anyway, I had called him *Cosmet*, so I let it go.

Alec yelled again and I called down 'Here!' and Luka gave me such a *look*.

LETTER FROM LUKA

I mean, I'd barely spoken to him for fifteen minutes and I didn't want to stop. I hadn't felt energised in so long. It was like every deadened nerve ending had come alive. Sometimes it seems like I stopped feeling anything when you died but there it was, suddenly: sensation.

ROISIN

'There you are – how was gazing into eternity?' Alec strolled across the grass, his arm looped round Theo's shoulders. I looked round to see his expression grow curious, and Theo step out from his hold. He always does that when meeting someone new. 'Who's this?'

ALEC

I couldn't see much of him on account of the shadows he stood in. A pale face in the dark, straightening up and stepping back from my sister. He held up his hands as if I'd accused him of a crime and he wanted to protest innocence.

ROISIN

'Just a bold rescuer of phones that get flung at me from a great height,' Cosmo said.

Luka laughed, and I smiled too. He was sharp, but there was something a little charming about him. At least in the way he spoke to her.

'Anyway, happy to help but I really need to take off. Enjoy the night, Starshine.'

He gave a nod to Alec and Theo, apparently forgot I was there, again, and pushed his hands into the pockets of his jeans as he walked away.

'Well, that was weird.' Theo came up and tucked his chin into the dip of my shoulder until I laughed and shoved him off. 'Was he bothering you?'

ALEC

Luka looked spectacularly insulted. 'He saved my *phone*.' She waved the object in question around like she might injure someone with it. She'd been smiling a moment ago. But that was my sister since Mom died. Moods that changed a mile-a-minute. 'He was just being helpful.'

I nodded. 'Sure. Well, at least you don't have to try to get the insurance to pay out on it for a third time this year. I'm terrified of the day someone lets you get a car.'

THEO

She made an insulted choking sound, but you could see her relenting. Alec has this way with people. Almost no one can stay angry at a smile like his. Although I've tried, once or twice.

But that's not important. He hooked his arm into Luka's elbow, leaning in to peer at her phone. 'Oooh, did you get his *number*? Fast worker, but really, that guy?'

ROISIN

'What's wrong with *that guy*?' she asked, shooting him a glance so scornful it could have seared on contact.

'He was wearing plaid,' Theo put in, quietly mind-reading. 'Alec has a personal campaign against the fabric as a whole. He thinks it makes people look like they parked their tractor down the street.'

THEO

'He'd best watch that.' Roisin tutted. 'The village where my gran lives is wall-to-wall tractors. Half of them registered in the family name.'

ALEC

'It's not the tractors – it's the aesthetic. Plaid doesn't suit anybody.'

'It suited him!' And with that, Luka totally gave herself away. And I thought well, *good*. It's good if she likes somebody. It's good for her to like *something*.

Of course, I wasn't going to say that out loud.

'Fine, keep daydreaming about your knight in shining farmer. Ready to go down to the hill?'

ROISIN

Wait – I just want to stop this for a minute. I want to ask something. I know that you two only met him for a few seconds that night, barely long enough to make an impression. But I just want to know, from the way he was, and the way she acted after, was there anything at all that made you think it could have gone the way it did?

THEO

Nothing.

ALEC

Nothing.

ROISIN

No. It kills me, but there was nothing at all.

LETTER FROM LUKA

We spent hours that night lying on our backs on the hillside, with Theo pointing out constellations and retelling the stories he'd heard in the Planetarium while we waited for shooting stars. When they came – tiny streaks of white so faint that you could think you saw one if you just turned your head too fast – you could hear murmurs from all around. People kept ruining the moment with a phone camera flash.

To me they looked too small and insignificant to wish on, but I was hardly watching. Too busy thinking about the wishes I'd already made in my last letter.

Is there really some magic to asking favours from the dead? Should I have started asking you for miracles a year ago, and if I had would I be living in a mansion right now, wondering what to spend my lottery winnings on next?

I don't think so. Honestly, I don't even know if he'll call. But he might.

Alec gave me a hard time about missing the telescope but I don't care. So maybe I didn't gaze into infinity that night, but it feels like I might have glimpsed a small part of the future that I can actually reach out and touch.

Something warm, when everything's been cold for too long.

We never saw the comet. Theo said we wouldn't with the naked eye, and eventually we got up and stretched out our stiff limbs to walk home.

But as we walked, I looked up and I swear Mom, I saw *something* crossing the sky. Bright and strange. More than just part of the meteor shower. Some streak of shining, unknowable promise.

Something to wipe out the old and establish the new.
I hope so.

I love you.
Luka

SIX

EPISODE OUTRO

THEO

Alec? . . . Alec.

ALEC

Mm? Oh – did you start the recording again? I don't want anything not relevant on there right now. It'll make things harder when I'm editing. Let me just –

THEO

This is relevant. Sit down a second. I've been thinking about it, where we started, and I think you missed out something important. Sit down?

ALEC

Okay, okay, make some room. So, go on. You're the producer now. What did I miss?

THEO

You missed an introduction. Alec . . .Tell me about Luka.

ALEC

Oh.

THEO

If it's –

ALEC

No, you're right. The letters say something but they're not about the Luka I knew, not for most of our lives anyway. So . . .

We grew up in Arizona – near Tucson for people who only know the place from songs. And for as long as I can remember we grew up without a dad. Luka remembered it a little different to me – she's just scraping a year older and she had some memories of arguments when he'd come back and take off again for months at a time. She used to tell me she'd come down in the morning and find things broken: a chair, or the jar Mom used to keep our allowances in, and that meant he'd stopped by.

She remembered the night Mom called the police, too, and that was the last of the visits. Her and Mom kept that between them for a long time, but it wasn't secret outside our house. The kids at school told me my dad was in jail. I was furious with both of them over keeping it from me for such a long time, but they were protecting each other as well as protecting me.

Luka and Mom were always each other's security. Luka was fierce about it. And most of the time she was fiercely happy, too. She had a hand in everything: she volunteered at a dog rescue with the neighbours' kids. They spent weekends hosing down German Shepherds and taking them out on hikes, and then she'd spend the week begging to be allowed to bring one home. She took ballet class and they put on shows I'd be forced to sit through every third Sunday.

Torture, but I forgave her after she took on the kids who used to tease me on her way back from class. I'll never forget how they looked trying to process a girl in a swan tutu threatening to take their teeth out with her fists. She'd have done it, though. No doubt.

That's how she was, overprotective. So it was hard for her when Mom started working at Arizona State, when she met William. *I* got the appeal – this sophisticated English professor with glasses and soft cardigans, and rooms full of books. I may not have known I was gay back then but that whole set-up's a *classic*.

Luka refused to get along with him. It didn't matter how he tried, and it wasn't because there was something wrong with him. We were just a team already and she hadn't planned on recruiting for new members. It got worse for a while when we moved here. Then it got better. She met Roisin. She was as popular as she'd always been. Suddenly she had a hundred things to do again, every social engagement under the sun – she didn't go back to the ballet but I considered that a blessing. William even got us a dog.

She hugged him the day he brought her home – the first time I ever remember her doing it. This German Shepherd puppy, all ears and paws. Bluebell.

And then Allegra showed up. Barely a year after we got here. Mom kept it quiet an absurdly long time – we're too good at secrets in this family – and when she told us we all took in a tightly held breath.

Luka was *delighted*. The baby was an automatic team member before she even arrived, and Luka helped Mom with everything. It was like Allegra was the embroidery over a rough patch in our fabric. She held us together and made us better at the same time. Allegra started ballet when she was five. Luka used to dance her round the kitchen. I never minded watching.

We felt happy. She felt happy. I . . . took a while, but I had secrets of my own. Secrets Luka picked out of me from the way I'd talk about you, Theo. You should know she was your first cheerleader. The first person who told me whatever I felt was okay.

That's Luka. Toughest person I know. She loved and *was* loved so much. You only really got to know her after Mom – after everything with Mom – and we were all changed by that. I know I was. I felt like a creaky building that had spent the night being battered by a really long storm, with roof tiles thrown everywhere, and leaks, and a tree in the garden that's tipped over and taken out a window. So you mostly got to know her after she'd survived the destructive force that losing someone is.

Like I said, she was always overprotective. She'd have fought for any of us, but with Mom's illness there was nothing for her to fight. I think William took the brunt of her helplessness. It unpicked so many of those careful stitches that had been holding the family together.

But she was still holding on to the rest of us. Still on her feet.

That was Luka.

You can turn it off now, I think.

SEVEN

MY NAME IS LUKA: EPISODE 2
'GHOSTS HAVE NOTHING BUT TIME'

ROISIN

So I said to her, 'All I'm saying is, you've got to try the pans.'

ALEC

Wait, Rosh, I cut off the start of the recording. Can we go back through where we are again?

ROISIN

Ah, okay, sure. So we're in school, lunchtime, about three weeks after that party at the observatory. We're in the girls' cloakroom with sandwiches, and Luka's in a black mood.

THEO

Which was the kind of mood she'd been in, on and off.

ALEC

But it had been on more than off, noticeably so, for a while. A while which, thinking back to it now, corresponded pretty well to those three weeks since the meteor shower. It wasn't that she was angry all the time – she just seemed to be swinging between lower lows and higher highs, and the lows were getting more common. The days she was happy she'd be *wildly* happy. She bought me a computer game, hugged our little sister and put up with her asking sixteen different questions all beginning with *why*, and ate dinner with the rest of us, even talking to William sometimes while we ate.

ROISIN

Some of the black days she barely even spoke to me. And she was getting in the kind of trouble with the school that had never happened before. Coming in late, wrong uniform, no homework.

ALEC

No homework?

ROISIN

I know. That should have been the real tell, from the start. I mean, Luka could be as much of a nerd as Theo when it came to History, at least. The little threesome they both had with the library was something I never quite understood.

THEO

Using the library together doesn't make it a *threesome* –

ALEC

I know I got jealous.

ROISIN

But it's one of the things I liked about her. Always had. She was popular, sure, one of those people who manage it without even trying, while the rest of us flounder around certain in the knowledge that *trying* to be popular is the ultimate way to fail, and that we can't help doing it anyway.

But she went to the parties she wanted to, and not the ones people went to just to be seen. She hung out with who she wanted, which was mostly me, and was nice to the people who wanted to hang out with us. She always tried to be kind. I think that was the key.

ALEC

That's an opinion you'd have struggled more with if you saw

the way she was at home sometimes. But school was often where I felt like I got my sister back. I didn't know about the homework.

ROISIN

She did nothing in lessons, either. Stared out of the window. Mocks were coming up right after Christmas and usually you wouldn't be able to wrestle her out of a book. Nobody even knew how important the mock exams were going to end up being that year, but it was always her plan to treat them like the real thing. Except, when I talked to her – offered to look at her revision timetable only *partly* so I could crib from her planning skills – she hadn't got one. She said she hadn't even thought about it. That kind of thing was unheard of, for her.

On the bad days it was like she hated being in school at all.

ALEC

And that morning was bad?

ROISIN

That morning was *so* bad. She arrived an hour late and slumped into the classroom in the middle of History, saying something about delays with the bus. That's Mr Tang's class and I think he'd had it with her by then. He started going on sarcastically about the state of the bus schedules lately, and how maybe he should call the company after class to ask why they could never seem to get one of his best pupils to her lesson on time. Or, he said, perhaps she'd like to try getting an earlier one for a change? On and on. He's got a tongue like a razorblade on him when he wants.

THEO

That's not wrong. I have him too. I know. But he's not usually unkind.

ROISIN

And I don't think he was trying to be then – he was just fed up with it. And Luka must have been used to having been treated with kid gloves. The way people do when –

ALEC

When you've lost a parent. You do get used to it, but you resent it too. It's like a constant reminder that something's fragile about you, that people think you're breakable. You want to tell them that treating you like glass doesn't make the world any less rough a place. It's honestly easier to just acknowledge things and carry on.

ROISIN

Well, I don't think she liked the soft-voice-sad-smile approach either, but she wasn't ready to be spoken to like that. We all heard what she said as she sat down. And obviously you don't swear at a teacher that way without being sent out.

ALEC

I spoke to her head of year about how they handled it. Well, I spoke to all her teachers for the podcast – but I think this answer bothered me the most.

MRS CATHCART, HEAD OF YEARS 12–13

I can't say I'd never had Luka in my office before, but it was never for disciplinary reasons, Alec, as I'm sure you know. She received a number of commendations. And then that terrible day when we had to call the both of you in for . . . well, of course you'd remember that too. All in all I'd call your sister an exemplary member of the student body before that year. And we were all well aware of your situation.

However, comments like that aren't acceptable. She had another lesson that afternoon, so I told her to stay in the library until then and get on with work. We usually send students who don't need to be entirely isolated there, where the librarian can keep an eye on things.

I'm told she was on her phone the whole time. Nothing

unusual about that, unfortunately.

I think I can say, looking back, that while her behaviour had taken a turn, there was nothing about it we wouldn't have put down to grief. And with grief being such a complicated, private thing, we wouldn't have wanted to intervene. According to my records she had been offered sessions with the counsellor and had turned them down.

It's all so very regrettable, and yet I really don't see that we could have done any more.

ALEC

It's all so very regrettable . . .

THEO

If it's all right for me to say it, the thing I think everyone gets wrong is feeling like grief has to be private. When I heard what had happened the day you and Luka were taken out of school, the first thing I wanted to do was run to your house and tell you I was there. That I'd be there even if you just wanted to sit in silence. Even if you just needed to punch someone. That I was always going to be there. We weren't even together then. I just . . . needed you to know that you weren't alone. But the teacher, and my mum and everyone told me you needed your privacy.

ALEC

So you waited, and told me the next week.

THEO

And pretty soon after that we were together.

ALEC

I don't know if you showing up that first day would have
been the best time. Honestly, I don't remember it. It's a haze
of people being angry with each other, and sad at each other,
and all of us sitting apart, lost together. After Mom died
things were a blur for months, and when they weren't blurry
then everything felt too sharp. Even breathing hurt. But it . . .
it really meant something, you showing up. Being there even
when it felt like I was barely there myself.

I know it was the same for Luka with Rosh.

ROISIN

She came and slept on my floor for almost a month. Your
stepdad gave mine a bit of money for food after a week of
it. We didn't talk about much, most of the time. I could feel
the gaps where conversation should have been, but it stalled
every time we tried to start it up again. And that was okay.
We sat and watched movies. We left the TV on into the night.

I wouldn't begin to pretend that I understand what grief like that feels like, or how to talk about it the right way. All I could do was be there.

ALEC

Being there is a lot. But Theo's right. People don't talk about grieving even though it's something everyone has to do sometime. It's left as this big surprise: *Hey, you thought burying your hamster was a punch to the gut? This one's more like getting run over by a truck.* Even with how rough it was when Mom was ill, I never understood what it would feel like when we lost her. If I hadn't had people who wanted to scrape me off the road when that truck hit me, I'd never have gotten back up alone.

Maybe if it wasn't kept so quiet, if people understood a little more – even if they couldn't comprehend *exactly* what it's like – then someone who's grieving might be able to talk more about it without just feeling like we're putting a burden on other people.

Teachers might feel like they could reach out, instead of wrapping a grieving student in bubble wrap and hoping they don't suffocate in there.

It's a thought.

ROISIN

You know, we still haven't got back to the pans.

THEO

And I had *no* idea what that was about, so I really need to know.

ALEC

Go on.

ROISIN

I caught up with her in the cloakroom at lunchtime, like usual. We never eat in the canteen on cabbage Wednesdays. I have a violent reaction to the smell. I'd brought her History notes and she asked if Tang had been really mad. Of course he hadn't. He spent the rest of the lesson looking guilty as sin while Luka became a legend via the whispers spreading round the class. So I told her that, but I also asked her what was going on. She leaned her head into my shoulder and said 'I'm just not sleeping. I feel like I haven't slept for a year.'

And that's when I said she ought to try the pans. 'It works for me every time. When it gets to two or three am, and some of the channels shut down for the night, all you've got to do is look through the adverts they start playing and

49

you'll find the pans without fail. Non-stick pans. Marble,
stone or ceramic. Pans you can stab with a breadknife,
should you feel an itch to do so, and you won't leave so much
as a scratch. Pans you can fry eggs in without needing butter,
if you're one of those people who values lower calories over
taste. Pans that probably release all sorts of toxins into your
bloodstream, but by *God* can you wipe them clean with only
a tissue. There are some nights when I can't sleep if I can
think, and I can't think if I'm playing infomercials. Try the
pans.'

THEO

I'd like to state for the recording that I've changed my mind
about wanting to know.

ROISIN

I'm telling you, it *really works*. Don't knock it till you've
tried it. And it made her laugh, if nothing else. She laughed,
wrapped an arm round me and murmured 'Love you, Roisin'
into my shoulder. She really did sound so tired. Exhausted.

I squeezed her back and said, 'Love you too.'

We ate lunch together and it was like normal, like
her mood had picked back up at least enough to drag her
through the day. Afterwards I went to the bathroom and said
I'd see her in the lesson. But she wasn't there.

THEO

I saw her walking out of school instead. Nudged Alec.

ALEC

We both saw him waiting for her at the gate.

EIGHT

LETTER FROM LUKA
17 NOVEMBER 2019

Dear Mom,

The first rule of buying-flowers-for-your-dead-mom club: someone will always see you with them, smile, and say 'Ooh, lovely, who are they *for*?'

You then have three seconds to decide whether to ruin their day.

I didn't ruin the day of the old man in the supermarket line this morning. It didn't seem like the right thing to do. I did shrug and roll my eyes so he wouldn't press any further though. There are only so many lies I can tell.

And I've been telling a lot, lately, but I'm trying to stop.

I don't lie to school any more when they ask where I've been. I just say, 'Not here.' I know they'll have called William anyway – like he's got a say in what I do. And I know they won't push me too hard about it because of my 'special circumstances'. The less I show up, the less I have to answer the questions.

I do miss going to lessons, sometimes. Like History. I think I just miss the routine of going in, sitting down, turning to the set pages and thinking about dead people I *don't* know for a while. It's fine when I'm there, but it takes so much effort to show up in the first place. I just don't have the energy for it, any more. I can't bring myself to care.

And there'll be plenty of time to catch up after mocks, anyway. Mr Tang told me at the start of the year I could get the marks I need in my sleep, so he can't exactly complain if I've decided to take him at his word.

I don't lie to William much – I just speak to him as little as I can. He only has to open his mouth and I get angry. I yell at him over the stupidest things, things I know aren't his fault, except in the way that everything's been his fault for years.

I still lie to Alec and Allegra when I haven't come home for the night, because it's easier to come up with an excuse than to have to say I just can't stand being in the house with them, pretending anything's the same.

It's different when I'm alone. I like spending time in the house then. I cling to the rooms that still have parts of you in them: photographs, your coat preserved on its hook, the little collection of snow globes you arranged on the bookshelves that nobody's had the heart to move.

I just hate the rooms you've been wiped away from – your things put in boxes and given to charity. It's like whiplash walking along the hall sometimes, between places you still exist and places where it feels like you never were. I think about how many times your feet walked the same stretch of carpet as mine, and I think where are they now? Where are you? Where are you?

But it's when everyone's home that the walls crowd in on me. When William's in his office and Allegra has her cartoons on, and Alec's on the phone or yelling at people on some gaming stream and everyone's acting like it's normal. Like we're normal, like we're a normal family when we're not. There's a hole in the middle of us and I don't know why I'm the only one who seems to keep falling down it.

Anyway, I lie to them. I tell them I'm seeing Ro.

I lie to Ro. I tell her I'm fine. I tell her I'm staying home.

In the mornings I get dressed like I used to, I eat toast like I used to, I leave the house, I circle round to the little supermarket in the street behind and I get a coffee that tastes like overboiled evil from their machine, and I wait until I know everyone else will have started their day.

Then I go back, go to my room, and that's where I stay. My day ends about 9:50 a.m. and I'm already exhausted.

If I can sleep for a while, the days go by faster.

I feel like a ghost in the house when I'm there on my own. I can cry and scream and wail and no one will ever hear me, or know it happened at all. Like a tree falling in a forest with no one to hear: if I exist unobserved do I exist at all?

You have to understand, I've got to do all this alone

because it wouldn't be fair for me to keep putting my sorrow on other people. It's been a year. You're supposed to be over something after a year, aren't you? You're supposed to stop dragging your friends down, or falling into silence in the middle of a conversation. I'm supposed to stop bleeding but I'm not ready.

I'd guess you were expecting a perkier letter after my last update.

Because, Cosmo.

Maybe you're assuming he never spoke to me again. That he was just a one-night brush with a cosmic future.

Well, you're wrong. And things are better. I just needed to establish the baseline darkness before I paint in the bright spots.

He calls me all the time. It's one of the reasons I started staying home, because he'd ring me at school when I couldn't answer, so I'd have to find ways to get out of the lesson with my phone buzzing in my bag, and there's only so many conversations with him I wanted to have in the school bathroom block. I'd tell him I was in a class but he still kept calling and he's got this way of talking me into anything once I answer. He always wants to see me. He even started picking me up at the gates. I got looks when I walked out of there with him, but honestly? I think I liked them. I've never been someone who got those kinds of looks before.

If I'm at home when he calls we can just talk for hours. He doesn't know he's communicating with a ghost, but he tells me it's good to hear my voice and I feel suddenly real again.

He works in a call centre, which is why he's free to talk so much. He told me that once he realised he could make outgoing calls and it meant no new incoming ones could get through it made the job so much less stressful. The rest of the time he's still getting yelled at about vacuum cleaners by housewives who he says should consider smoking a few bowls instead of getting so worked up about home appliances, but it breaks up his day.

And I like to feel I'm doing something for him. He does so much for me.

Like, lets me stay.

He's in a house share with eight other people, a crumbling old disaster building where his room is half of what used to be one room, and he has lace curtains up like someone's grandmother because the window looks straight out on to the street. And water comes up through the floor sometimes, and no one ever remembers to top up the electricity, and there's barely room for more than a wardrobe and a bed but it's okay. Because that's all we need.

And yes, we do. There, that's top of the list of things I only tell you because you're dead.

Anyway, the *problem* is that he has a sort-of girlfriend already.

I know, I know. That's second on the list of things I'm only telling you now because you can't look at me the way I know you would. But he says they're nothing to each other any more. She went to university when he didn't and treats him really badly now, like he's not good enough for her. He's going to break up with her as soon as she's finished her exams, because he doesn't want to screw anything else up for her, and I can't complain about that.

He tells me I'm beautiful, which isn't true, and that there's no one else like me, which might be true but I don't know if it's good. But in his mouth I believe those words. I believe them when he kisses them against my mouth. The way he talks about me sometimes - it's almost overwhelming.

And the days when he sees her and I can't stay with him are bad, but the rest make it worthwhile. He always says he expects me to leave him, that he can't believe I'm so good to him. Like he's surprised I'll wait.

Of course I'll wait. Ghosts have nothing but time.

Well. You'd know.

Love you, love you, love you.

Love,

Luka

NINE

WILLIAM BOOTH, STEP-FATHER

Of course I feel responsible. But there's only so much
control it would have been possible for me to exercise over a
seventeen-year-old girl who, despite my own feelings on the
matter, regularly reminded me she wasn't my daughter.
I knew she still visited Gabriela's grave regularly, as I did.

ALLEGRA BOOTH, 7, SISTER

The bus from school goes past where Mum is and every
Thursday Daddy meets it there and I get off and we go and
see her. And a lot of times there were already flowers.

WILLIAM

I can't ever give Gabriela all the things I wanted to. Now I
give her flowers. There are other visitors too, but the telltale
signs of a visit from Luka were often there in those days.
Orange roses.

ALLEGRA

Orange is her favourite colour, mine's green. Daddy always stands in front of where Mum is for a minute and then goes to sit on the bench just a little way along and I look at the flowers and sometimes at the names on the other graves. The first time I found a letter it had been blown on to Agnes Hedwig Stahl, who is ninety-nine, and her grave says 'the memory of you shall never pass away'. I thought it was for her, but then I saw it said 'Mommy' on the front the way Luka spells it, and the writing was the purple pen Luka uses, and so I picked it up.

ALEC

You *stole* it.

ALLEGRA

I never! I just kept it safe, and all the other ones I found. I put them in my sock drawer. I never even opened them all that time.

ALEC

Well, maybe if you rob a bank in future and just keep all the money in with your laundry basket, the police will let you off with a caution. I always wondered what made you start taking the letters home in the first place, though. You knew who they were for.

ALLEGRA

But Mummy can't read them now, and my teacher said that if I just *think* about the things I want Mummy to know, she'll know them. So if Luka had already thought them then it didn't matter if I took the letter, just to keep it safe.

ALEC

Keeping them safe is why you started your collection . . . ? It's okay, Allegra. We're all glad you did, now. I just want to know why.

ALLEGRA

The first letter was all soggy at the corner because Agnes Hedwig Stahl had a little bowl on her grave and it was filled with water. And the water was spreading up the paper almost to Luka's writing. And I didn't want to leave Luka's words there, on someone they didn't belong to, getting all wet and washed away. I wanted them. Because –

ALEC

Because?

ALLEGRA

Because she was leaving us. Luka was. She wasn't there any more hardly at all, like she wouldn't watch TV with me, and I couldn't get in her bed because she went out at night and left the door locked. And I just wanted some little bits of her to keep. Like I have Mum's necklace and her jumper and some books. I'd just have taken something from Luka's room but she shouts at me when I do that. But she wouldn't shout at me about this because she wouldn't know. It was just little bits of her.

ALEC

Because you felt like you were losing her too. You're stupidly smart, you know, Legs. The rest of us didn't figure out we were losing her until much later. She was always angry, and getting sketchier and sketchier about when she'd be around, but, if I'm really honest, sometimes it was a relief when she stayed away for a day or two. When she was mad about something she could be a lot to cope with, and she got mad so often. But still, we always assumed she'd come back.

WILLIAM

My thinking was that if I came down too hard on her, that would be what made her go. I wanted her to understand that, no matter what, there would be a place for her in this family. When I married Gabriela I didn't do it in spite of you and Luka, Alec. I loved the whole family. I felt lucky to be allowed to join. But I think Luka always felt like I was stealing something away.

ALEC

Mom. It'd been her and Mom against the world for so long. I don't think she knew how to let someone else in once Mom started to. But she was never pushed out. I know that, at least. She pushed herself.

WILLIAM

Still, I made mistakes in how I handled it, so very many of them. Letting her go in the hope she'd come back wasn't a line of thinking that I ever explained to her, and I suspect it seemed as though I didn't care. Looking back, I wonder if it felt like the prelude to abandonment.

ALEC

You wonder if she decided the only way to protect herself from more loss was to abandon us first.

TEN

ROISIN

She *never* let me meet him, you know. Not after that first
time. I heard about him so much that if we'd been given a
test on exactly what shade of golden-brown Cosmo Allen's
eyes were, then I'd be top of the class. *Like autumn leaves
with the light shining through them. Like dark honey.* I knew
what all his favourite films were, and his favourite football
players, and the ones he didn't rate. It was such an amount of
bloody nonsense that I couldn't believe she gave a shit about
it herself, so it was bizarre having it all it inflicted on me.

But it felt like the only way I could get her to talk to
me, so I learned how to be very sympathetic about the shit
computer he had that meant he couldn't make a pure fortune
as a top streamer, or bitcoin farmer or something, and how
much he hated it when they left the little hard bits of star
anise in his takeaway curry.

Will you listen to me? I still know it all *now*. There are
huge, valuable sections of my brain that'll be wasted on his
curry habits forever.

ALEC

She never even *talked* about him to us. I'd try to raise the subject sometimes – teasing or serious. It never worked. She'd clam up or fly off the handle and in the end it really wasn't worth it.

THEO

She talked to me, once.

ALEC

Really? You never told me. What did she say?

ROISIN

Was it about his preference for vindaloo over madras?

THEO

She asked me how I'd known I was in love.

ALEC

How you . . .?

ROISIN

Well, go on then. What did you say?

THEO

I don't think that part's vital to Luka's story, is it? But I suppose it shows what she was thinking about. And this was only a couple of months into everything. It was the middle of December, just before that night we were all in Costa to try all the Christmas flavours.

ROISIN

A festive ritual even Luka couldn't duck out of. It's always been a prime tenet of our friendship agreement: the both of us being obsessed with Christmas. We'd usually have made at least three trips to Winter Wonderland by then, and I'd have a gift drawer stuffed with tat from the Bavarian market to give to my various aunts, but it had been impossible to get her to keep to any kind of plan. In the end I went with a couple of the other girls, Shauna and Tiwa, and I felt guilty the whole time.

But letting her miss the last late Thursday at the Christmas Craft Market? Not an actual chance. I'd ducked out of school early myself just to make sure she didn't vanish on me, but when I got to the house there she was: ready to go. She had her hair tied up in silver tinsel, bright against her dark, and a few blue strands of the stuff saved for me.

'I always think blue's your best colour.' She twined it round her hands and set it carefully into my curls like a tiara. 'Your hair's *so* fair. See? You're an ice princess.'

I looked into the hallway mirror and couldn't deny the effect. I looked like one of the less corny characters from the local pantomime. 'That'll be ice *queen*, thank you. No sitting around waiting to be rescued for me. I have ruling to do.' And I swept her out of the door.

THEO

We went straight after school. Ate unwise hot dogs from the German sausage stand, then bought overpriced Nutella pancakes to take the aftertaste away. All the best festive traditions.

ALEC

By the time we caught up with Luka and Rosh, they were balancing a bag between them that was stretched wide by the spikes of a multitude of paper star lamps, decorated in Moroccan patterns. Rosh's eyes were wide and wild. 'They were on special offer. I got one for *every* aunt.'

ROISIN

Listen, if you'd a family as large as mine, you'd be thrilled about the bargains too. And the craft market does things to me. I can't explain it. Like, I never buy scented candles from the regular shops – they're overpriced and most of them do nothing but make your room smell like there's been a spillage at the chemical factory – but show me scented candles hand made in a shed by someone with a beard you could grow cress in and I'll want twenty. It's like catnip for people. That's why I was a bit hyped up – I was high on *Christmas*. I grabbed the nearest arm and gestured to the open doors of the coffee shop. 'Ready to caffeinate ourselves till it hurts?'

ALEC

'Not quite . . .' The Christmas Elf had quite a deathgrip, but we had another stop to make first.

THEO

I just put a hand on Rosh's wrist and smiled until she let go.

ROISIN

I'm telling you: sometimes I don't know my own strength.

THEO

'We just need to stop at a couple more places before they close. See you in there in twenty?

'Do tell me if the Irish Velvet Frostino is good enough to become Roisin's official new nickname.'

ROISIN

Luka saluted with a grin. 'Aye, aye.' And we went in together to order one of every artificially flavoured delight on the menu. Plus two of the Salted Caramel Yule Logs and a bag of fir-tree-flavoured popcorn. (I'll spoil it for you now: pure boke.)

It had been a couple of hours since Luka's mind had diverged from its singular track, which was a true Christmas Miracle, but while we were in the line she just couldn't help herself.

'Cosmo never drinks coffee from these places. He says they're glorified hospital waiting rooms with overpriced hot water. He gets coffee at McDonald's and pours it into a different cup when I want to come and sit in here. He says they can't exactly challenge him on whose hot bean juice he's drinking. It's not like they have coffee DNA tests.'

I let out a high keening noise as I leaned over the counter to pay the admittedly outrageous bill for our drinks. It got me looks both from the barrista and Luka.

'What?' she asked.

'I'm sorry – it's just the sound of my last three brain

cells weeping over being asked to give a shit about Cosmo's bad takes on coffee.'

'I thought the DNA thing was funny. Though –' she grinned at me, secretly – 'I've kind of missed having someone match me macchiato for macchiato. McDonald's coffee is *not* a genetic success story.'

'Then tell your boyfriend not to hog you as much as he does. I'm always around.' I slid the tray off the counter into my hands as she carried bags and snagged the two drinks that looked most likely to fall. 'I missed you too.'

'He's really not –' Luka said, and I think she was probably about to say *my boyfriend* given how long I know he strung her along for now.

He was her only conversation topic. She spent three nights a week at least at his place, as far as I knew. I didn't see what else he was supposed to be. But I cut her off.

'It's like we're in one of those films everyone hates because the only time any female characters speak to each other, they're talking about a boy. So I was just thinking maybe we could –'

'There he is.' Luka said.

And there he was.

THEO

We got to the chemists just before it shut, and I made Alec wait by the door while I picked up my beta blockers.

I don't know why – it isn't as if he doesn't know what I take. Blockers of all kinds have been a bit of a way of life for me for the last few years – these ones take the sharper edges off some of my anxiety. I'm just always waiting to be asked intrusive questions by the elderly pharmacist and I worry. Which I realise is ironic given what the prescription's for but . . . it's like I'm always waiting for him to hear something that will make him change his mind about me.

ALEC

Theo.

THEO

Not while we're recording. At any rate, we'd have been back in no time if he hadn't pinned me to the door on the way out and kissed me until the shop assistant cleared her throat. *So* embarrassing. But – reassuring too.

We headed back with our arms round each other, my chin tucked against his shoulder and his hand under my shirt at the waist. It was too busy in town to worry about who might be looking. The buildings above us were strung with stars and snowflakes and somebody had corralled a children's choir into singing 'Silent Night' on the steps of the church.

It felt beautiful, for a while.

I did too.

ALEC

You always should.

So that's what was keeping us. What was Cosmo doing in a coffee shop if he hated them?

ROISIN

Oh, he was just sitting on his phone, his stuff splayed across a table meant for four people while the rest of the place was rammed. In front of him he had a tall glass with the dregs of what I could immediately recognise as the Black Forest Gateaux Supreme. The leftover cherry stem in the bottom of the glass really gave it away. I had two of them on the tray I was carrying in his direction, with Luka shooting me nervous glances about going over, even though we both knew she wasn't just going to ignore him.

He didn't look up from whoever's texts he was smiling over, until she nudged his chair with her foot, and then he startled and looked up at her with a quick scowl that slowly smoothed out as she greeted him.

'Hey, if it's not the most beautiful girl I know. Are you stalking me or something?' He raised an eyebrow as he smiled. I thought the grin looked a tiny bit tight myself. Like he was keeping gritted teeth below it. 'Wasn't expecting to see you today.'

'We were just Christmas shopping. If you've been very good this year there might be something in these bags for you.'

She smiled pure sunlight down at him, while at the use of the word *we* he looked up and found me looking back.

I felt a little less sunny and put my tray on the table with a little bit of a thud. 'Honestly, living in the same part of town, shopping in the same places, what are the *chances* we'd ever run into you. Are these seats free?'

He picked his bag up reluctantly, from the seat in front of me. Luka slipped into the one next to him, looking like she'd won a game of musical chairs, and after a minute he leaned into her for an eskimo kiss, nudging his nose against hers.

'You look gorgeous,' he said, raising a hand to brush her cheek. 'But what's that tat in your hair?'

Luka reached up, her fingers tangling in the tinsel. That little bit of sparkle she'd smiled so much about before.

'Oh, it's just . . .' she said, and she pulled it loose. Dropped it to the floor. 'It's silly. You're not busy, are you? We don't have to bother you –'

He pulled her in against his side, folding an arm loosely round her shoulders. I don't know how a person makes a hug look smug, but the boy was capable of it.

'I always want to see you, Starshine, you know that. I just thought you said you had other things to do. If I'd known you weren't busy we could have been walking round together.'

In that moment I could have spat over how apologetic she looked.

'Oh, Rosh and I do this every year. It's just a day out to look at the lights and pick up some gifts before the shops get too wild. You'd have got bored by the time we looked at the third scented candle stand. *And* I wouldn't have been able to get you a surprise.'

They were looking at each other like they were the only people in the coffee shop, possibly the world. Cosmo started telling her he'd have to up his game if she was getting him gifts already, going on and on about how he'd have joined her if he knew she 'wasn't doing anything'.

I sucked the cream off the top of one of the hot chocolates noisily, trying to guess whether it was praline or mint below. It isn't the loveliest of feelings to sit there and hear yourself described as *not anything*.

'Well, you can join *us* now,' I said. 'Though it looks like you've got started on the taste test section of the evening already. How was the Black Forest? Marks out of ten?'

Luka grinned. 'Rosh takes all this very seriously.'

'I can see.' Cosmo pushed his empty glass slowly away from himself and looked at the cardboard cups and the slices of cake I was laying out. 'Is this your idea of a light snack?'

He said it with a look over my body that I'd seen too many times. Though I couldn't deny that the table did look ridiculous with everything laid out on it like that, and just two of us there. I know – I know – that if I'd said anything, he'd have told me it was a joke. But the way he said it, it didn't land like it was funny. It was a little too pointed.

There was that look.

Luka usually jumped to my defence when anyone gave me that sort of look. I could see her wavering.

Then Cosmo's lips twitched and he forced out a grunt that sounded almost like a laugh, pushing his glass further away. 'This was on the table when I got here. I don't drink the swill they serve. It's sugar in a glass and I can think of better things to spend my money on.'

He let that little rant sit a moment. Then there was that smile again, pushing dimples into his cheeks with the force of it. 'But don't let me stop you.'

I didn't think he really meant anything by it – not then. People say things without knowing the sore spots they're hitting all the time. But I settled in my chair feeling strange, and just a little smaller than before.

THEO

Alec was trying to bite my ear when we made it through the door, I think.

ALEC

Which is necessary information only because it meant Theo yelped and jostled a table as we went in, and half the people in there were looking at us before I remembered to pull my arms from round his waist. Cosmo saw, right?

ROISIN

He looked over, but he didn't react. I didn't know if he remembered the two of you, but I know he snagged his phone off the table and went back to scrolling through texts as Luka stood up to call you over, which I thought was strange.

THEO

He was still doing that by the time we made it over, flicking a look up at each of us as Luka introduced us to him again, but not much more.

ALEC

'Five of us, only four chairs.' I looked around to see if there was a spare, but Costa looked like the last shelter at the edge of the apocalypse given how full it was with exhausted people trailing overstuffed bags.

THEO

There was just a second's silence – it hung in the air.

ALEC

None of us really wanted him there. But he didn't even look

up. Just spread his legs wider and hunched over his phone. Then Roisin tugged at Theo's arm.

THEO

'We can make space. I call the cute one,' she said. I poked my tongue out at her and sat where she was patting her knee.

ALEC

I took the seat at the other side of Cosmo, dragging a couple of the festive cups over to me to try and figure out the contents.

ROISIN

'You're pulling them out of order – I've got a system, Alec! Don't mess with the system.' I started telling Theo what order the drinks were *supposed* to be in, reaching round him to arrange them. 'With a bite of yule log between each one, as a palate cleanser.'

THEO

'Perfect, Rosh. Love a bite of log.'

I didn't understand why, but I could see Luka looking rather uncomfortable as I passed a couple of cups over to her. She kept glancing at Cosmo, who was immersed in his phone, as though he was a complete stranger to us all. I thought perhaps he was unsure about new people. If anyone could understand that, I could. But still, even when anxiety's clawing at me, I try to say hello.

ALEC

'Shit, I forgot – look at these, aren't they disgusting?' I pulled out one of my earlier market purchases and tossed it on to the table. 'Cosmo, want to suck on one of Santa's sweet balls?'

ROISIN

He didn't look up until Luka reached over the table for them and shook them in his face, making a circus act out of trying to include him. 'Seriously? They've got to name these things deliberately to get teenage boys to buy them for their friends.'

Cosmo gave the pack a glance as she was waving them under his nose. 'Yeah, disgusting. I'm going to pass. But look at this –'

He showed his phone round the table, suddenly acknowledging that we were there with one wide sweep of his arm, face brightening in a way it hadn't even managed when he first saw Luka. 'Look!'

THEO

'It looks like an email,' I ventured. We couldn't see much more with the way he was waving it around.

ALEC

He clicked his tongue, talking as slowly as someone might if they were addressing a class of preschoolers. 'It's an email to say I've *won*. Unseen Screams? The film festival? I put in for two tickets for the uncut screening of *Blood of Omens*. Thought I hadn't got it, but it looks like someone's pulled out tonight.'

Grinning at Luka, he reached for one of her hands. 'You're coming, right? Got to take my lucky charm.'

ROISIN

I'd been eyeing him as I sampled an Eggnog Hot Chocolate (cocoa with a light aftertaste of baby sick – not a favourite: three out of ten). 'Didn't you just say it was tonight?'

ALEC

He was already pulling his jacket on, nudging his bag from under the table with a foot. 'Yeah. Perfect timing. I've got nowhere else to be.'

ROISIN

'But Luka does.' I was going to say it for her if she wouldn't.
'This is a tradition.'

She looked at me, and she was smiling but not in a way
I recognised. It was an odd, guilty thing. 'It's just trying a few
drinks, Ro.'

She'd said she missed it barely twenty minutes ago.
Missed this.

'But it's not just –'

ALEC

'Do you even like horror movies?' I asked Luka. I'd reclaimed
my candied balls and was focusing on laying them out on a
napkin in a multicoloured grid. Santa's balls have a touch
of 'taste the rainbow' about them, for the curious. I very
carefully didn't look up. Telling Luka not to do something
only ever made things worse. 'We watched *IT* together and
you wouldn't use the bathroom sink for a week.'

ROISIN

'You don't have to come.' Cosmo's voice was as gentle as
I'd heard it. He sounded nice. He even smiled across at me
and for a moment I could see why she had such a thing
about his mouth. 'I don't want to drag you away from this
little . . . thing you're doing. But it is a once-in-a-lifetime

opportunity to see this cut of the movie.'

ALEC

Like that was some kind of selling point. *Blood of Omens*
is bad enough it left me wishing *I'd* been killed off in the
opening scene.

ROISIN

'And if it gets too much I'll hold your hand.' He crouched
and whispered a second part of that into her ear, which made
her blush. I'd *never* seen Luka blush before.

She looked at me, and I sighed loudly at her. '*I* could
hold your hand over a festive coffee, if that's all it takes. Go
on, then. Go with him.'

THEO

Cosmo pushed a hand back over his short hair and grinned
round at us like the prize-winner on one of those adverts
with the giant cheques. 'Have I told you I love your friends?'

ROISIN

It was news to me.

ALEC

I raised my hand. 'I'm her brother. Just don't let her come out afraid of washing again. We live together.'

Luka ruffled my hair. 'Don't worry. We're still getting over your four-year soap-shy phase. Text me updates from the sugar coma, okay?'

I nodded, and she paused and bit her lip, looking at Roisin as though she was going to apologise again.

ROISIN

She didn't. She just left. I turned my head to watch them through the window, Cosmo tucking his hand into her back pocket as they walked.

THEO

We sat with our coffee cup carnage. 'Looks like it's just the three of us.'

ALEC

'Yeah, more and more, lately.'

ROISIN

'Balls.'

I slumped forward over the table as Alec poured a scatter of sweets into my palm.

ELEVEN

EPISODE OUTRO

ALEC

So what I wanted to ask about was how things changed between you and Luka, and when. I know how things went at home – like a slow gathering of clouds before a storm. But whenever I saw you two together things still seemed steady.

ROISIN

If you mean did we start having screaming fights, then no. We never have fought, somehow. There are girls I know who can be banging each other's heads into desks in the morning and brushing each other's hair by the afternoon, but that's never been how we were. Not to say we never disagreed on a thing, but we'd bicker – we wouldn't fight.

Part of that's me. I'm not much for loud dramatics which, to know me, you might be surprised by. I don't mind a raised voice. It's the anger I'm not so fond of.

And anyway, I think I was an escape from that.

ALEC

We've talked so much about Luka and trying to be there for her – it makes me wonder how much she was there for you.

ROISIN

Oh, Alec. That's all she was. Did I ever tell you how we met?

ALEC

Accents. You both had them and no one else –

ROISIN

And no one else did – at least ones the same as ours. Well, that's true. But we found that out sitting in the school canteen, me on my own trying to stare down my lunch.

I always say I hate eating in there because the food smells like it's already been digested once, and that's not untrue. But it's more that I used to have this issue about being watched while I ate.

The thing I've learned now is that if someone wants to find fault with you, they can always pick a reason. Any reason at all. So maybe it's your accent, or your hair, or your clothes, or your body. For me, for such a long time, it was all of the above. Every single thing.

At my old school it felt like I was in with a class of

vultures. They spent every day picking at me like a corpse.

People who want to feel better about themselves – some of them are like Luka. They make friends, they're good to people, and they earn back the results of that. And some people get confused. All I can think is it's a crossed wire somewhere in how they're made that leaves them thinking putting other people down's the way to make themselves look better. And there were a lot of people with their wires crossed at my old school. So I got followed constantly. Called all kinds of names, most of them prefaced with 'fat' or 'ugly'. I'd have my bag taken and gone through if I didn't keep it wrapped in my arms at all times. And because these people love to pretend they're helping someone rather than assaulting them, I started having my meals policed. Every lunchtime I couldn't get a spot on my own. I must have looked like the most popular person on the planet for everyone who wanted to crowd my table and comment on every last thing I ate.

ALEC

God, Rosh, I never –

ROISIN

Well, I don't talk about it. God knows I spent enough of my life thinking about those people, I don't need to give them space now. But it can mess you up no matter how you work on pretending not to care about it, you know?

That first day: new school, no one to follow me to the table. I was still convinced the moment I took a bite of cheese and tomato sandwich there'd be someone there to ask if I really *needed* that. And then this gorgeous thing sat down and leaned over and I was expecting every fear to be confirmed.

'Oh my God, I *love* Miles Riva.'

I must have blinked at her wildly for a good minute before I remembered the quote from one of his songs that was printed across the front of my shirt. *Darling, you're my daylight.*

How I hadn't remembered I don't know. It had been a war that morning, getting ready in the dark. Up early enough to put my face on and torture myself with all the ways my clothes would be wrong. I didn't usually like to wear things that hinted at what I liked, or loved. It would just be one more thing people could take and turn against me. But I'd tossed my whole wardrobe on to the floor by the time I got to it, and the shirt *does* look good. Faded blue, low scoop neck, from his last tour.

And maybe some small part of myself was deluded into thinking it might call to someone with something in common.

I never, ever thought it would really work.

But we talked for the full hour of lunch, while I ate my sandwich unremarked on, and she had two desserts because the vegetarian main option at the counter was dire, and never once implied that she was being 'naughty' for doing it.

I can't tell you – to have someone look at me and notice something they liked rather than pick out all the things they could hate about me, it felt like a miracle.

That we liked each other in a dozen other ways was something we only found out as the days went along. But we never ran short of things to talk about. We don't have the same sense of humour, but we've got the kind that overlaps. So we laughed all the time. And I think when other people see you laughing, they can't think of you as weak.

I'm not saying nothing ever got said. I'm an Irish girl with a mouth that never stops and a body just a fraction too wide to frame in that perfect Instagram image. People are going to say things sometimes. But Luka was always there with just the right reply when my brain froze. She got the whole story out of me early on and it was an effort to keep her from marching across to my old school over it. She was so fierce – it felt like nothing could ever touch her.

Nothing except that great bloody guillotine that came down on your family.

It's so unfair, Alec, on all of you. I don't know if I've said that, or if I've said it enough, but whenever I think of all the things I can't imagine not being able to go to *my* mam about – it's *so* unfair. You're two of the strongest people I know, Luka and yourself. But some things would break anyone, and anything I can hold for you while you're putting yourselves together feels like the least I could do.

So never think Luka wasn't there for me. She was, always. Until him.

TWELVE

MY NAME IS LUKA: EPISODE 3
'THE MOST WONDERFUL TIME'

LETTER FROM LUKA
23 DECEMBER 2019

Dear Mom,

I was thinking about getting you an actual birthday card today.
I know combined holiday and birthday gifts were the bane of
your life, so maybe they'd be the bane of your death too. But
somehow picking out something in foil with CELEBRATE! on
the front feels like a disingenuous thing to leave on a grave.

Kind of like the way that hanging glittery things on trees
and decorating the windows falls flat this year too. We've done
it – later than we used to. You used to start plotting the tree
as soon as we closed the door on the last trick or treaters.

Last year, last minute, we picked up a store-bought fake
tree with decorations already hung on its branches. It felt as
artificial as every smile I tried on for that whole winter, so it

was kind of ideal. The tree was this perfect, tinsel-covered lie in the corner of the room, telling anyone who didn't know us well that things were normal. Thinking about it, I can only now see how hard I've tried to be like that tree.

I can't help wondering how many people spotted I was artificial too. Just a vague, plastic approximation of a real girl.

This year, for Allegra, we're trying to get some tradition back, but it feels like a bad idea already. I had no idea how hard it would be to open up boxes full of the decorations you collected for the last twenty years. There's even a shoebox that travelled all the way from Arizona, with a squashed Santa that Alec made out of yogurt pots, and a plaster of Paris star I painted MOM across, from point to point.

There's a white bauble with a portrait of Bluebell on it that was the dog's Christmas gift to the family the year we got her, and the silver-filigree angel Grandma Camila made you take from *her* collection the day you left home. There are snowglobes we picked up in Disney and a blue-glitter Big Ben to commemorate our first Christmas in London. I caught the smell of your perfume in the tinsel and immediately shoved it back in the bag to try and keep hold of it.

So many memories packed end to end in a few small boxes. I love every one of them. I never thought things I loved could hurt me so much but unpacking each of them was like running a blade across my skin.

It took three days just to get the tree done. You always decorated (you always let Allegra think she decorated, then

91

took down and redid her disaster scene late at night). No matter how many times I rehung tinsel and restrung the lights I couldn't get anything looking the same. It kept ending with Alec and I snapping at each other over all the things that were *wrong*.

So we let Allegra do it, and this year we're keeping her chaos intact. After last year's fake perfect, this year's barely contained explosion seems somehow right too.

But it's still hard to look at, you know?

Anyway, I'm still trying to figure out what to do about the whole actual day.

Everyone else thinks plans are settled. We visit William's mom in the morning and drop off gifts for her old lady circle at the retirement village. William and Alec get in the kitchen and pretend they have any clue what they're doing with a turkey (Alec's been watching the Food Network on a loop and now he's mad we don't have a giant deep fryer). I unwrap and microwave a festive vegetarian bake. At some point Theo comes over: he'll spend half the day and then go home for Hanukkah business in the evening.

Roisin will FaceTime me at least sixteen times to complain about each of her aunts and cousins separately. That's the same as every other year.

But this year there's Cosmo.

He asked me to spend it with him. He's not going home. I don't think he and his mom see eye to eye on much, so he told me he'll just go over to pick up his gifts and then get out before anyone gets nasty. And the rest of the day he'll be stuck in his tiny room in a dirty house with a few half-strangers who haven't gone home either.

I don't want that for him. And it's not that I wouldn't be fine pretending Christmas isn't happening at all. It'd probably be a relief to spend the day in his room with no nod to festivities except the remains of a tub of seasonally wrapped chocolate. I could do that.

But I'm not sure I could do that to them.

Alec's already permanently pissed at me, and William's stopped saying anything when I turn back up after a couple of days MIA, but his silence is noisier than the questions ever were. I've stopped pretending I'm leaving for class most mornings. I just . . . don't go. I'll pick it back up after the holidays, before mocks. Once I've given myself a break. I think I was far enough ahead of everything that catching up won't be a problem. Maybe I'll just be less bored.

But even if I'm not their favourite person, I know Alec at least wants me there. Just like those baubles in the boxes are a little bit of you to me – I think I'm a little bit of you for them. Maybe I hurt to look at, sometimes, but I'm carrying memories no one wants to give up.

It is *weird* how much losing somebody feels like losing your memory. All the shared moments I had with you feel less tangible now we can't remind each other of them, or bat back and forth private jokes. I've realised that memories aren't the same when they're not shared. If they're just yours, all they really are is stories. I'm nothing but stories now.

And I need to be there to share those with Allegra. She's only had a few years of building her own memories, and she'll never have the chance to make more.

So I want Cosmo to come to Christmas.

I want to share something good with him.

I just know I can make it through the day if he's there for me to roll my eyes at when William insists on reading out cracker jokes at the table, as if the whole point of them isn't that everyone already knows the punchline. If he's there, I can ignore the parts I need to. He makes me feel good about myself, while William and Alec leave me feeling like some kind of traitor for trying to exist away from them.

If he's there, maybe I can get past all the little, painful memories and make something new.

I'm going to ask him. The question is, do I tell them or not?

I hate to leave you on a cliffhanger, Mom. I just really haven't made up my mind.

Love,
Luka.

THIRTEEN

ALEC

That Christmas I thought for a minute that things were going to be okay. I keep saying that, don't I? Every time something didn't look like it was going to turn into the complete disaster I expected, I thought that was the moment. We'd come through it. We were all going to be fine.

THEO

What was the disaster you were expecting?

ALEC

I didn't think she'd be *there*. It's a long time since I haven't been able to sleep on Christmas night. It used to be because I was afraid Santa wouldn't show. That year it was my big sister who I was worried might skip out on proceedings. I had visions of Allegra running in the next morning and finding her bed made and empty.

But she'd been okay. She was home Christmas Eve. She was *nice* Christmas Eve. We all sat in the kitchen, ostensibly trying to string popcorn but mostly just watching Allegra eat it, and talking about how we used to do the same thing back in Arizona, and how popcorn tastes better in the States, somehow. Mom used to dye it with food colouring, and instead of tinsel on the trees we'd have rainbow strands that she policed with extreme prejudice every time one of us wandered by looking hungry.

Bluebell hung out, hunting for scraps, and even William ducked his head in without getting it bitten off. We had a playlist of the worst Christmas songs ever.

THEO

So Gaga's 'Christmas Tree' over and over?

ALEC

Yeah. Allegra spent all evening telling anyone who'd listen that her Christmas tree was delicious.

Anyway, that wasn't a disaster. I could really see Luka was making an effort with her too, even though she was being clingy. You couldn't blame the kid. I felt like being clingy myself. I thought about asking Luka why we couldn't just keep things like that. Keep them good.

I was *sure* she was going to vanish in the night.

THEO

We spent most of that night on WhatsApp, chatting and watching *Elf*.

ALEC

Until you pulled your usual trick of falling asleep ten minutes before it ended. Honestly, I think you prefer being left in suspense. Do you pull the last few pages out of books too?

THEO

Perhaps it's an unconscious thing. If you never find out the way something ended, you can always believe it was happily ever after.

ALEC

I guess you have a point, but still – it's *Elf*. It's not like it's gonna end with a reindeer massacre.

Anyway, after I realised you were down for the count, I went and stood outside her door for a while. Just stood there, in the dark of the hallway. I couldn't hear anything from her room, which either meant she was sleeping or she'd gone. And I didn't have the courage to check which.

I fell into bed and must've crashed for a few hours, because the next thing I knew Allegra had landed on my back, trailing gifts from her stocking and yelling at me to wake up because Santa had been. And Luka was sitting on the end of my bed, smiling at us both. A Christmas miracle.

THEO

I've always been just a touch jealous of people who 'do' Christmas. I think that's a common thing when you have a family that celebrates something else. At school, since kindergarten, December has always been about nativity plays and learning carols, with only the occasional sympathetic nod to those of us from other traditions who don't get gifts on Christmas Day. I used to be interrogated over it by other children who didn't know if they were horrified or sympathetic, only pacified by the news that Hanukkah at least meant books and money. And I suppose it made me uncomfortable because then I felt more 'different' than I did already.

When I met you, I realised your family 'did' Christmas the way I'd only seen in Hollywood films. All out.

ALEC

That was all Mom. Someday, when things are . . . steadier, I'm going to invite you over for a real Mom-style all-out holiday with us. I think, of everything, that's one part of her I want to inherit. The way she loved things shamelessly. And the way she loved bringing people together to love it with her.

Last year it was never gonna be the same. But we were doing our best. We visited Nana and her circle of old ladies that I'm pretty sure is some kind of wise women's coven at Willow Haven Home. Allegra had made them all cookies with their names on, and Luka danced the ones who wanted to around the common-room floor.

Allegra danced too, but since she'd decided to wear her nativity-play star outfit for the day, she was too spiky to hold too close. It was great. It was all great, until we got home for lunch and you were outside the door.

THEO

With Cosmo.

I still can't believe she hadn't told you he was coming.

ALEC

Not a word. She hadn't even mentioned him, which shouldn't have been a surprise, since she barely talked about him at all when I was around. I think Rosh was the official keeper of The Cosmo Tea, and she told me even she didn't know this was the plan.

THEO

He walked up while I was trying to balance my gift pile on the step, and I nearly fell over at the same time that all my bags did. Perhaps I shouldn't have been so surprised – you'd invited me, so it made sense that Luka would be able to bring someone. I just . . . knew that you felt tense about him. I was baffled that you wouldn't have mentioned he'd be there.

He didn't smile. In fact he was so expressionless that I wasn't entirely sure if he'd recognised me. He must have been standing there for a minute before I'd turned around, and the look he was giving me felt awfully blank. But then he said, 'Have they decided not to let you in?'

He flashed a set of teeth behind his smile, as though that was a joke, and in fairness it was probably meant to be. But to me it felt as though his tone didn't match up.

Something about him always made me feel nervous. I've wondered since if that's just hindsight trying to repaint things with what I know now. But I think my memory holds true. It was that way right from the start.

I was explaining that you hadn't got back yet just as the car sailed up the road like a rescuing chariot.

ALEC

It's a Honda Civic. Let's not go too far.

I saw you as we were pulling into the drive.

THEO

By the time you parked I could see everyone looking at Luka.

ALEC

I'd certainly turned her way. I had a couple of questions to ask. Questions like: 'What the hell?'

She looked the way she always did when an argument was about to start. Not sure whether to defend or attack but prepping for both. 'What the hell what?'

I didn't want to wave my hands toward where you stood, or make it too obvious, but I was dumbstruck. 'Were you gonna mention this at *any* point? Don't tell me it's a surprise to you too. I can see from your face it isn't.'

'Did I have to mention it? Cosmo's my friend. You've never complained about Roisin coming over before.'

'You didn't invite her over for the first time *secretly* on *Christmas*. Don't you think not mentioning it is *kind* of a tell that you know how weird that is?'

She leaned right over into the front and hissed at me, 'It's not a *secret*. Apparently I just overestimated how welcoming you're willing to be. He's got nowhere else to go. And didn't you tell me last night it was good to see me happy again? This is what makes me happy, Alec. Maybe at least try to give him a chance.'

She shot a look at William, as though she was daring him to say something, then sat back and ruffled Allegra's hair

101

before opening the car door on her side and sliding out.

THEO

She called out to me first. 'Theo! I'm *so* glad you came.'

Then she stopped in front of Cosmo, so close she had to tilt her chin up to look at him and, well . . .

ALEC

Yeah, we all saw the kiss. Then he ducked in and whispered something that made her giggle. That was the weirder thing to watch. My big sister's never really been a giggler. In the back of the car Allegra gasped and started giggling too, asking us who *that* was. I rolled my eyes and leaned back to look at her.

'That's Cosmo. He's Luka's boyfriend,' I said.

William turned off the engine. I could see him take a deep breath as he watched them, then he added, in a low, stern voice, 'And we are all going to be *very* nice to him.'

THEO

The effort was obvious. By which I mean the smile you pasted on as you looked across at me seemed like very hard work.

William nodded him a welcome as he came over, then

clapped me on the shoulder and said something about being sure there would be enough roast potatoes to go around. Allegra rushed up, bold until she got to William's legs, then hid behind them.

'Hope he likes burnt ones,' you called from the car.

Wait, should I use 'you' now, or Alec?

ALEC

If it's just the two of us talking, you is probably fine. It's more confusing when it's all three.

THEO

At any rate, you ushered him in, and he was set up on the couch and given a tray of Allegra's more broken cookie attempts to call his own. William went to the kitchen to finish the lunch, and we both sat on the floor to start construction work on a doll's house that seemed as though it required a degree in architecture to put together.

ALEC

We weren't ignoring him. We weren't making too much fuss over him either. If I got up, I'd offer him a drink or a mince pie.

THEO

I guessed he must have been nervous. You would be, in your girlfriend's house for the first time, wouldn't you? Christmas Day is a very in-at-the-deep-end way to meet the family. I remember thinking that Luka's invitation to him must have been last minute, as he'd turned up with nothing but himself. Not that I'd have expected him to have brought gifts for everyone –

ALEC

Like you did –

THEO

Yes, well I *know* you all. And I enjoy gift giving, even if it's not exactly my holiday. But I think I'd have found it difficult to arrive with nothing, not even a card.

ALEC

Like he was the gift.

THEO

Luka was nervous. That much was obvious from the way she was talking, filling in gaps in the conversation.

She introduced Cosmo to Allegra – Legs – Lego, saying everyone tended to pick a nickname for her.

'Not *strangers*,' Allegra told him, cautiously.

'Lego, this is Cosmo.' Luka smiled, making them shake hands. 'Now you're not so strange.'

ALEC

For once I think Allegra's *why* questions were a godsend. If you're ever short of small talk, just get a seven-year-old to start questioning the meaning of life. She got through whether Cosmo liked her cookies, why some cats have long hair, and a brief history and description of every Christmas gift she'd ever received before Cosmo asked if we could have the TV on.

He'd been pretty patient until then. Not fake-enthusiastic, the way that people used to dealing with children know how to be, but he didn't brush her off either. It made me think he might just have given us a bad impression before. He never asked *Allegra* any questions, though, like most people do with kids. Just let her ask a million about him. It was like watching a hard-hitting interview where the presenter is relentless and the topic is whether or not the interviewee likes cats.

I didn't blame him for wanting a break.

Luka was setting up her tablet, signing into FaceTime with Roisin. I knew they'd leave it connected all day, the way they did at night sometimes: just checking in from time to time through their window into each other's worlds. Distantly, I could hear Roisin mid-flow: '*And Granny says the pastor's donkey's died, so I said, "What's a man keeping a donkey in the middle of town for in the year of our Lord 2019?" I mean, Luka, we've got a Starbucks here now. It's a whole new era. And she says it was an old sad creature he adopted from the sanctuary who'd loaned it out for the Nativity scene each year, and now I'm spending my Christmas depressed about a donkey, would you believe it?'*

I stood and scooped Allegra off the floor. 'Come on, lets go find something else to wear and then you can watch *Frozen 2: The Snowman Strikes Back*. Again.'

She grabbed my hand, complaining that *wasn't* what it was called, and that she wanted to stay in her star costume, until I pointed out that her spikes wouldn't fit at the dinner table.

As we left I could hear Rosh still in full flow.

'*He was called Figgy Pudding. The donkey, not the pastor. Honestly, it's a local tragedy.*'

THEO

And you and Allegra vanished up the stairs.

A minute later, Luka got to her feet. 'Okay, I just need to go to my room so Ro and I can unwrap our presents together. Give me ten minutes, and then you can come up to unwrap *yours*.'

The look on her face as she said that definitely wasn't meant for me. I hid a grin as she leaned down to kiss Cosmo on the cheek, and he caught her wrist and pulled her closer to murmur, 'You're way too good to me, Starshine.'

She laughed and got up again, squeezing my shoulder as she walked past, while I acted like I was deeply invested in fitting together the jigsaw-puzzle pieces of Allegra's Doll's House of Doom.

Then it was just me and him, and my mind was racing through attempts at working out the right thing to say. It had felt like he'd been off with me while we were waiting outside, but I'm the first to admit that anxiety sometimes makes me read people more negatively than I should. I didn't want to judge anything, when he was probably just nervous too.

Taking a breath, I looked up to ask if he wanted to help. Right at the same time, as if he'd been waiting, he said, 'You can look if you want to.'

I could feel my forehead creasing into a frown. 'Sorry, what?'

A sneer cracked his face apart, lips drawn back around teeth, and for a moment his expression was so predatory that I imagined rows and rows of sharper teeth behind those, like a shark's. 'I said, you can look if you want to. I've seen you looking at me.'

The accusation left me stuttering.

'Y-you really haven't . . .'

'Anyway, what are you?' he asked quite casually, then leaned back, folding his arms behind his head, as if he'd just tossed out a ball and it was my job to catch it. And I . . . froze.

I didn't ask what he meant. I've been *me* long enough. I knew exactly what he was getting at. Neither did I want to give him the chance to elaborate, in terms I already knew I wouldn't enjoy.

ALEC

Theo, if you don't want to –

THEO

No, I do want to. I think it's . . . if not an important part of everything that happened, then at least significant. Another signpost we should have paid more attention to at the start.

I'm anxious, yes. I'm careful around new people, for good reason. I expect looks sometimes, and I'm used to comments. But I know who I am, and, anxiety or not, no one gets to make me question that.

I asked my teacher to tell the class to use my real name when I was eight years old, and since then I've known that it is entirely possible to be scared and brave at the same time. In fact, I think one might be a prerequisite for the other.

So I took a breath, and I smiled at him. A smile can be

a remarkably disarming weapon, particularly when coupled with a wide-eyed expression that pretended to have missed any traces of malice in his voice. It's my usual strategy, since I'm not quite built for fighting. Kill with kindness. Most people feel too ashamed by that to keep going.

'*Oh*, sorry, did you not get my name? I didn't mean to be rude. I just assumed you'd remember from the coffee shop. But I should have thought – so many new people must be overwhelming. I'm Theo. I'm with Alec, like you're with Luka.'

He spluttered into a cough. I hadn't realised I was making such a startling comparison. In fact, I'd thought I was being generous. 'Not *quite* like us, though, are you?' he said, his lips curled as though he was swallowing down something nasty. 'I mean, you're nothing like *me*. All right, what *were* you then?'

And I could feel my heart start rabbiting in my chest, the way it does when I can see a confrontation coming. But beyond the nerves, it all just made me feel so weary. I'd given him every chance to leave it, and me, alone.

'If you're trying to ask my pronouns, you might want to put it a bit differently.' I dipped my head but made sure my voice carried enough for him to hear. 'I was always Theo, if that's what you're wondering, even if other people used to call me a different name. Was that what you meant?'

Cosmo's sneer had settled into something smug but not satisfied. I don't think I'd quite given him what he wanted.

With that shark's smile, perhaps he wanted blood.

When he finally spoke, the teasing tone was gone from his voice. It had turned as hard as flint. 'Yeah well, *Theo*, whatever you are. Like I said, you can look, but if you try to touch I'll take your hand off at the wrist.'

ALEC

Jesus. I should've –

THEO

Don't do that. We can't go through all this with you pinpointing the things you should, would or could have done. We could *all* drive ourselves crazy with those, and the truth is we don't know if any of it would have changed things. When you can't fix something, all you can do is try to stop it happening to anyone else.

ALEC

You're right. That's what I'm trying to do, recording all this. It's my only way of fighting back against how useless I felt. Feel.

THEO

I know.

I felt useless too. I wanted to run, but I wouldn't let myself do it without coming to my own defence first. It was like my fight and flight instincts both kicked in at the exact same time.

So I stood up. I smiled. I hadn't stopped smiling for a second. And I said, 'Cosmo, I don't think I'd want to touch you if you were hanging off a cliff.'

Just as Luka walked back in.

She looked so hurt. I couldn't say anything to her. I didn't know what to say. So I just jogged past and up the stairs to find you, while I heard her behind me going, 'I came to get you for your present. What *was* that?'

ALEC

The second I saw you, I knew something had capital-H *Happened*. I told Allegra to go and help her dad in the kitchen.

THEO

And I didn't know what to say to you, either. I didn't want to ruin the whole day. But I've never lied to you about anything that mattered. 'Please don't *do* anything. I'm *fine*. I just . . . I don't think Cosmo's particularly okay with me being trans.'

ALEC

You smiled at me, the way you always smile when something hurts. I hate that smile.

THEO

It must have taken me half an hour to talk you down from doing or saying anything to him directly. Not that I didn't appreciate the desire, but it was a difficult enough day already. Neither of us wanted to tear the whole thing apart. We decided we'd keep as much distance as possible while he was in the house, and talk to Luka later.

ALEC

Difficult as things had been, I knew and trusted my sister. She loved me, and she loved you too. I thought she'd have to understand if we could just talk to her without him there.

THEO

But when we left your room you veered across the hall and into hers anyway.

ALEC

Good intentions are no match for instinct. She wasn't there.

But her tablet was, propped up on a shelf by the door.

THEO

We were turning to go when I saw Roisin staring out of it, muted, with her hands pressed up against the screen like a mime trapped in a box. I jabbed at the volume, and she started to speak, gesturing furiously.

'God, that boy is such a penis. He's worse than a penis. He's a collection of penises in a bag. Alec, you have *got* to get him out of your house.'

FOURTEEN

ROISIN

She'd left the tablet on while she brought him up to her room. Because I had my doubts about the boy and she wasn't daft enough not to know it. 'I just want you to see how he really is,' she said. Then she muted me and went off to get him.

Never mind that I had as much interest in watching the two of them coo at each other through their mutual gift exchange as I had in attending a memorial for a local donkey.

Less, in fact. Poor Figgy Pudding had never put a hoof wrong with me.

I was only half paying attention by the time she got back with him, too busy trying to keep one of the smaller cousins from using her brand-new paint set on my face. But I could hear them talking together in low tones that didn't sound like festive joy.

'It's fine, Luka. Not everyone's going to love me.'

'It is *not* fine to speak to you like that. Theo's technically a guest here today too. I've never seen him be that rude to anyone – what on earth were you talking about while I was gone?'

Luka paused to give a wary look out along the hallway, then I watched her close her door. Cosmo had his hands pushed deep into his pockets, his head slung low. He looked like a little boy getting in trouble at school.

'Look, I really don't want to cause a problem. Today's hard enough for you already, I'm here for *you*. To support you, not fuck things up –'

Stepping forward, she shook her head and ran her hands down his arms. 'You could never. This family's fucked up already, that's all. Just tell me what happened, please.'

He rumbled some gravel out of his throat and nodded. 'Theo just . . . he told me I shouldn't be here. Said *he* was invited because Alec was serious about him, and he and Alec were nothing like you and me. I don't know why he'd think that . . . that I'm not –'

He broke off. I couldn't see Luka's face but when she spoke she didn't sound angry any more. She sounded so careful.

'Are we?'

Cosmo lifted his head, his eyes dark and wide. 'Serious? Starshine, no one's ever meant more to me. I wanted to tell you . . . me and Kelsey are over, finally. I did it a couple of days ago. It wasn't easy – I've told you how crazy she can get – but she's finally out of our way.'

ALEC

And right there's when the three of us found out Cosmo
hadn't been dating my sister at all. She'd been staying at his
place, with everything I was sure that entailed, and the whole
time there'd been *Kelsey*.

ROISIN

Let's say it wasn't cementing his reputation *well* with me.
And I couldn't believe Theo would say a thing like that,
either. He's a bunny rabbit in a softer bunny rabbit's clothes.

THEO

Hey, I'm here.

ROISIN

And you're only proving my point.

But perhaps I could have overlooked it all for how she
obviously felt about him. They had that way of looking at
each other, like they were the last people in an empty world.
Like he'd slung the moon into the sky for her.

I wonder now if Cosmo looked in the mirror the same
way. As if he was looking at the only person who mattered.

Luka was telling him it was the best gift he could have
given her and he was – oh, saying something romantic, I

suppose. I missed a bit when one of the small gremlins I'm related to decided to stab me in the eye with her paintbrush. By the time I got back he was mid-flow.

'So maybe they'll accept us more now you're my girlfriend. I don't know, though. I get now what you meant about no one here understanding you.'

She had her head resting against his shoulder. 'They try. I know they do. It's just –'

'It's just they're grounded, while you're a galaxy all of your own.'

Really, you couldn't fault the boy's lines. He could have written a book of the things. Luka smiled up at him.

'But not *on* my own, not any more.'

'Not any more,' he said, wrapping his arms round her. 'I'm always on your side. And any time you want to get out of here just say, okay? I don't think I'm as welcome as we thought.'

'What did you tell Theo, when he said all that? Something must have made him reply the way he did.'

Cosmo took on that apologetic air again. 'Ah – I'm not proud of it. I said you and I were a lot more real than he was.'

Luka visibly caught her breath, stepping away and turning to face him. 'Cosmo, that's not okay –'

He was acting like he'd just told a bad joke – sheepish but not ashamed.

'I know, I know. You can't blame me for being

defensive, though, right? It's just hard to pretend he's normal when he's like . . . you know. When he's not what he looks. But it's his business, or whatever. I just get wound up when someone goes for me like that. There isn't much that means something to me, except you. I'll say sorry or something later.'

I could see her checking herself. Or maybe I'm imagining that now. I felt like I was watching her swallowing the sharper things she'd have said if she was really herself. When she replied she was speaking slowly and deliberately, as if she was checking every word. 'Whatever he said doesn't matter. Being wound up doesn't matter – it's not just about saying things like that. It's about thinking them. Even the way you're talking now. There's nothing not normal about Theo. It matters to me you understand that. So if you can't, then –'

He already had his hands up, palms out as if he was gentling a dog. He cut her off before she could finish. 'Hey, hey, you're right, I'm . . . yeah I guess I'm an idiot about these things sometimes. It's not something I know a lot about. Grew up in a house where you'd get a smack for even sounding like a girl. It was a stupid comment, that's all. I didn't mean anything. But if it means something to you then I'll learn about it, all right? Promise. I'll google a TED Talk if it helps.' He tried for a laugh, but it landed flat.

Luka looked up at him for what must have been a full minute before she nodded. 'I'll ask him to talk after dinner, okay? You'll have to apologise and explain. And I'm sure Theo will apologise too.'

Cosmo didn't seem convinced. He looked away as she fell silent. I watched Luka bite her lip as she cast round for something else to say, how to change the subject to something brighter. It hit her the next moment. 'I still haven't given you your gift.'

That brought his attention back. He smiled at her, tipping his head to one side. 'Sure you still want to give me one?'

Then she laughed. 'Mhm. Pretty sure.'

She slid a small wrapped box from the bedside table and turned round, holding it out to him.

His mouth twitched downward at the corners just for a second as he looked at it. He took it like it might bite, and seemed confused as he unwrapped first the paper layer, then opened the silver cardboard box inside.

'It's a bracelet,' he said.

I'd been there when she'd bought it from one of the craft market stands. Her eye had been caught by a series of chunky silver chains like the ones he already wore, but she was sold by the extra twist. A little black gem of a thing embedded into the clasp.

'It's a meteorite fragment,' she told him, beaming. 'And then they engraved the coordinates of the place we first met under it. Which was easy, because it was right under the prime meridian. We met under a shower of falling stars, at

119

the centre of the world.'

It was so romantic. It killed me how romantic she was. What a bloody waste.

'Oh,' he said. And he picked it out of the box with two fingers and added it to the rest of the jingling collection on his wrist. Shook it a moment, then turned it to look at the clasp. 'Yeah, it looks cool. Thanks.'

His voice was flat as a lake in summer.

This kind of enthusiasm is why you should never waste a good idea on a boy.

THEO

Hey –

ROISIN

I'd say no offence, but the both of you know it's true.

So he said *Oh*. That's his big reaction. And then he said, 'Is that it?'

She pulled her hand back as if he'd slapped it away, reaching up to push her fingers back through her hair. I watched her worry the ends into knots. 'Don't you like it?'

'No, it's great. Yeah. You're amazing.' Not a single shred of feeling made it into his tone. Then he scuffed his feet on the carpet and turned away to stare out of the window as if the gift was too disappointing to look at. 'I thought I'd mentioned that game I wanted, that's all.'

'That game . . .?'

With him not looking at her, she let more show on her face than she should. I know Luka, and for all the attitude she has sometimes – with William, with you Alec – she likes to get things right. I think there's maybe a part of her that never quite feels good enough. She sighed and stood behind him as though she was a maid awaiting her instructions. 'You talk about a lot of games. I thought this would be more . . . but if you don't . . .'

'I said it's great.' The words snapped out harder than I think he intended, because the next second he'd turned to her, put a hand on her shoulder. 'Sorry, sorry, babe. It's just a stupid game. It's just – you know I said Mum never bothers with much, and I broke up with Kelsey so . . . I'll get it myself when rent's not round the corner. I'd just been wanting something to distract me. You get how it is, finding this time of year hard. The chain's great. It's fine. I'd love anything from you.'

Reaching up, Luka wrapped both her hands round his wrist. She tilted her head up to look at him. I couldn't see her face and I wasn't sure I wanted to. She was tangled in what he was spinning. 'Well, it's only a small thing, the bracelet. There's no reason I couldn't get a game for you too.'

'You would?' Like magic, he was instantly Captain Perky again. 'Might be cheaper in the Boxing Day sales. But it's still going to be like sixty pounds . . . I don't want you spending everything on me.'

'That's okay.' She was nodding, like that was pennies. 'I'll tell you a secret. Most of our inheritance from Mom's locked up in savings accounts for each of us, but I've got some I can access. It's going to be for uni but I dip into it now and then. When it's important.'

Cosmo smiled slowly, and for a moment he looked sweet, and unsure, and not a calculating weasel at all. 'And I'm important?'

'You're *so* important.' Her voice was so warm.

'Great, then I'll show you the ones I want. They're on my Amazon list. I'll just send you the –'

William's voice came up the stairs, then. Yelling something about potatoes. Luka sighed and yelled back 'One minute!' and Cosmo pocketed his phone again. I saw him roll his eyes while she was looking away. Then she turned back and there he was, glowing like sunshine again. 'Dinner?'

'Dinner,' she said, smoothing her hand down his arm to twine their fingers. 'Are you going to be okay with Theo and everything?'

Cosmo shrugged his shoulders. 'I don't care what people think of me if they're not you. I'll be fine with Theo. And your brother.'

'Alec?' She blinked, drawn away from pulling Cosmo up on any more of his bullshit. 'Has he said something too?'

'Only through his little attack dog. It doesn't matter. It's just, apparently, you're only with me for the attention. That's what they think this whole thing is. Some sort of "poor me" thing now that you're not getting enough sympathy any more. You not showing up at school, seeing me, not playing the perfect sister all the time. All an act, that's what your brother thinks. Or Theo said it, so I guess it's come from your brother and not your stepdad. He seems all right.'

William's voice came through again like he was answering a cue. Less patient this time. Luka looked down at her hand in Cosmo's. Her knuckles were white with how tight she was holding him.

'We've got to go,' she said. 'Come on.'

They swept out, and there was nothing until the two of you came in. Just an empty room and me working hard not to throw my tablet across the floor. That's all he said.

THEO

A bag of penises.

ALEC

A whole stinking bag.

FIFTEEN

ALEC

We pounded downstairs with me ready to grab him by the collar and dump him back out on the doorstep.

THEO

Which I was still suggesting might be a little too much. But then we got down there and the table was laid. Allegra was standing on the chair beside Cosmo, reverently placing a paper crown on his head, and when she saw us she called out 'Three kings! One, two, three! Come here, I need you!'

ALEC

We were only the three kings if it was one of those fantasy series where they bloodily murdered each other to get their hands on the throne. But my little sister could diffuse the bitterest of feudal disputes, and I couldn't steal her newest playmate out from under her little fists, so somehow a couple of minutes later I found myself sitting opposite Cosmo while William dumped piles of blackened potato on to my plate and, across the table, Luka was looking at me like she could sizzle off my skin with a glare.

THEO

Allegra was singing carols between mouthfuls, having insisted on sitting between us. I shot glances round her at Alec when I could. He was silent and I could almost imagine there was steam rising from his skin, rather than from the gravy.

ROISIN

Meanwhile I was tucked in Theo's jacket on the iPad, white with fury. I'd expected to overhear a confrontation, so that long silence came as a frustrating surprise.

ALEC

I'd gotten used to being the one keeping conversations going, when Luka was in one of her worse moods and William was too worried about stepping on thin ice if he opened his mouth. But now that both me and Luka were openly furious with each other there was nothing to say that wouldn't turn into an attack.

Even Legs' singing trailed off after a little while.

William's attempt to spark interest by reading out a cracker joke smacked into a wall of silence.

THEO

I smiled at him. It wasn't his fault.

Finally he put his hands flat on the table and asked, 'Is everything all right?'

ALEC

Letting out a slow breath, I was working up to forcing myself to say *fine* when Cosmo opened his mouth.

'Vegetables taste like the kitchen caught fire, but the rest's great. Thanks, Will.'

THEO

William blinked at the nickname but smiled. He was about to say something when –

ALEC

'You don't have to eat them.' I didn't even look up at him but I couldn't force my mouth to stay closed. The effort was making my teeth ache. 'In fact, you don't even need to be here, so if you're staying, maybe you shouldn't complain about it.'

THEO

I murmured Alec's name under my breath just as Luka said it out loud.

ROISIN

It came clearly through the muffler of Theo's jacket.

'*Alec* – what gives you the right to talk to him like that?'

ALEC

'What gives *him* the right to even be here? I didn't invite him. Did you, *Will?* Pretty sure you'll find the rest of us barely knew he existed, considering the way you hide everything related to him.'

Luka slammed her glass down on the table hard enough to shake it. 'So now it's a problem when I invite someone here *and* a problem when I stay away? Since apparently you get to be judge and jury of whether I'm behaving acceptably, maybe you should tell me what I *can* do.'

Cosmo put his knife and fork down on his plate and quietly folded his hands in his lap while we were going at each other, bowing his head and saying nothing. It pissed me off even more the way he made himself look pious while it seemed like I was attacking him unprovoked. It just made me want to be more vicious. I had to goad some kind of response out of him so she could see what he was really like.

'It's not a problem when you invite *someone* here, just this asshole –'

THEO

William stood up. He and Allegra were the only two at the table completely blindsided by all this. Until dinner everything had seemed civil, if not cosy. 'Alec, that's *enough*,' he said. Allegra climbed into my lap and I wondered if I should put my hands over her ears. If I should cut in and say something.

It felt like my fault, but it didn't feel like it was my place to try and fix it.

ALEC

'*Me?* You think I'm the problem in this situation?'

I'd turned to look at William, as if he should have been able to pick out the heroes and villains in this movie without knowing the plot. Luka twisted to face him too. It's a sibling thing. Any argument needs to be won by a parent figure telling you who's in the right. Anyway, she cut in with her point before William could get out more than a word or two.

'No, apparently the problem is my boyfriend. Since I'm not allowed one for some reason. Do you want to explain that to me, Alec? Everyone's always been fine with you and Theo –'

THEO

With Allegra tucked into the crook of one arm, I'd reached a hand across her chair to catch hold of Alec's, but he snatched it away and stood up. For a minute I thought he'd go straight across the table.

'He is *nothing like Theo!*'

It was what Cosmo had said to me, turned backwards.

ROISIN

It was what Cosmo said Theo told him.

ALEC

And I knew immediately it was the wrong thing. I'd confirmed his lie. But I couldn't – I just couldn't stop. 'Don't even compare them!'

THEO

'*Alec.*'

William and I said it at the same time, both of us standing up. I went to Alec, taking both his hands, as Allegra ran over to her dad and did almost the same thing.

William doesn't thunder. He has a patient, soft voice entirely designed for giving lectures on romantic poetry, but I suspect this was as close as he got. 'I don't know what's going on here but you both need to stop.'

At the same time I was trying to make Alec look at me, murmuring 'Let it go. Let it go for now. It's okay.'

ALEC

'It is *not* okay, for God's sake. I don't want him in the house.'

Luka looked at me. 'Great. One thing we can agree on.'

She reached out to pick up her phone from the table, and paused to put her knife and fork into a neat alignment on her almost untouched plate, as though signalling to some invisible waiter that the meal was done. We were all done.

Except Cosmo. He was still just sitting there, head bowed like an altar boy. The way his head was tilted, only me and Theo would have been able to see the corner of his mouth that had curled up into a smirk.

THEO

'Can I still go with you?' Luka asked him, and he finally moved, jumping to attention at her side and looping his arm around her. Even knowing what I did, it looked chivalrous. And if he could take *me* in, what chance did she have?

He said, 'Of course. Like I said, always.'

ALEC

If both my hands weren't caught up, I don't know what I'd have done. I wanted to hit him and see if he'd look so pleased with himself then. But I looked at Theo. I looked at Allegra, and William.

I sat down and stared at my goddamn gravy until they both moved away from the table.

THEO

Cosmo didn't have much to take with him. He hadn't come with anything. As William muttered some kind of apology, tempered with his clear lack of understanding of what was happening, I stayed on my feet and put myself half in front of Alec. I watched Cosmo all the way to the door. Watched him tell William he was sorry if he'd been intruding, or if he'd said anything that could be taken the wrong way. Watched William reassure him. William said it was just a delicate time.

Luka looked back at me once. That was all. I felt my heart wrench with the things I didn't know how to say and she . . . she looked like she was about to cry.

It felt as though it was all my fault.

ALEC

It wasn't.

ROISIN

Really wasn't. If it hadn't been you he'd have found another place to stick the knife in and twist it.

THEO

I know. Logically I do know that. But it was me. And I could feel it, right between my ribs.

ALEC

And then they were gone.

SIXTEEN

MY NAME IS LUKA: EPISODE 4
'EXIT WOUNDS'

ALEC

Luka put us all on radio silence after that. Until New Year's Eve. Roisin still has the WhatsApp messages on her phone.

ROISIN 13:41

Luka

Luka

Luuuuka

Lulu.

Ulurulu

Looby Lu

Loodles?

ROISIN 14:23

Can't believe you're still leaving me on read

LUKA 15:01

Can't believe you're expecting me to answer to Loodles

ROISIN 15:03

Well apparently, you do

Is this really you? Luka? My Luka? It's been 84 years

LUKA 15:12

Damn it, I guess you're right, I do

And sorry. I know I've been shitty at replying to anything lately. It's been a weird week. I missed your face

ROISIN 15:36

Tell me about it, I went to a donkey funeral

You missed me? I missed YOU. Right down to the nose on your face. Darling, you're my daylight

LUKA 15:41

Don't quote Miles Riva at me. Now I feel worse.

Down to the pores on the nose on your face.

You're back now, though, right?

ROISIN 15:42

Come now, you've never seen me with a visible pore.

Home and dry. Finally. Honestly, don't know how it rains so much in Ireland. It's like the whole country's in a fight with the sky

LUKA 16:11

I wouldn't put it past it. Is Cinderella going to the ball tonight?

ROISIN 16:13

Ball?

You mean Tiaras and Tinnies at Tayeesha's? I'm going. Are you going?

LUKA 16:14

Of course, we talked about it forever ago

Don't know what I'm wearing, though. Having a crisis. What time do you want to come over?

ROISIN 16:15

Oh I didn't think you still were

I'm at Tiwa's is all

Do you want to come by?

LUKA 16:43

Why wouldn't I be?

You're getting ready with Tiwa?

ROISIN 16:48

She asked me so

You can come here?

LUKA 16:52

All my clothes are here. Tiwa's half a foot taller than me. It's not like we can share

It's fine

I just thought we talked about it ages ago

ROISIN 16:53

Maybe, but you've left me on read all week. I didn't know what was happening

Come round to Tiwa's. We've got Prosecco so cheap I swear it's mislabelled lemonade

LUKA 16:55

I can't go round there. I'm getting picked up here

ROISIN 16:56

Picked up?

LUKA 17:11

Cosmo. He's not even going to drink so he can get us home

Ro

No one except Allegra's even talking to me. Can't you just come

ROISIN 17:23

I can't just walk out on Tiwa

I'm sorry

Text me photos. We'll do long-distance dress consultations

You'll look fine. You know you could put on a sack and everyone who saw you would be out hunting for a sack of their very own the next day

Okay?

You can't expect me to just hold plans for you. I didn't know

Luka?

Show me your options

LUKA 17:48

No, it's fine

I'll see you there

ROISIN 18:04

Cosmo's coming

Tonight

Call this a heads-up

Don't you dare ignore my messages, Alec Booth

Will you just TALK to her, please? I think she's hurting

ALEC 18:09

Trust me, she wouldn't like anything I have to say

SEVENTEEN

ROISIN

Tiaras and Tinnies at Tayeesha's is a time-honoured tradition, where 'time-honoured' means she did it for the first time last year and the rest of us decided it was a whole lot better than seeing in the new year freezing in the queue for one of the clubs in town. Tayeesha's place is on the river, and it's one of those eco buildings, all wood and glass. Has to be worth a fortune. I think her dad's something fancy in phones.

None of which anyone cared about, as the systematic process of wrecking the place had already started by the time Tiwa and I showed up. Just after eleven and you already had to step over the bodies of the fallen and the fornicating on the way to the door.

ALEC

We'd got there early. Partly because I needed to get out of the house the second I heard Cosmo would be coming anywhere near it, partly because Theo's got a freaky obsession with turning up to parties at the exact time he's invited, and cannot physically understand how much people hate that.

THEO

It makes no sense, that's why. Why not invite people for when you want them to arrive?

ALEC

Because then they'd get there an hour after you want them.

THEO

Which makes no –

ALEC

Which is *why* you invite them an hour before. Literally everyone knows this, The. And this was a party, a *New Year's* party. People were going to be showing up all the way from ten through to three am.

But no, we got there at nine thirty on the nose and spent half an hour helping line every surface in the kitchen with cans. Soft drinks too, for the Theos of this world.

THEO

Beer tastes disgusting. Change my mind.

ALEC

By ten the music was kicking in and people were throwing themselves around to it. The couches we'd pushed to the edges of the living room were draped with people from school. Most of the crowd were from Luka's year but one of Tay's sisters, Lyta, is in ours so there were a bunch of faces from my class. Unlike most house parties, the sheer sense of occasion meant almost everyone there was making at least some kind of cursory effort when it came to outfits. A jacket over jeans at least. Maybe a bow tie. There was a smattering of suits, while the rugby contingent all showed up in tiaras. And the dresses – not worn by the rugby team, unfortunately – went from barely there to *you shall go to the ball*.

THEO

We'd gone monochrome. Alec in a black suit and me in white – just something from Primark I wouldn't regret having wrecked when I inevitably walked out looking like I'd been to a Holi festival.

ALEC

You looked like the angel you are. Just short of a halo.

THEO

No halo, and no tiara. Neither are quite my kind of thing.
But how often do you have the chance to see in a new decade
as well as a new year – I mean, *every ten years*, but besides
that not being terribly frequent, 2020 was *different*. None
of us will be here to dance our way into 2121, after all. I'm
aware that there's no logical reason that repeating numbers
would make a year unique, and any significance I felt was
just because human brains can't resist reading meaning into a
pattern. But I think that everyone felt as if this one would be
important. Or, perhaps, just that it should be.

Our generation missed 2000. 2020 was supposed to be
our big year.

Though I still wasn't seeing it in with a tiara.

ALEC

I had a tiara. Kind of. It was one of those basic golden-plastic
headbands with the year on. I don't know if *I* felt 2020 was
going to be special. I guess until the week before I might've
hoped it would be *better*, at least, but the whole fight with
Luka and the fact she was barely speaking to me now had
stamped that idea down already.

I felt like it was going to be strange. A whole decade I wouldn't have a mom for. The first without her. Those are the kind of markers you notice but you don't talk about because it would kill everybody else's mood.

I guess . . . I guess I was going into it just hoping we'd all survive. Which, that night, didn't seem like it'd be too much to ask.

ROISIN

Tiwa and I had gone the ballgowns route. She was wearing the same dress she'd bought to go out as Belle for Halloween. A bright yellow concoction, with skirts that swept out around her like a dome. Her hair and skin glowed, clear and dark. Disney or not, there was no doubting she was a princess.

I went with blue for my outfit. Luka was right – it's my colour. Especially in winter, when I'm embracing pale and interesting instead of trying to tan myself into something a little less ghostly. I'd ordered the dress from one of those discount sites you see on Insta that are so cheap they're probably money laundering operations, and by some miracle it turned out to have been made for me. From the V-neck to the mermaid cut that skimmed every curve, I adored the thing. It was a no-apologies kind of an outfit. I wore that dress like it was an announcement.

But I didn't feel right.

Turning up to a party not knowing what last-minute

thing Luka had picked up to stun everyone in, let alone if she'd even *be* there made everything seem off-kilter. Like that party game you play as a babe where you have to cut up a chocolate bar with a knife and fork while wearing oven gloves: a simple, obvious thing made more difficult than it should be.

Now, I'm not saying I should have dropped everything and ditched Ti the moment Luka asked me to. I'd been messaging the girl all week with as much response as I'd have got from chatting up a brick wall and it wasn't fair to expect me to make no plans at all. It wouldn't have been fair on Tiwa to drop the ones I had with her all of a sudden either. She's just as much our friend. Most days it wouldn't have been a fuss for Luka to come over to Ti's anyway.

The only problem I could guess at was that boy. I was bracing myself for being nice to him because I know how this sort of thing works – I mean, I thought I knew. The worse you talk about someone's toxic-waste monster of a boyfriend the more determined they get to drink his poison. So I'd be sweet to him, to both of them, and give Cosmo the chance to show his own backside.

That was the plan.

ALEC

My plan was to avoid them. Not completely selfishly – I still hadn't figured out how to talk to Luka about any of what had happened at Christmas. The couple of times we'd been in the same room together all it took was me drawing in a breath for her to look at me like I'd drawn a knife at the same time and she was waiting to see what I stabbed at next.

I couldn't deal with her thinking I *wanted* to hurt her over all this so, after a couple of weak attempts to discuss it, I just stopped trying.

When I was less angry. That's what I told Theo. When I knew I could put my side without blowing up. I'd talk to her then.

I'd wrecked Christmas. I didn't want to destroy her New Year's, too.

THEO

The guilt was incredible. Alec and Luka's relationship had been halfway back to normal before Christmas. If I hadn't said anything perhaps it would never have gone so sour. And I'm perfectly used to ignoring the ignorant things people say. Why I didn't just do it then, I'll never know.

I think it's because . . .

Because I felt safer with Alec than I've ever felt before, anywhere. I'd always felt safe in that house. I desperately didn't want to lose that feeling.

Still. If I'd just ignored him . . .

ALEC

Remember what you're always telling me about shoulda, woulda, couldas, sweetheart? There's no point in dwelling on them. I'm glad you didn't ignore it. What happened wasn't your fault. It wasn't mine. He walked in that Christmas determined to destroy things.

ROISIN

Just like he did that night. New Year's Eve. Mark and Tiwa were the ones to see him arrive, and even they could tell.

TIWA OJO, 17, FRIEND

I had known something was going on. Ordinarily Roisin and Luka are joined at the hip, so having just one of them over had been strange. Although this had become more common, recently. For a month or so Roisin and I had spent more time just the two of us, as Luka vanished more and more.

I remember telling Roisin it was as if the tables were turned.

ROISIN

I sent a message to Luka saying: *I'm here, just look for the belle of the ball. Or actually, the belle of the ball is who I'm here with and she's going to abandon me in T-minus 3, 2, 1 . . .*

Mark's here. There she goes.

TIWA

It's a long-running joke that I only have friends when Mark isn't in the room. Hardly my fault when he's not from our school and I can only see him when my parents think I'm with someone else.

ROISIN

Absolutely no one holds it against her, and Mark's a prince, but when she's with him Ti simply cannot multitask. I knew I'd be a single pringle at that party a heartbeat after arriving, so I wasn't going to complain. Besides, being at a party alone means leaving with new friends. Or that's what I told myself. Determined not to have a terrible time, I decamped to the kitchen, where everyone goes when they've no one else to talk to.

TIWA

Luka arrived in the eye of a thunderstorm, if the look on the face of the boy with her was anything to go by. Roisin had given me his name and a short history. I knew that Ro didn't approve, but only a little about why. Mark and I were talking in the hallway and I raised a hand to greet her, but she didn't see anything but him. Of course not – he was in her face the whole time.

I don't recall every word of it, but he was speaking to her as though she'd dragged him into the party by the hair. Throwing a tantrum my baby nephews would be proud of. About alcohol, for the most part. He was saying, 'How long are we supposed to stay here?' and, 'If we stay here, I can't drink. It's New Years Eve and you don't want me to be able to have a drink?'

She had her hand on his arm, reassuring him, but she looked upset. 'If we can just stay for a bit? I won't drink either – it's been ages since I've seen anyone, Cosmo.'

I murmured to Mark that perhaps we should step in.

MARK RILEY, 18, FRIEND

It was a weird place for a domestic. Like, I know how things can go after a few drinks but most people don't start out the night at each other's throats. Ti was worried so I turned round to watch them. I wanted that lad, Cosmo, to know someone had an eye on him, but he didn't seem to pick it up. He was going on at her, at Luka, like: 'It's all about you, though, isn't it? These are all your friends. It's like you didn't even think about who I wanted to see.'

TIWA

She looked so apologetic. I wasn't used to seeing that
expression on her. She said, 'I didn't think you had plans' as
quietly as a mouse.

MARK

Yeah, I didn't like the way she looked like something was her
fault. The way he was snarling at her wasn't right. I suppose
in some lights the stuff he was coming out with could have
looked flattering. He was saying, 'Maybe I just wanted to
spend the night with you, did you think of that? Just you.
We spent Christmas with your family and look what
happened. Maybe it would have actually been a nice day if
we'd just spent that together, too. Your family didn't even
want you there, when I do. I always want you with me,
Luka. I don't understand why you don't want to spend time
with me after everything I do. I drove you here, didn't I? And
now I can't even have a drink.'

TIWA

Mark moved at the same time that I did but in a different
direction. I bustled straight into the two of them, the smile
bright and wide on my face, and wrapped my arms round
that girl. '*Luka,* here you are after what feels like forever.
And you look beautiful, of course.'

MARK

I just put a hand on his arm. The one she wasn't holding.
'You all right, mate?'

It wasn't much, wasn't anything really, but the fire went
right out of him as soon as he was looking at me, not her. I
thought it might.

TIWA

She was telling me she hadn't made much effort, shooting
glances at him. But that couldn't have been nerves, surely.
Luka Booth, concerned over how someone else thought
she looked? Unheard of. Roisin often said that was her
superpower: appearance-related invulnerability. Where the
rest of us fretted and fussed, Luka simply arrived and was.

We should never have believed it would be so simple for
her. For anyone.

She tugged at the hem of her dress: black, close-fitted
and dotted with tiny silver stars. Perfect on her. 'I was in a
rush – just grabbed the first thing.'

That sounded like the Luka I knew. But then, another
of those looks in Cosmo's direction.

I tugged her arm and she was free of him. 'Come on,
we'll find Roisin before someone convinces her up on to a
table.'

ROISIN

Honestly, you do your finest TikTok routine along the picnic tables at *one* barbeque and they'll never let you live it down. I'd moved on from the kitchen by then, though. Like I said, being alone at parties is a perfect way to pick someone up.

Unfortunately I'd picked up the human equivalent of a persistent cough. Just could not get rid of the boy.

ALEC

The space downstairs was getting rowdy. It was a combination of having no room to move without crashing into someone, and a playlist that would've challenged anyone to keep their limbs inside their own vehicle. Theo and I vacated when it became less about dancing and more trying to avoid accidentally being punched in the face.

THEO

Upstairs was a different kind of risky, however. Trying doors up there was an assault course in finding out which of your friends hooking up would leave the worst mental scars. We compromised.

ALEC

We sat on the stairs.

Huddled in with Lindy Brinton and Ellis Robins, and a couple of the rugby boys who'd taken part in a chugging challenge earlier and now couldn't walk straight. Aside from people stumbling up or down once every couple of minutes, it was the safest place in the house.

THEO

Not exactly conducive to quiet conversation, though.

ALEC

Which is why when Roisin's voice came from behind the wall, it was obvious she was *really* trying to make herself heard.

THEO

It's never the *best* sign when the first words you hear of someone's conversation are

ROISIN

'I said *no*.'

For his benefit, I was saying it again three or four times as loudly. For the tape the boy in question was Alfie bloody Newly. His dad's a Tory on the local council. He's tall, sleek, blond, and that night he was unbelievably wasted.

ALEC

Alfie Newly is stupidly pretty.

THEO

With a reputation for being pretty stupid.

ROISIN

Careful – I've a problem with his methods, not his taste.

ALEC

Rosh, you were a vision. Nobody would've been stupid for wanting to get with you.

ROISIN

Well, thank you for that. And of course, the problem wasn't his wanting to get with me so much as *where* he wanted to get me. He'd spent a good five minutes insisting I should go back to his house with him. His parents were on a boat on the Southbank, apparently. He was swearing up and down that if I'd just go home with him nothing was going to happen. He wouldn't push it. He just wanted to *talk*. All of which, of course, sounded entirely unsuspicious, along with being a wildly boring time if it were true.

So I said, 'Alfie, you're pushing it *now*. I'm not going back to your place tonight, and if you can't demonstrate at least a vague notion of how to take no for an answer then I'll not be going *anywhere* with you. Literally ever.'

THEO

Alec and I climbed over the others on the stairs and rounded the corner to intervene just in time to see that you had it handled.

ALEC

Too-keen Alfie was already saying his sorries, backing off and trailing away toward the dance floor, looking forlornly over his shoulder and promising to be back once he'd got you another drink.

THEO

It would have been almost sweet if you could overlook how creepy he'd been just moments before.

ROISIN

Which I couldn't, even if it seemed he had the message now. I turned and slung an arm around two sets of shoulders.

THEO

We wrapped ours round her waist.

ROISIN

'All right, boys. For your next trick you're going to make the lady vanish.'

ALEC

But we didn't.

THEO

There was no next trick.

ALEC

Because that's when she appeared.

EIGHTEEN

ROISIN

Tiwa swept her through the chaos in the room towards us like it was all part of a waltz. It was like watching one of those period ballroom scenes dropped into the middle of a club. Luka looked somehow smaller than she should have, although maybe that was an effect of being caught up in Ti's enormous yellow skirts. She was dressed in black, and smiling, and blessedly alone.

ALEC

And in that instant I knew my own plan was fucked. Avoiding her would've been one thing, but can you imagine how bad it would have been if I'd turned and walked away? I wasn't about to do that, even if he'd been with her. And he *wasn't*. Maybe he hadn't come. Maybe they'd broken up. She was smiling. I smiled too.

THEO

I admit it took everything I could muster not to wallflower my way off somewhere, perhaps find a secluded spot behind everyone where the glare of attention would be kept well off me. But, as Alec said, once we'd been spotted the prospect of walking away was far more horrendous than any alternative. I let my hand loosely circle his wrist behind Roisin's back as we faced Luka – a three-person chorus line.

ROISIN

'You look like you're about to break into a round of the cancan.' Luka's smile was a fragile, hopeful thing. I guessed she was worried how Alec would be with her, as if I wasn't ready to stamp on his foot if I needed to.

ALEC

Hey. I was on my best behaviour. 'You caught us – we're the entertainment for the evening.'

ROISIN

I peeled away from the pair of them to hug her. 'They're idiot boys helping me avoid another idiot boy and I'm grateful for it. Would you believe what Jai Daunt said about Alfie being obsessed with me turned out to be true? I'm so glad you're here. Let's go and sit down – are you coming, Ti? With three of us I'd lay bets on our chances in any fight for sofa space.'

ALEC

'Just three of you?' I raised my eyebrows. Roisin pressed her foot lightly over mine. 'I mean – just the three of you. Of course. Sounds cosy.'

ROISIN

I just didn't want her to have to be on her guard all night. And if something had happened with Cosmo, I knew she'd only say if we were alone. When it came to Alec just then, she was always going to be feeling like she had a point to prove.

'Girls only, no boys allowed.'

TIWA

There was one boy in particular I had come specifically to see. This whole thing was not my relationship drama.

'But Mark's waiting . . .' I checked Roisin's glare and sighed. 'All right, just us three.'

THEO

'That's right. I'm so glad we're all on the same page,' Roisin cooed. I don't think she knows just how much like a mob boss she can sound when she's getting things done. I can't fault Alfie Newly's interest. It can be kind of hot.

Anyway, Roisin stepping forward had left Alec and I holding hands in the middle of the room. Untangling our fingers, I tucked mine back into my pockets and nodded at Luka. She nodded back at me. We both smiled. It felt like . . .

If not forgiveness, it felt like a start.

ROISIN

Elbows locked with the girls, we marched away grandly to bully someone off a sofa. Luka was laughing and as I stopped and asked Dean Jones if he'd become one with the sofa somehow, 'cos he'd been sat on the thing so long, she leaned in to speak against my ear.

'I need to hear all about the donkey.'

'Do you mean Alfie or Figgy Pudding?' I asked, tugging both her and Ti down with me as Dean fled.

THEO

'Okay, that wasn't awful,' I said once the music was back to creating a sound barrier between us and the girls. 'Why do you think he isn't here? Wait – I need to go to the bathroom first, debrief after. But are you all right?'

ALEC

I laughed and darted in to dot a kiss to his cheek while no one was looking. 'I think I'm okay. Go get in the queue before you're *not* okay. I'll be in the kitchen.'

THEO

Rule one of needing to pee at parties. Start queuing the moment you even begin to think you might need to go. Preferably half an hour before that.

As I got upstairs and found a line snaking round the corner, crowded with people who looked like they were enduring various levels of pain, I became aware I'd made a grave mistake.

ROISIN

It had been a mistake thinking she was here alone. It quickly became clear Cosmo was lurking somewhere in the depths of this party, and she was only away from him because of Ti. She asked me if I'd seen him.

TIWA

I hadn't considered it was so important to get her away from her boyfriend. It just seemed the natural thing to do – allow them a little time to cool off and they could both enjoy the party. When Mark and I argue, ignoring him for a while always works for me.

'He won't be far,' I said, thinking I was reassuring, 'Mark was giving him a tour.'

Looking around the room, I couldn't see a trace of my own boyfriend anywhere, so with a sigh I settled to hear what this Cosmo saga was about.

'You said he and your brother don't get on?'

ROISIN

While I was slouching and Tiwa was arranged to not crease up her dress, Luka sat bolt upright on the edge of a cushion. I've never been reminded so much of a mouse in a nature documentary, standing at attention, trying to catch a hint of a dark, feathered cloud wheeling in the sky.

If I could figure out how that boy had made her so nervous, I'd catch and pluck him.

'Alec really upset him at Christmas.' She corrected herself: 'He upset both of us. I ended up leaving . . . which I hated. I know it upset Allegra, but we couldn't stay there. And since then – he tried to tell me Cosmo said these things I *know* he wouldn't have –'

TIWA

'How do you know?' I admit that I was interested then.

I could see Roisin frowning at her, and Roisin is one of the most trusting people I know. She didn't trust this Cosmo. 'I mean, how do you know what Cosmo says is true and what Alec says isn't?'

She knew her brother best, after all. It could be he was often like this. But she paused for too long for her words to have any certainty. 'Cosmo told me about it first. And he wasn't the one acting like an asshole at the meal.'

ROISIN

'But what if Cosmo was just covering his tracks?'

I leaned forward, unable to let this opportunity go too easily. I couldn't tell her I'd listened to their whole conversation or she'd be too up in arms over that to hear another word from me. Besides, what I'd heard proved nothing about what had really been said that day. Technically I didn't know any more than she did. But if I could only make her question this a *little* . . .

'If he knew he'd said something, wouldn't he want to get his story in first? You said yourself, that's what makes it seem real. But what if that's just what he wants you to think?'

TIWA

It was too much.

ROISIN

I could see that right away. I came over as desperate to make him look bad, and before I knew it she had her eyes narrowed my way. '*What if it's what he wants me to think?*'

It wasn't so much the anger as how hurt she looked that got to me. I couldn't stand it.

'God, Alec's got you drinking the Kool-Aid, hasn't he? You sound like a conspiracy theorist. But no, that's fine. It's great, Rosh. You think I'd like the kind of person who'd not only *say* a thing like that but be so deliberate about it that he'd have his lies planned in advance? *Seriously?* I don't know why everyone's so pissed off about someone liking me for once.'

TIWA

Roisin bowed her head. I watched her jaw work a moment before she spoke. 'Maybe because *we've* liked you for ages. And you don't seem happy.'

Luka looked at me. I nodded my head.

Her voice, when she spoke, was completely hollow. Empty. 'Well, I don't know when I seemed happy before. I don't know what the problem is, Rosh. You're not missing me. You've got other things to do.'

ROISIN

She stood up with me hot on her heels, because I was not letting her walk off on that note. 'That is *not* fair, I've texted every day –'

'You've been *fine*,' she said, looking between me and Tiwa like tonight was our trial and conviction all in one. 'He was right. We didn't need to come.'

ALEC

In the kitchen, I wasn't surprised to find that the beer wall I'd helped build up earlier had been laid siege to. There were a few scattered cans to choose from, a selection of cheap wine boxes if you wanted to be fancy, and plastic bottles of emergency cider that had clearly been recruited as back-up from the all-night garage. I was just trying to pick a can that didn't look like it had been shaken up for a prank, when I swear I felt the hair at the back of my neck stand on end.

'Does he not like holding your hand?'

Cosmo leaned over me and tossed a crumpled beer can into a stack of them on the floor, then opened a fresh one with a crack and hiss right by my ear.

He stayed where he was, half a step behind me. I didn't look round, but I put down the bottle and let my hands grip the edge of the countertop to keep them from doing anything else.

'I just saw him drop it as soon as anyone was looking

at you out there. Like you had the plague. Does he not like people knowing?'

The plan to avoid him hadn't worked. Ignoring him wasn't going to work either, unless I wanted to shove my way past. I turned and we were practically nose to nose.

'Knowing *what*? Is my relationship really the only thing you can find to pick at? If you're asking what I think you are, everyone who matters here already knows I'm gay.'

THEO

That's the position I found them in as I popped my head round the doorway. If I hadn't known any better I might have thought it was the prelude to a kiss. The easy request for Alec to get me a drink without anyone else's backwash in it stuttered in my throat.

ALEC

Cosmo's gaze slid across to where Theo stood in the door. Then he turned back to me and he smirked. 'Are you, though?'

I pushed away from the counter, past him, and stalked toward the door.

THEO

Towards me. I put my hand out, then thought better of it – of what it might make him say. Before Alec could reach out to take it, I tucked both hands into my pockets.

I didn't know why, then, but Cosmo laughed.

ALEC

And that's what made me turn back round and punch him.

THEO

The drink in his hand hit the wall and showered the room in sticky droplets at the same time that Cosmo stumbled back and kicked his way through the heap of discarded cans. There was an instant reaction from the other people loitering in corners of the kitchen. A couple who'd been tucked into the curve of the breakfast island, wrapped round each other, ducked and yelped. A girl who'd come dressed as Barbie for no reason I could understand screamed, while a couple of the rugby lads approached Alec with their hands out, palms down, muttering 'Whoa, whoa, mate.'

ALEC

'Whoa, whoa' never diffused any situation I've ever heard of. As other people were drawn in by the noise, Cosmo surged forward and had me back against the countertop, his hands in my shirt. I could feel other people reaching in, trying to push or pull us away from each other, but not before I got my elbow into the centre of his chest.

I pushed forward. He fell back and pulled me down with him, and then we were both on the floor. Knees and elbows. He got on top of me somehow and I was trying to kick him off when I saw his fist coming down.

Someone caught his hand before it could fall, and before I could think I'd raised myself up to retaliate and someone caught mine too.

THEO

As the room filled up I got pushed forward from where I'd been frozen until then. I tried to get through to Alec but there were too many moving parts in the way. A net of arms seemed to be reaching in to get them off each other.

'*ALEC.*'

It wasn't my voice. It was Luka's.

ALEC

She came into a tableau of Cosmo being pulled away from me, across the floor, while two people had hold of my elbow, keeping my fist still but stuck in the air.

Cosmo wiped his wrist across his mouth, smearing

167

away the remains of the beer I'd spattered across his face. He might as well have been wiping blood from his mouth. Luka looked between us, him then me. 'How could you?'

She pushed her way through. People let her, eager for the next episode in the drama. I could see some of them getting out their phones, starting to film thirty seconds too late to catch the main event. She crouched down with him, shutting me out of her line of sight.

THEO

'I'm sorry. I'm so sorry he's like this. You were right – we shouldn't have come.'

I was still forcing my way through to Alec as Luka and Cosmo passed me on their way to the door. He smiled at me. She didn't even look my way.

ALEC

I'd got to my knees by then. Should've called after her. Should've said something, made my case. But I didn't know what to say. I didn't know anything at all.

THEO

I got to him, put my hands out, a hand at the side of his face.

ALEC

I pulled away.

THEO

I –

ALEC

I'm sorry.

THEO

I know.

ALEC

But I couldn't be touched by anyone just then. I got up and I walked away.

TIWA

I found Mark by the front door, in the hall almost where I'd left him. Alec was with him. This time I had Roisin in tow, her make-up newly fixed and a series of wild rumours on our heels.

'What happened?'

MARK

'I was just telling Alec. I missed everything but the exit, but it seemed like they'd made up, at least. Had their arms wrapped round each other, her apologising and him stroking her hair, saying it was all right, not her fault.'

Ti tucked herself in against me and it was seeming like things were getting set right again.

Roisin grabbed Alec's face in both her hands. 'I heard he *hit* you.'

ALEC

I still wasn't in the mood to be touched but I let her.

'I hit him.'

ROISIN

He gave me a grim, half-proud smile.

I tutted. 'Alec, you can't always be stealing my thunder. And they're gone?'

Mark nodded. 'I guess he's driving her home.'

ALEC

They went on talking, I think. Roisin unstuck her fingers from my cheeks and turned to ask something else, but the world had gone to white noise in my head.

'Driving?'

I thought about the empty can he'd thrown on to the pile. The second that he'd half downed in a few long swallows before I sent it flying, each one of them an ugly glug beside my ear.

I wondered how many there had been before that.

'He was driving her?'

ROISIN

Mark shrugged. 'That was what the fight was about when they got here so I assume –'

He was cut off as Alec raced out and down the driveway, pulling out his phone. But the two of them were long gone.

NINETEEN

EXCERPTS FROM A LETTER FROM LUKA
5 JANUARY 2020, SOME PARTS LOST DUE TO
WATER DAMAGE

Alec's name came up on my phone over and over, the whole
drive. I just wasn't in the mood for his apologies or his reasons
or him telling me that what I'm doing is wrong. He lost his last
chances with me in that kitchen.

I was expecting Cosmo to be mad about it, like he had
every right to be, but he was . . . warm. Pleased. Happy to
be with me, in a way he hadn't been all evening. I should've
listened to him all along – things really are so much better
when it's just us. I thought Roisin had actually wanted to see
me tonight, but it was just another chance for someone to tell
me I should be alone.

Well, I've had enough of that, Mom. This last year's felt
like enough loneliness for a lifetime.

Ro's name interrupted the constant buzz of Alec trying

to call me.

So I turned off my phone, and asked Cosmo if we could go back to my house before his.

THEO

Roisin came and told me. They'd both tried calling and calling, but Alec wouldn't stop. No one had a number plate – no one even knew what car Cosmo was driving, and how likely was it that the police were going to act on a report of someone driving after a can and a half on New Year's Eve? There would be far bigger things to worry about.

LETTER FROM LUKA

He tensed up before I explained, but then he slid an arm round me with that smile that always undoes any hope I have of not falling in love with him. He pressed kisses to the side of my face as he drove, while I kept reminding him to keep his eyes on the road.

At the house the lights were all out. I knew neither William or Allegra would've been able to keep their eyes open until midnight. So we crept in and he helped me empty my room as silently and swiftly as I could.

THEO

I found Alec in the road. The rain that was just starting already flecked his hair and gave his skin a strange glow under the street lights.

Taking a breath, I risked putting a hand on his shoulder. He didn't pull away.

'You can't fix everything. Not tonight.'

Behind us the house erupted into sudden cheers and whoops and I realised I'd forgotten the supposed purpose of the night. Inside they were welcoming in a new year, perhaps a better one.

He drew in a sudden, noisy breath, and turned to wrap himself round me, his head buried against my shoulder. I closed my arms round his waist and pretended I couldn't feel him shake.

'Not tonight.'

LETTER FROM LUKA

We brought the last bag down, a few clothes folded over my arm, and I shut the front door behind me. As I left, I imagined a thick blanket of snow falling behind me and wiping all traces away. As if I'd never been there, and nothing bad had ever happened. But there was nothing but the grey, drizzling rain.

Cosmo stopped me in it, just before we got back into the car, checking his watch.

Funny, I'd forgotten what the night even was.

'Starshine, you just made my whole year,' he said, and he tilted my head up and kissed me into a new one.

TWENTY

MY NAME IS LUKA: EPISODE 5
'GROW THROUGH WHAT YOU GO THROUGH'

LETTER FROM LUKA
15 JANUARY 2020

Dear Mom,

I almost decided to get fancy and write this one like a formal letter, address in the top corner and everything. Why? Because I'm writing to you from my house. The official (new) residence of Luka K. Booth, Esquire.

It's happened insanely fast. Just over one week ago I was sitting on the saggy mattress of the creaky bed in Cosmo's tiny musty room in the flatshare, watching him play his way through some of the new games I got him for Christmas. *This* week I'm sitting on a saggy mattress on the floor of the flat we moved into two days ago – just him and me.

Next week we should have a bed and a new mattress too. And plates and dishes and spoons and pans and sponges and toilet cleaner and all the stuff you don't realise you're going to need when you get your own place, because at the old one they've always been there. I'm adulting like my life depends on it, but the whole thing's been a revelation.

Firstly, that I could afford it. I always figured the money you left had to be held back for university, but talking to Cosmo I realised that student finance loans are practically free money, and it was crazy I wasn't going to take one. It makes more sense *not* to pay for studying upfront. Which meant I could give Cosmo the money to put down the deposit, and cover everything we need to get set up in style. Then he can pay the rent from his wages, and I'll get a job too, until September when that loan comes through.

It means I'll need to study closer to home than I was planning, but it doesn't matter where I go so much as who I'm with, and I just want to be with him.

I can't believe we have our own place.

We did a wild IKEA run, filling two carts and then half unfilling them again to remove all the pointless things we'd picked up just because we could. But I got some planters, and on the way back I stopped at the market for plants to put in them. We're on the third floor, so no garden, and the windows only open halfway, but I'm going to be a plant mom, Mom.

I got two polka-dotted begonias, and a baby monstera with its new leaves only half unfurled. A dragon tree, a hanging neon Pothos with luminous green leaves like a highlighter pen, and a tiny rubber plant about as big as the palm of my hand.

And a bag of compost to pot them in, in the sink to catch all the mess. Cosmo says I'm building an army.

I wanted something to take care of. The building rules say no pets, but if I give each plant a name it's almost the same, right?

I'm thinking of Heather and Veronica for the begonias. But do you think Heather'll get confused being named after a different type of plant?

This isn't my usual kind of letter to you, I know. I know I must sound crazy. But you know why?

Mom, I think I'm happy.

And Cosmo's being amazing. I can't believe we've officially been 'together' less than a month. It feels like we always have been, somehow. Or maybe just that there was always a space in me where he was supposed to fit.

He makes me want to be a better person. To make an effort every day, when before I could have lain in bed and let the days drift past me without noticing. I get dressed every day, because I don't want him to see me slobbing around in my PJs. I'm even wearing make-up. Just a little. Not my usual thing but he talks about how other women look so put together with some on – not trowelled on, like Roisin (his words, and I told him off for them) but subtle.

And I know he appreciates it when I do.

I mean, he *really* shows me.

I've never felt this beautiful in my life. I've never felt so important in someone else's world, like it would be an emptier place without me. Except, perhaps, with you.

What do you think about Toothless, for the dragon tree?

So I'm happy, Mom. I'm happy. I'm going to give myself a couple more days like this and then take the risk of replying to Roisin's text messages, because that's the one thing missing. Other people. As much as I think Cosmo might be happy if it was just us – and maybe I could be too – I've been thinking about her. Maybe I rushed into being angry with her. I know it must seem like everything moved too fast. But I think, of all people, she'll be happy for me.

I'll message her before mocks start next week, so there's no awkward moments when we're back at school.

So, Heather, Veronica, Toothless. Sully for the monstera? Two left to name. I'm painting a sign to put on the window behind them. It says *Grow through what you go through*. I think it's something both I and the plants can relate to.

I'll update you on all forms of growth next time.

Love,
Luka

TWENTY-ONE

DAVID TANG, HEAD OF HISTORY

We did have to call Luka in for a meeting after the first day of mocks took place without her in attendance. With Mrs Critchlow – Luka's usual head of year – out on maternity leave, it fell to me to try to keep track.

Of course, every year there are students who don't turn up for mock exams. For some of them the very word 'mock' seems to suggest that they treat it as a joke. Some students view study leave as an extension to their holiday time. And of course we always have cases of sickness, all too often turning out to be chronic cases of nerves that keep students away.

Luka Booth should have had nothing to be nervous about. Since she joined my class two years ago her work had been of an extremely high quality, even when her attitude failed to match the same standard, and I'm told this was consistent through most of her other classes. Overall she worked hard and was diligent and thoughtful.

Beyond that – in spite of everything – she's always struck me, simply, as a nice girl.

We were all aware of the difficulty of her circumstances, and to some of us the change in her attitude wasn't a great surprise . . . I lost my own father when I was five. Too young to remember much about it, but I do recall the thick layer of grief in the house. Something heavy that settled on every surface – on my mother's back – for years afterwards. Grief isn't something that attends to a schedule or is easily overcome.

Her attendance had been spotty for months. And while I may not always have been patient while listening to clear lies and excuses, when I reached out, it was with no intention to offer anything but support. I called her stepfather.

WILLIAM

New Year's Day had been a blind panic.

I'd been aware of the atmosphere in the house – hard to miss the sensation of running smack into a wall of ice when attempting to communicate with either of the teenagers with whom I shared a space. It was all the more obvious, then, when both of them had absented the place.

I thought it not unexpected, at first. Allegra woke me with the news that Luka and Alec hadn't come home, and I pictured them asleep on the floor at someone's party. I'd spent enough morning-afters like that myself, you realise. I didn't come out of the womb in a tweed jacket with leather patches sewn on to my elbows.

ALLEGRA

Daddy groaned and rubbed his hands all over his face and said, 'Happy New Year, darling. Pancakes?'

I'd been worried, but you can't be worried and have pancakes too.

WILLIAM

Alec, I thought, would have gone home with Theo, whose family had been gradually opening up to their nascent relationship in a way I could only find encouraging.

Luka – well. I admit I found less to encourage me about her situation. Alex had laid out for me what he believed were mitigating circumstances for the episode on Christmas Day, but without speaking to her I tried to keep an open mind. As ever I thought it best to give her the freedom to make her own mistakes and return of her own accord.

My mindset on that changed somewhat on finding the door to her bedroom swung wide and the room itself ransacked. Essentially empty. When children pass perhaps sixteen you tend to stop worrying about them running away from home. You shouldn't.

ALLEGRA

We didn't get pancakes. Daddy was on the phone to Alec, shouting, and then on the phone just listening to it ring with his head in his hand. I didn't like it. It was a bad day.

ALEC

It was a bad day.

I came home mid-morning and helped William put Luka's room back into some sort of order, just in case it turned out that leaving with half her belongings had been some sort of prank, or accident. Just in case she changed her mind.

It felt like I was burning up inside, but there was nowhere for the fire to go. She wouldn't answer her phone. None of us knew where Cosmo actually lived.

WILLIAM

Alec asked if we should report her as a missing person. Quite apart from the general lack of concern with which I suspected the story of an absent eighteen-year-old would be treated by the police, she wasn't missing. That was the absurdity of it, of course. We knew very well where she was. But not *where she was*.

ALEC

The next day I wrote her an email calling her a selfish bitch. I posted it to my Facebook status too, and tagged her. She didn't view it.

The day after that I took the post down, ignoring the confused messages and emojis left by assorted distant relatives. I emailed her to say I was sorry, and that if she'd just come back we could work things out.

I said she didn't even have to come back. She could just tell us where she was.

I said she could just reply.

WILLIAM

Days passed without a word. It felt very much like a punishment for all my past failings with her.

ALLEGRA

We went to see Mummy.

WILLIAM

I visited Gabriela daily, ostensibly with the excuse of seeing if Luka had been there too. In reality I brought my guilt with me and laid it down with my wife like wilted blooms. The one thing I should still have been able to do, after failing to save her, was keep her children safe.

ALEC

And then Tiwa called to say she'd had a reply to a text.

We'd all been texting. All of us getting left on read for eternity. I wasn't getting read at all. I don't know why she responded to Ti in the end and not Roisin, or Shauna, or Theo, or me. The message sent to her had just said, *Everyone is worried. Please just let us know you're okay.*

And her reply said: *I'm good.*

And then, after a few minutes: *Tell everyone I'm fine. See you at school.*

WILLIAM

It was a relief, if a small one.

ALEC

It just made me more mad. Because up to then I could just be worried. I could be scared for the sister I loved, who'd vanished.

Once I knew she was okay, all I had left was to be angry that she'd abandoned us.

And then she didn't show at school.

DAVID TANG

The information Luka's stepfather was able to give was both scant and telling. In a moment it changed her status with the school from deliberate truant to a safeguarding concern.

I sent a letter to her house, where I knew she wasn't, as a formality, requesting a discussion with her and with a personal assurance that, in extenuating circumstances, allowances for retakes could be made.

We questioned her classmates. Futilely as it turned out – they'd all already been spoken to by her brother.

I was also worried about her brother. The boy had been holding his head above water admirably from what I could see, but how long he might stay that way with all the additional weights being slung around his neck, I couldn't say. I asked his year head to keep me informed. And I asked that I be told if Luka was seen at the school in any capacity at all.

I didn't hear from her again.

TWENTY-TWO

ROISIN

We called it Operation SCUM. Seeking Cosmo Ugh Men.

THEO

I thought it was Secret Cosmo Undercover Mission.

ROISIN

Look, exactly what the words were doesn't matter. It was the acronym that counted. SCUM. We were on a mission to track Cosmo down. Secretly. And undercover. And, yes, okay, maybe you were right about the original operation title.

THEO

Mhm. It was only secret and undercover because we'd decided not to tell Alec. Not because we didn't think that he'd want to know, or that he couldn't handle it but –

ROISIN

We thought he couldn't handle it.

THEO

He just had so much to deal with already. I knew he never stopped thinking about her, and if he ever managed to then the constant questions – from friends, from school, from Allegra, would just set him off again. Really, I didn't want to weigh him down with one more thing.

ROISIN

And he'd have treated it like a military operation.

THEO

He'd have taken it so very seriously. Not that we weren't – but we only had a limited amount of information and we knew it might not work out. He was so desperate for something to hope for that I knew he'd have thrown everything into trying to track Cosmo down. He wouldn't have *slept* until we found him and if we didn't . . . Honestly, I dread to think. I so wanted to give that hope to him but couldn't bear also being the one to strip it away. It didn't help that I still felt responsible.

ROISIN

Both of you felt responsible, Theo. William felt responsible.
I felt responsible, for pity's sake, and I'd at least managed to
stop short of punching anyone in the face. Luka disappearing
made everyone question where they'd gone wrong. It was like
we were trying to pick one specific cloud out of a storm and
blame it for causing the flood.

THEO

But it's true that the guilt made everything harder. Alec and
I didn't talk about it much. I suspect we both imagined we'd
find our darkest thoughts mirrored in each other if we looked
too long. I was sure he must have been thinking how much
easier this last year would have been without me in it.

Not that it could ever have been easy, of course. But I'd
been . . . in the way. By trying to be there for him I'd moved
into the space where Luka would otherwise have been.
Should have been. If he hadn't had me, they'd have had each
other.

ROISIN

You do talk a load of old balls, you know.

THEO

It's how it felt. And I've no doubt he thought I blamed him
for throwing that punch. He never did tell me exactly what it
was over.

We still saw each other just as much. Neither of us was
accusatory. It was just . . . quieter between us. He'd insist
he was fine if I ever asked, and while I knew how deeply
wounded he was, I was hardly going to push him to bleed
for me. We filled the time with films and games – general
nothingness. But I could feel the tension in him, under his
skin all the time. He felt like a clenched fist.

I'd stay over when I could, which wasn't as often as I
wanted. My parents kept reminding me to focus on my work.
I think I started to drive them crazy, but it mattered that I
saw him as much as I was able.

It mattered because, while Alec would never say he was
anything but fine if you asked him straight out, sometimes –
just sometimes – when the lights were out and I was halfway
to sleeping, I'd feel him press his face into my shoulder and
the silent tremors as he started to cry.

ROISIN

All of which is why we left him out of SCUM meetings.
I only had a few scraps of information, mined from the
endless quantities of tedious nonsense Luka had forced me
to sit through in the days when Cosmo was her only topic of

189

conversation. If only I hadn't switched off so much during those personal Ted Talks I'd probably have had an FBI agent's board full of information on him – little push pins with red thread winding between everything from the colour of his pants to his favourite meal deal sandwich.

Here's what I actually had:

He worked in a call centre, where he spent his time being shite at his job and texting her under the table.

I thought it might have been somewhere that sold electrical goods. Not computers. I mean washing machines, hoovers and the like. I could remember a comment she'd made about him being the housewives' choice.

He hated fun, joy, and expensive coffee, and would take her to Maccy's to get a cup of cheap black water instead, the old romantic. Maccy's near where he worked? Maybe.

THEO

It's called triangulation. You take locations you know the unsub's been to and use them to draw lines around his territory – he usually lives somewhere in the middle of the range. I learned that from *Criminal Minds*.

Although, I still don't quite know what 'unsub' means.

ROISIN

All right, Inspector Apfel. We were triangulating. Which meant

adding in the Picturehouse, the cinema he won his tickets to –
that must have been a regular haunt.

His favourite football players were no help. All
Liverpool, which just showed he was a fickle, feckless creature.
We weren't going to triangulate him by way of Merseyside.
But she'd mentioned he played five-a-side in the park. I knew a
couple of bars and a club he liked going to, too.

And my star witness for the prosecution: she'd told me
about stopping by a twenty-four-hour food and wine place –
Stop-N-Shop – when she met him after he'd had a night shift
at work. And, yes, they did night shifts at his call centre. It
seems the housewives never sleep or stop vacuuming.

THEO

Or house husbands. Let's not maintain the gender
stereotypes, shall we?

It took some time. It turns out that you can't just type
'call centres, Greenwich' into Google and come out with a
handy list. Many of them are strange, stealthy operations that
work under assumed names like 'Strategic Communications
Ltd'. After calling all the washing machine suppliers I could
think of, and speaking to faux-friendly staff who all seemed
to think they were dealing with a test caller and potentially
being recorded, I established that it's common to find these
places outsourcing their customer support to hub operations.

ROISIN

So Theo kept up his calling and searching the city via street view, while I decided to take it to ground level.

I went to McDonald's.

You *can* put those into Google and come up with a handy list.

There were only two prime suspects in my investigation. One was on a retail park in Charlton, sitting pretty beside a couple of supermarkets and – relevant to my interests – some electrical goods retailers.

It was my second choice for two reasons. Firstly, Theo had already found out that not many of these places do their customer service calls internally, let alone in the actual store.

Secondly, one of those supermarkets was twenty-four hour, and why would you opt for overpriced alcohol and out-of-date twiglets from Stop-N-Shop when you've a budget supermarket at your door?

The other was the one down by the *Cutty Sark*.

Close enough to where we first met the boy to have given me goosebumps. I went for a look around.

THEO

Ro was keeping me up to date with her search as I alternated between Google-sleuthing and revising some History chapters. At times the two seemed to overlap, as she fed me lines from tourists disembarking the *Cutty Sark* and pouring into nearby pubs and restaurants.

ROISIN

The comments are always hilarious. *But why were the boat's ceilings so low, Randy? Do you think they made sailors shorter in the olden days?*

I don't usually spend too much time in the area. Besides the market, so much of it's a tourist trap: chain restaurants, souvenir hawkers and the like. It's very pretty. But it's like anywhere in London – step out of the interesting, pretty places and you'll see a shift between where people visit and where they live and work. I walked up past Waterstones, a whole wall of picture books in the window, past banks and Chinese takeaways until I found McDonald's, then let my instincts guide me on where to go. A bit further out from the pink buildings, pubs and comedy clubs. Taking a sharp turn at Tesco I walked round the corner and straight past some sandy-bricked office buildings, most of them with tinted glass and fancy cars outside.

And opposite: ye olde Stop-N-Shop.

None of the buildings looked like a call centre. Whatever one of those looks like. I think I was expecting something like a college: loads of bored-looking students standing outside smoking, or pretending to smoke because it got them an extra five-minute break every hour. There was nothing like that, though. I read every office name as I went by. Most buildings had them on brass plates. Some had two or three.

I texted the names to Theo as I found them, letting him do his Google-fu.

THEO

B-Live – that appeared to be an entertainment company. Not them.

Figment – I couldn't narrow it down, but there were no call centres listed under the name.

The Rent Agency – exactly what it sounded like.

Widen-the-Net – a start-up of sorts.

Conduit –

Wait . . .

Conduit Communications: we aim to be a conduit between you and your customers, providing people-focused solutions and 24-hour support.

Despite a website comprised of jargon and descriptions that didn't actually describe anything, the words *24-hour support* caught my attention. I ran a couple more searches and found job adverts for the company that made it clear their staff would be 'taking inward-coming calls and providing support for a number of high-profile brands'.

It had to be the one.

I abandoned my half-done notes on tsarist Russia and texted Roisin that I'd meet her there.

ROISIN

Which of course wasn't going to happen. I wasn't about to stand outside Cosmo Allen's potential office like a lemon, waiting for him to come out and catch me stalking him. Not a chance. I told Theo I'd meet him outside the Lost Hour.

THEO

Even on a chilly January evening, gangs of drinkers clogged the pavement outside the Hour. I found myself performing a complicated dance towards the door, sidestepping and taking two steps back, then reeling to the other side until I was in front of the blue-framed glass and about to step in. And that's when someone clotheslined me almost hard enough to knock me on to my back.

ROISIN

Me. It was me. And for the record, I've a mean right hook as well. But on this occasion no violence was intended. I just had to stop Theo from walking in there. I grabbed hold of his arm as soon as he found his footing and pulled him in against me, just to one side of the door.

'What the he–'

'Shut up a minute and *look*.'

Someone else stepped around me and pushed their way through the door, letting in a row of four or five others all heading to the bar for another round. From our angle we were afforded a perfect view across the brightly lit interior to where Cosmo was sat with his arm round a girl who'd tucked herself into his side. As we watched, she laughed up at him and affectionately rested her head on his shoulder.

Theo caught a breath and turned to me as the door swung shut.

'That was –'

THEO

'Your man himself,' Roisin said, nodding gravely.

Cosmo, that was Cosmo. I closed my eyes, screwing them tight before opening them again, as if to assure myself they were functioning as expected.

I was still looking up into Roisin's blue ones.

'And that was . . .' I started softly.

ROISIN

I nodded again.

'That, Theo, was not Luka.'

TWENTY-THREE

ALEC

They both told me not to, but the first thing I did when Theo and Roisin turned up at my door with their spy story was call her.

When she first left I'd called all the time, sure her resolve would eventually weaken enough for her to answer me, but it never happened. I even borrowed other people's phones – Theo's, people from school whose numbers there's no way she'd have known. Somehow she did. She screened me from every angle and eventually my own resolve was the weaker one.

But hearing he was *cheating on* her, maybe a month after having found out he was cheating *with* her? That set me on fire all over again.

I called. And called. And called and called and called. She turned her phone off and I rang through the goddamn night so she'd have a thousand voicemails to delete in the morning. I called until I fell asleep – having told Theo and Ro to go home, since I was no kind of company – and I called again when I woke up. I called during breakfast, ignoring William's requests for no phones at the table.

I called her on the way to school and right up until I had to hand my phone in before the day's exam. The paper was a blank to me. I filled it in somehow but God knew what with. My mind was a series of numbers and an endless ringtone.

And then, when I emerged blinking from the exam hall to grab lunch and claim my phone back, she called me.

'Is something wrong?'

The first words she'd said to me since New Year's Eve and *that's* what they were. I froze. Or – the world froze. I was just staring at the phone, not quite sure I wasn't hallucinating.

Is something wrong?

It sounded like the world's biggest joke.

I laughed, in case I was supposed to, turning and pitching myself back against the wall in the art corridor until the weight of my own body was too much for either my legs or the wall to hold. I slid down to the floor, tugging a poster of *The Snail* by Matisse down with me, just as crumpled as I felt.

'Hey. Yeah, Luka, I guess a few things are wrong.'

She sounded – maybe frustrated, maybe just worried. It was hard to tell with her voice just a distant signal down the line. 'I mean, is something wrong at home?' she said. 'You must have rung two hundred times.'

'Yeah,' I said. And I could hear my own voice echoing

hollowly, being broken down into a bunch of vibrations, an electric echo, and sent across to her. That's how I felt. Broken down to my smallest components, flinging myself out, just trying to reach someone. 'If you were worried, maybe you could've picked up after the first hundred.'

There was a sigh. The crackle of her breath too close to the receiver. But then her voice was softer than I expected. I'd been waiting for a snap, or for her to simply disconnect. I figured I might have undone my two hundred calls' worth of work in one sarcastic comment.

I hadn't. She said, 'Alec, please. What is it?'

'We miss you at home, you know. Allegra misses you.'

A long, long silence.

'Even William probably misses being the arch nemesis in your superhero origin story.'

I waited then. Let the silence drag out as long as she could bear before she had to break it.

'I miss you too. Please, Alec, I don't have that much time. What's this about?'

Briefly I wondered how she could not have much time. She wasn't at school. She wasn't seeing *anybody*. What would be taking up her time now? Except me. And I knew I should get to the point.

It was strange how hearing her voice had just knocked all the air out of me. My energy – my fury over all this – was flatlining. I just wanted to string this moment out and hold her there as long as possible.

Twisting a hand back through my hair, I tugged hard, hoping the pain would pull me back to the fire I'd started my telethon with. It got close.

'It's about Cosmo.' Tripping over my words, I rushed out 'Don't hang up!' as if I could manifest her pausing with her finger over the button.

She was letting me talk, so I guessed I'd better talk. 'Whether something's wrong depends on your perspective. There's just something you ought to know about him. Like, did you know he was out with another girl last night?'

I was analysing every silence like it could predict the future. She paused then. And then asked, 'What do you mean?'

'I mean, we *saw* him –' I'm not going to mention it was Roisin and Theo, or their plan. The whole thing sounded extreme even to me. 'He was in the Lost Hour with her. Tall, blonde, face contoured like something out of a Picasso painting.' But it was probably obvious which part was Roisin's contribution to the description.

'And just one more thing –'

When we were kids we used to watch *Columbo*, this old detective show that played in syndication on daytime TV, and whenever the viewer thought the old guy was out for the count on his investigation, he'd throw in that line before revealing his most devastating discovery, the conclusive proof of guilt. I thought I was being cute. *Just one more thing*.

'A whole gang of his friends showed up right before we

left. It's weird, though – they were all calling him Colin. Had he *told* you Cosmo wasn't really his name?'

Case made, I stared across the wall at a portrait of Jane Grey awaiting her execution and listened to the blade drop on the other side of the line, pretty sure I'd sliced cleanly through everything she thought she knew about the guy.

'So he was with a girl,' Luka said, eventually, and I hummed a yes. 'Blonde, tall and I guess being affectionate with him? Was he kissing her or something?'

'It hadn't reached that level of PDA when everyone arrived. He had an arm round her. She was resting her head on his shoulder and looking into his eyes.'

It was enough. I thought it was enough.

'You know how I look into your eyes when I'm speaking to you, Alec?' she said.

The question blindsided me, a little. 'You haven't exactly been talking to me recently. But obviously yes.'

'That was *his sister*, you creepy little asshole. Is there a reason you think he should tell me every time he sees his sister? Did you warn Theo any time you and I went out, just in case I leaned against you and it looked weird? Or does that sound as gross to you as it does me? What exactly do you think you're trying to do here?'

Her voice was cold now, cold and sharp-edged, a blade turned back on me. And I was stumbling.

It was true, they hadn't kissed – both Theo and Roisin had been clear about that. They'd both told me not to call

201

Luka yet, to wait and see what else they could find out. They'd said they *seemed* like they were together, but less than ten minutes after they'd started watching, the whole gang of them – Colin/Cosmo, the mystery girl and their friends, all piled out of the bar and Theo and Ro had hidden in the nearest shop doorway to avoid giving themselves away.

I was sure they'd seen enough, but they must have misunderstood. I must have misunderstood.

'I was trying to protect you,' I said at last.

'Bullshit. You know exactly what you're trying to do, and none of it's actually about me, is it Alec?'

'It's *all* about you –'

'So why are you making it all about you? Sure, I *get* you don't like Cosmo – and of *course* I know his real name – but what about *you* not liking him means he's bad for me? I like him. Even if he did say something stupid about Theo, or something that got misinterpreted or whatever, why does that mean I should cut him off? He's never said anything hurtful to me. He's never hurt me at all. You know what is hurting me? Dealing with all this from you. But I get it now. You're jealous, right? You're jealous because I'm happy with Cosmo, and because I can't even bear to look at you right now.'

I made myself listen without trying to protest.

I listened until the line clicked, and I was dropped back into a silence I didn't want to analyse.

TWENTY-FOUR

MY NAME IS LUKA: EPISODE 6
'SHE DIDN'T SEEM LIKE THE TYPE'

LETTER FROM LUKA
21 JANUARY, 2020

Dear Mom,

Where do I even start?

Okay, good news or bad news first? Since I get to pick for you, I think we're going with the good: Heather, Veronica, Toothless, Sully and the previously unnamed Athos (for the Pothos – it's a Three Musketeers joke) and George the baby rubber tree are thriving. They each have a share in two window ledges and spend their days enjoying the watery winter sunshine and my Spotify playlists.

George might be small but he's really into classic rock. Huge Blink 182 enthusiast. I think he'll be a badass when he's bigger.

I bought them a leaf mister recently. I'm getting pretty

invested in their care. So far plant momming's the brightest part of my day.

Which sounds like the rest of my days are dark, doesn't it? Well, that's not true. They're just a little complicated.

So I guess I need to get to the bad part. The rumours are true: I did not attend my mock exams. Any of them. I haven't even been near the school. I just know the minute I show my face there they'll haul me into an office and get straight on the line to William to come collect his errant 'daughter', or Alec will trap me in a stationery closet to yell about his problems with my life choices. As if he's not half the reason I've had to make them.

Let's save that for later. So, school.

The thing is, I meant to go. I studied . . . Not my usual amount, but I don't have all my books at the new place yet and I don't want to go home for the rest. And Cosmo doesn't love it when I ignore him for a textbook all evening either. But still, I already knew most of what I'd need for the papers. I did Google deep dives. I studied. I had every intention of getting up the morning of that first exam and heading back to school.

And then I didn't.

I stayed in bed. It wasn't even because Cosmo thought going in for a 'mock' exam was pointless, though he did say even the name makes them sound like a joke. He was at work. I just couldn't make my body function. I couldn't make my arms and legs do the necessary movements to get myself upright and dressed and on my way.

And I realised that somewhere deep down I think it's all pointless, too.

Maybe it always was. And I don't want to blame this change of heart on you. It's just that it's hard to feel there's a point in anything without you here. Like, what's the point of exams: working for them, taking them, getting the marks I've been predicted, when you're not here to be proud of me? And why bother going to university if you won't be there when I graduate? There's *so many* important things you're not going to be there for – I didn't realise how much I did because I knew how much you cared, before. Who's going to care what I do now?

After you died I got told I was making you proud all the time. For dumb, basic things like still getting up and brushing my teeth and not throwing myself into the grave during your funeral, I guess. For not a hundred percent falling apart after the worst thing that's ever happened to me. *Your mother would be so proud that you can still walk and talk and feed yourself, Luka, that you haven't gone completely off the goddamn rails.*

It's bullshit. It's bullshit. You can't be proud of me any more. You can't be anything, except dead.

Even writing this letter is bullshit, but I don't have anyone else I can inflict thoughts like this on. There's no one I can tell quite how dark I feel sometimes. Just how hard it is to make myself move.

So that's it, that's why I missed the mocks. I guess if you

can't be proud of me you can't be pissed at me either so I should feel less guilty than I do for saying all this.

It's fine. If I start to care, I can show up for the real exams in summer. Maybe I'll even make myself go in and ask about it. It's not like it's going to make any real tangible difference to my life not to have done this practice run.

I didn't call Roisin either yet. Yet.

I really am going to. I just need to wait till Cosmo's out because he thinks it's a bad idea to get back in touch with people yet. With how toxic it's all been and the way they drag me down. I love that he feels like we can take on the world together – just us – but I need other people in my life, too. For the subjects he doesn't like to talk about and for . . . just everything. I need Ro . . .

And it's not like he doesn't have friends, right? I mean, that's the elephant in the room. Alec and his phone call. That girl.

I asked Cosmo about it. I waited a couple of days after Alec's call and then I asked him while we were washing up after dinner, so it didn't seem like I was making too big a deal out of it.

'Do you have a sister?'

I'd made the explanation up on the spot, but the longer I let it settle the more it felt like it must be true.

He frowned. It was a little weird, almost like he didn't know what to say. He probably just wasn't expecting the question. Then, instead of answering, he asked why I wanted to know all of a sudden. I said I was just curious. That I'm interested in his life. It's strange when I think of how little I really know about all the parts that don't involve me. He laughed, but not like it was funny. Like he'd tasted something bitter. Then he said, 'No. Only child.'

I said, 'Oh.' And stuck my hands back under the suds.

It had been bugging me. I *hate* that I let Alec stir up trouble when that was what he was so obviously gunning for, but he'd succeeded in getting under my skin. So a minute later I went back to it.

'It's just someone told me you were out the other night with a bunch of people and a girl who looked like she could be your sister. I didn't know you went out.'

He stepped back from me. He looked so hurt. 'Do I have to tell you everything now? We've moved in together, spent a fortune because you needed somewhere to go. Is that not enough? Do you want to put a tracker on me too?'

I tried to tell him no. I told him I was 'just interested' again, although even to me that line was sounding fake, and he shook his head and spoke over me to ask who it was that told me.

I didn't say. He asked again, and after a minute I said it was Alec.

'My biggest fan Alec? Great. Well, that should tell you all you need to know.'

He left the kitchen and slammed the door while I stood there regretting everything, including who I'm related to.

I never should have let Alec get to me. Never. It's like Cosmo says – he only says that he wants what's best for me to try and get what's best for him. Right now he'll say anything to get Cosmo out of my life. He doesn't understand.

Later, I went to find Cosmo to say how sorry I was. I didn't mean to accuse him of anything. He rolled his eyes rather than reply to me, and I was about to give him some space, but he reached out and took my hand to pull me down on to his lap.

He just doesn't like to talk about his family. That's what he told me later, to explain why he'd been so off. He's got painful memories. None of them talk much.

I told him I know how *that* feels, and he laughed and I knew everything was better again. He leaned in close to me and tilted my chin up so our eyes met. I love the way he looks at me. Like he can see beneath my surface. 'That's why we work,' he told me. 'We're so much the same our souls are tangled up together, Starshine. It's you and me versus everything.'

The night at the Hour was just people from work. I knew that's all it would be. The girl's called Lucy and she's really beautiful, he says – and he wouldn't say that to me if he was interested in her. She flirts sometimes, but he wouldn't go there, even if blondes are his usual type. She sits one cubicle over and she has a boyfriend who works there too. So it's fine. He told me everything to make sure I wouldn't worry about it any more. I just haven't met his friends yet because he likes to keep work separate from his personal life, and I can't say that sounds unfair.

So what if his name's not Cosmo?

The night we met still feels fated and I guess, like me, he feels that name was part of it too. People have nicknames. It's not weird.

To me, he's always going to be Cosmo.

Like cosmic.

Love you, Mom. I hope you're not too proud/pissed/ whatever but I'm going to operate on the theory that death makes you okay with everything. Totally zen. At least it makes you easy to talk to.

Speak soon,

Love,
Luka

TWENTY-FIVE

ALEC

I navigated a few days on autopilot. Trapped in my 'Robo-Alec' persona, as Theo nicknamed it. He saw a lot of it, after Mom. And he's one of the few people who ever managed to get through the programming and reach me.

It's a state where I can function, move around, respond if people talk to me but I'm only carrying out the basic necessities. My mind's shut down. I didn't tell Theo and Ro how the call with Luka went. Not really. I just said they'd got it wrong and things didn't go well. Not a lie. Not inaccurate. Not carrying any personal detail or emotional depth. The robot's response.

And then, sometime near the end of January, I came downstairs to find William glued to news reports from China.

They'd grounded a whole city the day before. Eleven million people got sent to their rooms and told to stay there. It sounded weird as hell.

And watching it on TV for a few minutes while I finished my cereal didn't make it seem any more real. The

BBC had grey-looking, grey-voiced people talking gravely about the scale of the sickness and loss in this one single city. I don't know how much I actually listened at the time and how much I remember because they played the same footage over and over for months afterwards. But they were having to build new hospitals at breakneck speed because there were so many sick people that they'd run out of places to put them. That didn't sound possible.

Even weeks later, when we'd all started paying more attention, I couldn't take those facts and think about them in a way that felt like it was real life. A strange new sickness that people had picked up at the market and brought home with them along with their grocery shopping? A city bigger than London turned into a prison to try to prevent tiny virus particles getting loose and carrying their sickness to the wider world? Sure. I probably I saw Matt Damon in that movie once.

'It couldn't happen here,' William muttered, and now I think I know what he meant. He meant we'd never put up with it here. It could never get that bad for us. That this was something that happened to unimaginable, not-quite-real people, in a land far away. As callous and awful as that sounds now.

I wish I'd taken one minute to think about all the things I'd have called unimaginable just two months ago. Eighteen months ago. All those impossible nightmares that had been busy coming true.

But I forgot about the whole thing five minutes later.

I looked away from the TV and switched my brain back off to head to school.

THEO

It's funny. I barely even remember people talking about it that much, at first. Not for the first few weeks. It's not as if our school's a melting pot of searing political debate, but we're not completely unaware. People are always sharing slides or videos with bullet points on socials. I know there's an idea that teenagers don't 'do' news, when the truth is we get it in fifteen-second bulletins of the actually important parts, without all the middle-aged hot takes. I know about oppressive policies in parts of the world my parents think are just cheap destinations for a package holiday.

But there wasn't much out there for this. Maybe it was just that no one had processed it yet.

ROISIN

There was one kid in my year constantly on about how it was going to be the zombie plague and how in less than a month London would come over all *28 Days Later*, with no one left in the place except Will Smith and his dog.

I might be mixing my movies. You get the point. Everyone thought it was a big joke. There's some irony in looking back on that, now.

ALEC

Mr Tang mentioned it in History that week, since I suppose future historic events are also part of his job. He told us his family have friends in the city that got quarantined, and he even read us messages they'd sent about what the atmosphere was like, and how scared they were as the sickness started to take over. That got people to listen.

Then he told us someone in the year below had asked a Vietnamese girl if she had 'the plague' that morning, and he said that there would be serious consequences for anyone even thinking about turning a national tragedy into an excuse for racism. Along with a compulsory Geography test.

Funnily enough, Tang's personal stories and that all-too-imaginable little racist comment was what started to make it feel real.

THEO

Although still not quite like something that could touch us. Whenever the obligatory question was asked – can you *imagine* something like that happening in London? – the whispered answer in the back of my mind was always no. No. Absolutely not. No, not at all. Of *course* not.

ROISIN

I could imagine the zombies more easily. Because people

213

know how to handle zombies, don't they? Aim for the head.

But listening to the news reports my da and sisters had on all the time, it seemed as though no one had a real clue how to handle this virus thing.

ALEC

It stuck around in the background of conversation, a bit. A strange, distant story where people were being flown back from China and locked up in hotels to quarantine. A couple of people tested positive, somewhere. But then mock results came back and Wuhan fell right off the radar for a while. People had priorities.

I did as expected. Not a disaster, but nothing to stick on the refrigerator. Which was fine. This family always had one member suited for academia and she wasn't coming to the phone any more. Meanwhile I phoned it in and didn't quite disgrace myself.

THEO

Two Bs. One C. One A*.

Two Bs.

One C.

ALEC

Theo, on the other hand.

THEO

You have to understand, I just don't get less than As. My predicted marks were a solid wall of them, concreted with tiny stars.

I understood that half of my year would have been delighted with half of my results and I feel awful for saying I couldn't be. But I couldn't be. My parents wouldn't be. The university I had my heart set on, with applications less than a year away, wouldn't so much as give me a second look with marks like those.

And my best result had been in the subject I was intending to drop at AS level.

For the first time in my life I felt scared to tell anyone what I'd got. I was so unutterably disappointed in the marks. Disappointed in myself. And the worst thing –

ALEC

The worst thing is that Robo-Alec didn't even notice.

THEO

No. The worst thing was that I'd honestly tried. Yes, I'd been spending as much time with Alec as I could, and I couldn't say that a small part of my mind wasn't constantly reserved for him. But I'd done the work. I'd almost certainly revised more than usual to make up for any distractions. It just wasn't good enough. I wasn't good enough.

And while I didn't blame him for his own distraction, the only person I really wanted to talk to about it had other things on his mind.

Nothing had changed between us – not in any clear, abrupt way - but nothing was quite the same. His coping strategy had begun to affect how we were together. Everything felt distant, quiet and mechanical. I still went over. We still watched films. He slept fitfully, and I studied the ceiling until my mind calmed. But the silences between us had grown and grown until talking felt uncomfortable. Especially after the phone call. It was clear it had worsened the rift between him and his sister and I silently added it to the list of things I was at fault for. But we didn't talk about it.

I could wrap my arms round his waist, press my face into his shoulder, breathe him in as deeply as I could and still he felt unreachable.

I couldn't fix it. I couldn't risk making anything worse. I pushed down my own worries and settled into silence with him.

ROISIN

Then there was the day I went to eat lunch and found myself on a table alone.

Luka had been out of commission all term, obviously. But that day Tiwa was off sick, Shauna had a netball match and anyone else who'd usually join us seemed to have drifted to other tables.

I could have done that too, of course. Drifted. I could have done it easily. Just across the way I could see an empty seat next to Jan, who was my lab partner in Chemistry all through GCSEs and made decent company when he wasn't getting a little overinvested in how many fingers he could shove through a Bunsen flame without them blistering.

And on another table were Blessing and Riza, who'd been Saturday crew with me at Boots last summer. We could have reminisced about the joys of endlessly rearranging eyeliners.

I could get up and sit with anybody I wanted. There were dozens of people I knew, even if we weren't quite at the stage of sharing all our secrets and ironically exchanging coin necklaces split into two parts.

Except I'd sat at the empty table now, and the idea of standing again was suddenly impossible. It would make me feel *more* noticeable. Standing up would just make it really clear that Norma No-Mates had been left all on her own.

I realised I'd got too used to being joined by others – I'd let myself believe that meant I'd changed, become unafraid, when at the heart of me was someone still terrified by the idea of being turned away if I was the one asking to join.

Sitting there like the last lemon in the fruit bowl had me frozen to my seat. I didn't look up so I didn't have to see the looks I was getting, and in my head the whole room was watching by then. I could imagine the comments. On what I was wearing. On the food I couldn't make myself eat. I used to hate being crowded by unfriendly faces at the lunch table, but my own mind became unfriendly when I was alone.

I'd finally decided to abandon lunch altogether and make a break for the door when Alfie Newly slid into the plastic chair opposite.

Alfie bloody Newly.

For a moment I could almost have kissed him.

THEO

At lunch I went up to the Year Head's Hallway – the YHH – to keep an appointment I'd booked in for myself back on results day. I'd been winding myself up about it ever since, until it felt like every sinew in my body was pulled tight enough to snap.

ALEC

He told me where he was going and I didn't even ask why. But, Theo talks to teachers all the time. I've always imagined that half those meetings just consist of him sitting at the end of a long table while every teacher we have takes turns to tell him why he's their favourite.

But I know there are other reasons too.

THEO

Well, you always knew I had counselling sessions.

ALEC

Yeah. I had a few myself after Mom . . . So when you vanished that lunchtime I didn't ask about it. I wouldn't have wanted to be asked.

But I hadn't even checked what your grades were. It had been two days of everyone asking each other, and I didn't notice that you were going out of your way to avoid those conversations just as much as I was.

I'd looked at my own marks, shut down any part of me that cared about them, and forgot to care about anyone else.

THEO

You had lot on your mind.

ALEC

That's a bad excuse.

THEO

Not to me.

I'd hardly allowed myself to feel anything either – just let the winch of my anxiety wind tighter and tighter. Up in the YHH I had barely sat down on one of the squeaky plastic sofas to wait before Miss Bright put her head round the door, gave me a crimson-lipsticked smile and told me she was running twenty minutes late, if I wouldn't mind waiting.

The door snapped shut before I could even respond.

It wasn't a terrifically long time to have to wait. But it was as if, after holding it all in for so long, I'd somehow worked myself up to melt down at that precise, carefully scheduled moment, and so – as soon as she'd shut her door again and I was back in the dim hallway, alone – I did.

ROISIN

'If you tell me to go away, I'll go away.'

Alfie's opening line to me at the canteen table was said with his eyes wide and his chin raised up high like he was ready to take some knocks on it – a brave little soldier. I made a great show of drawing in a breath as if I was about to tell him exactly that.

220

I wasn't. I mean, really, who could be that inhumanly uncurious? I needed to know what he wanted. More than that, I needed the company.

'I should,' I told him instead – eyebrows arched, expression aloof, giving nothing away. I'd gladly have listened to him read the local train timetable to me if it kept me from sitting there alone.

I know, I know. But becoming a strong, independent woman takes work, and eating alone happens to be my own personal Everest. I was ridiculously grateful to have someone there with me.

THEO

I hate to cry at all, let alone in public, but I was too far gone to stop, even when I heard the swing door at the end of the hall open and let me know that I had company.

I was embarrassed to be sobbing. Embarrassed not to be tough enough to handle everything the world threw at me. As embarrassed by my sense of failure as I was to be taking it all so seriously.

I put my head in my hands and hoped they'd think I was distraught over being expelled for delinquency, not just feeling like my future was crumbling over a single C. I couldn't seem to stop my shoulders shaking, though.

That is, until someone put their hand on one of them and said, 'If he's screwed things up with you too, I swear I'll punch him in the nose.'

And Luka sat down at my side.

ROISIN

Alfie leaned across the table.

'Perhaps you should. You would have every right to ask me to leave. What . . . little I remember of my behaviour at that party was deplorable.'

I tilted my head and frowned at him. *Deplorable.* Not for the first time I wondered what period drama he'd escaped from. I constantly had the sense that he should have been wearing a cravat. 'It wasn't deplorable – it was *harassment*. You seemed to be frustrated that I wasn't about to let myself get in a situation where anything deplorable could happen.'

His cheeks pinked first, a colour that spread out to stain the tip of his nose, then his ears. 'It absolutely wouldn't have. I promise, Roisin. I –' he leaned in more, until I wasn't certain he wasn't about to face-plant straight into my sandwich – 'I've never been deplorable with *anyone.*'

Which I still think is the strangest way anyone's ever told me they were a virgin. And he was *still talking.*

'I only wanted you to come with me because, I'm – I'm just not all that good at parties. You may have noticed. I'm much better when talking to someone one on one, preferably without a soundtrack of someone explaining what they're doing with their horse on the Old Town Road.'

He winced, and despite myself I shot him a sympathetic smile. He swept the fair hair back from his face (even his forehead was pink now – I had no idea a person could change colour so completely so fast) and took a deep breath. 'And honestly, I've wanted to talk to you for a very long time.'

THEO

'You're still talking to me, then,' I said, after I wiped tears and any other unpleasantness from my face with the palms of my hands. Pretty vile, but given the lack of other options, somewhat better than sitting there dripping.

I must have been looking at Luka as though she might have been a mirage. She pressed her lips together and nodded carefully. 'My brother's an idiot, but you're probably the best decision he ever made.'

I hiccuped eloquently, still barely believing she was really there.

'This isn't to do with him?' she asked.

'No. Sort of? Not really.' My eyes were threatening to leak again, so I screwed them furiously closed. 'It's about a lot of things. I messed up my exams.'

'Hey.' When I squinted just enough to focus my watery vision, she was smiling wryly. 'Join the club.'

ROISIN

'*You've wanted to talk to me for a very long time?* No offence, Alfie, but that's the kind of thing elderly wizards say when they have a quest for you. Is this about a quest?'

I couldn't think of one single solitary reason Alfie Newly would want to speak to me. Except perhaps to let me know I'd got toilet paper trailing from one leg of my jeans, or to ask if I knew the pages we needed for homework. Luka used to say he had a crush on me. She'd say she caught him looking all the time. I'd say it was so much rubbish she should take herself to the dump.

'What was it you've been wanting to talk about?' I asked finally, in spite of my better judgement. This would be where the joke came in.

'I – I'm not sure, really. It's a general sort of want.' His eyes were the startled blue of puddles that someone had splashed through. 'Sometimes I just want to tell you that I really like your smile.'

THEO

'I just had a meeting with Tang,' Luka said. 'If I didn't make some kind of contact with him they might have kicked me out altogether, but I *can't* come back yet. I can't pretend to be normal. Can't deal with the questions. It's too much . . . It's worse now I know everyone's been talking about me. I heard Alec's been a one-man Spanish Inquisition.'

'He's so incredibly worried about you,' I told her, and she sighed, looping her arm round mine.

'Maybe I'm not the one he needs to worry about. Does he even know you're here?' As I shook my head, she went on. 'You'll be okay on the grades part, you know. Tang told me we could write off my mocks – as long as I get back on track now I'll still be fine. I need to check in with him for work that I can take home, and I need to let him update William that he's seen me and I'm alive or whatever, but it's going to be okay. For both of us. Okay?'

I pulled in a breath so deep I had to straighten up just to fit it in. 'Okay.'

She wrinkled her nose. 'You're not okay, are you?'

And I deflated again. 'It just feels more and more like everything's starting to slip away.'

ROISIN

I don't know how to handle lines like that. At least, not directed at me. All I had to offer in response was the sound a balloon might make as the air escapes it. A sort of curious squeak. *Really?*

Brave soldier, he marched on with his smile-based commentary. 'And that I've noticed you're not smiling as much recently. I was wondering if that had anything to do with the ongoing disappearance of Luka Booth.'

He'd been paying closer attention than I'd ever

imagined. I tried to cut in with an 'Alfie ' but he wasn't to be stopped.

'Which is *why* I'm talking to you today,' he said, and swept his hair back again. 'Because I wanted to, but also because I just saw her upstairs outside Tang's office.'

My jaw fairly well hit the table, though he had the courtesy not to mention it.

'She's back in school.'

I slid my chair away from the table with a screech of metal that made the whole canteen turn and stare, and, honestly, I couldn't have cared less.

THEO

'Talk to him,' Luka made me promise. 'I mean, sure, sometimes you practically have to perform a vaudeville routine in front of Alec before he'll notice something's happening, but I know he'll care.'

I smiled weakly. 'Good advice. I don't suppose you've considered taking it yourself?'

'And give up my Number-one Hypocrite badge? No way.' Luka smoothed down her jumper before standing. 'Look, I love him, but we're both stubborn and things are complicated. It'll happen eventually, but right now I just really need my own space. I don't suppose I can ask you not to mention you saw me?'

'You can ask,' I told her, letting my expression explain

what my answer would have to be.

She rolled her eyes. 'But you'll do it anyway. I know, I know. Then . . . just tell him not to worry. And, Theo . . . if Cosmo said something shitty to you then please know I'm sorry. I really am. I'm working on smoothing his rough edges, and his ignorant edges too.'

I opened my mouth to tell her it was okay. And I'm glad I was interrupted because it wouldn't have been true. What he'd said wasn't okay, and if I acted like I didn't care, why should he?

I barely got as far as taking a breath.

ROISIN

I have never felt so much like I was starring in one of those films that ends with a dramatic dash to the airport as I did at the moment I flung the doors to the YHH wide and saw her standing there with Theo.

THEO

Miss Bright opened the door to her office and peeked her head round at the exact moment that Roisin announced her presence with rather more flair.

ROISIN

'LUKA BOOTH, AS I LIVE AND *BREATHE*,' I declared, with a hand fluttering over my heart. The dramatic effect was only slightly dampened by my being a tad bit wheezy from all the stairs.

THEO

'*Girls –*' Miss Bright tutted, her voice as close to a warning as it ever got – 'keep it down out here, please.'

I saw her pause as her attention caught on Luka, then she moved on to me. 'Theo, sorry about that – I was taking a phone call. But I'm sure this won't take long. Why don't you come in?'

Not quite certain what sort of scene I was leaving behind me, I followed instructions. And Luka was right. Miss Bright told me that half the reason for mock exams was to learn where and how I needed to be stronger for the real thing, and in that respect I might as well call my performance a success. I'd given myself a learning opportunity. She told me she had no doubt everything would be better in the summer.

And she asked me if anything else was wrong.

A few minutes after saying *no* with varying degrees of red-eyed believability, but with all my crying thankfully done, I was back out in the hallway, strangely quiet now, with no sign of a throwdown or a joyful reunion left behind in Roisin and Luka's wake.

There was nothing out of the ordinary at all.

Except Alec waiting by the doors at the end of the hallway, looking at me with an expression I'd never seen turned my way before.

'I heard Luka was here,' he said. 'You saw her, didn't you?'

The panicked feeling that had begun to calm in my chest started to kick like a rabbit against my ribs. I nodded. Yes.

He nodded too. 'Yeah. Thanks for telling me.' He turned and walked away.

TWENTY-SIX

ROISIN

We got the bus into town. Headed to Costa. The same as
we had after school a million times. Except that it was the
middle of the day and we'd not seen each other for a month.
We weren't laden down with notes to bring back marked
with coffee rings, and there was no gossip to share. Half the
gossip in our class now was about her. I should have broken
the ice with that rumour about how she'd joined a cult.

Bunking off school for one afternoon wasn't something
I was feeling guilty for – particularly since she'd missed the
whole term so far. Though I did feel a little bad about leaving
Alfie sat at that table, his mouth hanging open as I made a mad
run for the door. Something told me he'd understand. And
when did I start feeling bad about Alfie bloody Newly anyway?

The bus was mysteriously busy for the middle of the
day. I'm very familiar with busses, by virtue of having a da
who tells me he's handed in his notice at the taxi service every
time I ask for a lift, and no money for driving lessons of my
own. Afternoons are the dead hours of a bus route, whereas

mornings are grannies, schoolkids and commuters, and early evenings are the same in reverse.

That day, though, it was standing room only among grans with trolleys and mums with prams and one old fella who'd decided spreading his whole Tesco shop over four seats was just fine.

Being pressed to the opposite window gave me a chance to study her a minute. Not so much trying to notice the differences about her as trying to figure out the one staring me in the face. She was wearing make-up. A bucketload of it, and that's by my standards. Her cheeks were contoured razor-sharp, lines of highlighter and blush layered finely enough to make a YouTube tutorial proud. *Contour*, though. Even on the rare days she decided to bother with the trivialities of mascara and eyeliner, I'd never known Luka to fuss about a contour. She had the kind cheekbones you could ski off as it was. Honestly, you could have hated her for it.

As I looked then, I could see why she'd never gone for it before. It made her look too angular. All hollows and ridges and strange new terrain. I almost found myself squinting to make sure it was really her.

And I'm sure all this sounds like a lot of talk about something incredibly unimportant, but it wasn't. It just wasn't. I love my make-up, but it's about putting the best version of myself out there for the world.

Luka looked somehow like she was trying on someone else's face.

At least her coffee order hadn't changed. I was worried she'd suggest popping round the corner for a cup of black water from the burger clown's place. For a moment, as we'd walked down streets I'd last visited on that ill-fated Cosmo-stalking trip, I thought she was going to call me out on it. It felt so much like retracing my steps that I expected to see him round every corner. The great elephant in the room himself.

Had I wanted to get off on a terrible footing, I'd have asked *How's Colin?* The minute I saw her, instead of throwing my arms round her and demanding to know if she had any *idea* what kind of a nightmare school had been without her. Who else could I perfectly time an eye-roll with the minute Miss Thompsett started talking about her fiancé? Or telegraph warnings to that Mr Brynn from the Maths department's deodorant levels were running distressingly low? Who else was I supposed to *sit with at lunch*?

'Roisin,' she'd said, peeling herself out of my grip enough to look at me properly, there in the dingy light of the YHH.

'I know, I know. It's not as if we're conjoined twins.'

'But we are conjoined,' she said, and smiled, linking her arm with me. 'I just can't stay here right now. Escape with me?'

And how could I ever say no to that? So there we were. Costa.

We piled coffees and fruit toast on to a wobbly tray and made our way across the café, until she paused. 'Remember the last time we were here?'

Ah yes, the first time Cosmo had kidnapped her.

'You never did find out how we scored Jingle All the Latte,' I pointed out mildly, and she grinned.

'There's always next year, when they'll rename the drinks and serve the exact same thing again.' She set the tray on a table and settled herself down in one of the deep-padded armchairs, looking up at me. 'I missed this.'

'I think you said that last time too.' I dropped myself down to the chair beside her, watching for a reaction to that.

She didn't flinch. 'I know. And I know it's my fault. I've been meaning to call and say . . . I understand you were just trying to look out for me at the party. If everyone hadn't been on my case already I wouldn't have had the reaction I did. The thing is, you've got Cosmo wrong. He's not a bad person – he's just . . . insecure. And that makes things difficult, sometimes.'

As far as I was concerned, I didn't have Cosmo wrong in the least. I'd learned a long time ago that most people are cruel to others to from having to look too long or deep at themselves. Unkindness stems from insecurity and possessiveness springs from being afraid of what you might lose. We're all cracked, fragile, pottery pieces of people. It's just some of us choose to break others rather than risk admitting our own damage.

'Difficult how?' I asked, trying to make the measly butter pack they give you spread over two pieces of bread as my stomach reminded me of my abandoned lunch.

'It's like he thinks everyone's against us. And I can't exactly blame him with the way Alec has been. Do you know he rang me up trying to convince me Cosmo was cheating?'

My toast freezes in mid-air, half way to my mouth. 'Really?'

'I knew he hadn't, but Cosmo's been worse since I asked him about it, and I feel like it's my fault for not . . . I don't know, not trusting him enough? I don't think it's that he doesn't *want* me to see people – he just worries what you'll say. Like I might believe something I shouldn't. Or maybe that I'll choose you over him.'

Thank God for a mouthful of food allowing me time to process that. I almost spat it straight out.

'You'd think you spending every minute with him lately would set him straight on that.'

'You'd think.' She looked into the middle distance. 'Sometimes it's like the more time we're together the worse he gets. I even think he's jealous of the plants.'

'The plants?' My eyebrows raised.

'Oh my God, Roisin. I'm a natural with them. We got a new place and he jokes that I'm trying to turn it into a jungle, but I really like having something to look after.'

'I thought he couldn't afford to move from that one house with the revolving roommates?'

She looked hesitant, an expression I didn't understand. 'Well, now it's both of us we can. He keeps an eye on all the money. And if everything goes to plan and he doesn't decide to take another gap year we'll have two student loans coming in September. I've got enough to keep us going until then.'

'How have you?' Toast forgotten, I frowned across at her. So far as I knew, she didn't even work on weekends. But that was when she was Captain Coursework. 'Have you a job now?'

'Not yet, but I'm looking, and –'

I cut in as another thought occurred, 'And you won't be able to combine student loans if you're studying in two different cities. Is he going to Bristol with you?'

Another of those hesitations. I noticed she'd been breaking her toast into breadcrumbs rather than eating it, and half wondered if she planned on leaving me a trail to follow. It felt like the Luka I knew was somewhere just out of reach. Like I was sitting with a hologram. A close approximation of the girl I knew. 'History at the University of Greenwich has a good reputation.'

'But it's not what you want! What you always wanted!' I must have sounded like a parent. I didn't mean to. I watched as her defences rose.

'People can change, Ro.'

That much I could see. I was noticing more changes all the time. All of them since she took up with him.

My phone trilled and I glanced down at it. A message from Theo asking if I'd seen Alec anywhere.

I tapped back *No, I'm not in school*, and at the same

235

time there was a ping across the table and Luka was looking down at a screen of her own, before automatically reaching to hook her bag into the crook of her elbow.

'I need to get going. I lost track of the time. But I'll call. I promise. We can actually make some plans now everything's settled.' She bit down one corner of her lip, looking away, but she added, 'I'm sure that'll be fine.'

'Okay,' I started, 'then how about –'

'I really have to head out.' She was moving while she was talking, and I was still sitting there with coffee and toast barely touched. 'I'm so glad I saw you today. I've missed you so much. I'll call.'

And as I stood to at least hug her or something, she'd turned and gone to the door.

I followed her that far, and a couple of steps out on to the street, to watch her grow smaller and smaller as she walked down to the figure of a boy who was leaning against the wall there. He flipped his cigarette to the floor and looped an arm round her shoulder, tugging her in.

She didn't look back.

TWENTY-SEVEN

EPISODE OUTRO

TIWA

I told everyone their rumours were nonsense.

SHAUNA COATES, 18, FRIEND

Yeah, as if this last year hasn't proved that everyone loves a good conspiracy theory. Luka was big news before the virus, before the US election and all that madness.

TIWA

It was just fascinating to me. Anyone can be popular, can have friends, until there's a story to tell. And then they're a mouse in a nest of vipers.

SHAUNA

There was the cult one – Jeremy Danvers said he'd seen her

outside Charing Cross Tube recruiting people to the 'true path'. Then after the party and that fight Cosmo got into she was apparently in with a drugs ring, being sent out to county lines.

TIWA

And then, when she'd been spotted back in school, but hadn't returned to classes –

SHAUNA

An affair with a teacher. Katie Harris told Mr Tang she'd testify that Luka was a nasty skank so that he wouldn't lose his job. She was really confused to be given that detention.

TIWA

But no matter what the story, no matter who believed it, I kept waiting to hear one thing. *She didn't seem like the type.*

That line you hear when someone's committed murder on a quiet street.

SHAUNA

Or robbed his grandma. Kept his wife and kids locked in the cellar. *He didn't seem like the type.*

TIWA

He seemed so nice and quiet.

SHAUNA

Nothing out of the ordinary about him.

TIWA

He just didn't seem like the type.

SHAUNA

But even when the truth about Luka was pretty well known
– she'd all but dropped out of school, she was estranged
from her family, living with some boy somewhere – nobody
seemed to say that about her. Nobody thought it was out of
the ordinary. They just let her disappear.

TIWA

Maybe there was something wrong.

SHAUNA

Maybe she needed help?

TIWA

Yes. I think that may have been the problem. Someone like Luka Booth in need of help? She just didn't seem like the type.

SHAUNA

So eventually people stopped talking about her. The truth wasn't as exciting as the fiction had been. And anyway, no one had been able to talk to her. No one even knew where she was.

ALFIE NEWLY, 18, SORT-OF FRIEND

Almost no one.

TWENTY-EIGHT

MY NAME IS LUKA: EPISODE 7
'BITTER LITTLE CELLS'

LETTER FROM LUKA
14 FEBRUARY 2020

Dear Mom,

I can't stop watching the news.

I've never really sat down to watch a news report before but it's somehow unavoidable when you've only got five channels to choose from. I've given up on Netflix because Cosmo tells me the kind of things I watch are 'brain drain for bimbos'. He hates every actor in every new series and grills me on why I like them, even if I tell him I don't.

Which means I'm down to just the terrestrial TV options now. The picture's fuzzy and the news seems to be on 24/7 but at least I don't have to explain whether or not I'm hot for the weather man.

So there's a city in China where this sickness has broken

out, and even though they've tried sealing it off from the world to keep the infection in, it won't stay put. It's escaping in trickles and droplets and coughs, one respiratory system at a time.

It's called a coronavirus, or maybe Covid-19 – no one seems settled on which. A couple of people here have had it.

Someone in France died from it today. From little virus particles that hitched a ride all the way across the world. It's weird to think about, but that must be how all infectious disease works now. Maybe the cold I had last month was a visitor on a world tour, too. After your cancer, I think I'd started to think of disease as being some part of yourself that turns against you, a cluster of bitter little cells.

But not viruses. They're tourists.

I'm just obsessed with all the footage, especially of this one cruise ship being quarantined in Japan, with people pressing their faces to windows and holding up handmade banners as though bedsheets and sharpies are their only way of communicating with the outside world.

I think I'm so hung up on it because I'm starting to feel a kind of kinship with them when it comes to that.

Cosmo has my phone.

It's my fault. He woke up while I was texting Ro at some crazy hour of the morning because Miles Riva had added a surprise UK date to his tour, and tickets went on sale at midnight. She finally got through the queue and snagged some at maybe two am. I must have made a noise or something. Something happy. Whatever I did, it disturbed him. It woke him up, and he got the wrong impression.

Like I say, it's probably my fault. I didn't explain properly – just rolled my eyes and tried to ignore it. And then I told him he was an idiot when he wouldn't leave it alone. When he started demanding to see who I was *really* talking to. He was grabbing for my wrist and it was irritating me that he'd just expect me to show him something private like that, so I slipped out of the other side of the bed and dragged half our blankets with me, saying I'd talk to whoever I wanted. I'd just do it somewhere it wouldn't bother him. I meant the bathroom, or the kitchen. That was all. Not that I was leaving.

I just meant the kitchen.

But I shouldn't have snapped that way. I get defensive so quickly. Claws out. It's something I need to work on.

He followed me. Half naked, just in his underwear, and he usually looks so vulnerable like that, with his pale, pale skin and the little trails of dark hair that stand out against it. He looks so . . . private and mine.

I wasn't expecting it when he got me up against the wall. He pressed me there, hands spread wide across my shoulders, leaning his whole weight in on me until it felt like my collarbone could snap. He said, 'What did you call me?'

He was hurting me. I told him he was hurting me, but it was like he didn't hear. 'Is that what you think I am, Luka? Maybe I am an idiot for trusting you.'

Even when he saw it was Roisin on the phone – he moved

243

one hand long enough to take it from me – he asked me if I was making fun of him. Me and all my friends making fun of him behind his back. As if I've even spoken to more than a couple of people besides him in the last two months. As if I ever do anything but defend him.

He asked me if I was going to leave him.

I said no.

He screamed it in my face.

I must have been crying – from the shock, not pain - but he held me there by the shoulders until they started to ache and

I'm *not* scared of him.

I would leave if I was scared of him. I have vivid dayglo memories of Dad's visits. Of the way they started out exciting and ended with you screaming at each other while I hid behind a chair. Worse were the ones that ended with him closing the door so all I could do was listen with my ear pressed to the varnished wood. I remember that kind of terror in Technicolor detail, right down to the look on your face the next morning each time he left.

I'm not like that. And Cosmo's not Dad. He's nineteen and he wouldn't knowingly hurt me, not for the world. He wasn't himself. I know that. I know.

But for a moment . . .

Anyway, things are better now, and he's been sweet to me ever since. Ridiculously sweet to me. From the moment he came back to himself that night there were nothing but

244

apologies. He kept checking he hadn't hurt me or held me too hard. It was like he didn't even recognise himself. That's proof too, isn't it? That it was all just the shock of the moment.

I know how hard it can be to keep everything you feel under the surface. I climbed back into bed that night and told him that, still shaking, and he held my face and said, 'See? We're the same. We're the same. It's just you and me, Starshine. Versus everything.'

This morning he filled the bedroom with balloons, red and white and pink. I'd almost forgotten it was Valentine's. He's bought me clothes. They're not exactly my style, but he spent so much money on them I don't have the heart to ask for a single receipt. He made me try everything on so he could call me beautiful over and over. And there's a necklace. White gold, shaped like a star.

I haven't worn anything but your pendant since you died, but he wasn't to know that. So I've taken it off just for today. I'm wearing his star.

He even bought me a new plant, and I know he doesn't understand what I see in them. She's my first vegetable plant – or fruit, really: Demi Tomato. So he really *is* trying.

I know he still feels guilty about what happened. Sometimes I've caught him looking at me with the kind of startled, immobile shock of a rabbit watching a hawk. It makes me feel strangely powerful, that I can make him nervous that way, even if it's not what I want from him.

But he took my phone that night and he's probably

forgotten about it, but I just don't know how to ask for it back.

The thing is, Mom . . . the thing is that sometimes I think all I want in the world is for someone to prove they love me most. More than anything. I just want to be everything to one person, the way I felt like everything to you. And I think maybe Cosmo's right. We're the same. Because maybe inside him there's the same strange, grasping creature, needy and desperate, and the other night was just it starting to claw its way out, vicious in proving its hold on me.

And if that's true, then maybe I brought it on myself.

I just have to prove to myself what he's proving to me. That he's everything I need. I think I can manage that.

Love,
Luka

TWENTY-NINE

ROISIN

It went silent for days.

THEO

He was silent for days.

ROISIN

A few of my messages sat there on read. The ones from that night, when I thought she must have fallen asleep mid-conversation. Then the texts I sent next morning: *HOW can you SLEEP when we're GOING TO SEE MILES??*

I won't tell him you chose sleep over him obviously, but he'll sense it from the stage and like me best.

Seriously, did I dream getting those tickets?

Checked my bank: if it's a dream at least Da's going to have less of a fit. WORTH IT.

They weren't read. None of them were, for at least a week.

THEO

It must have been over a week before Alec talked to me again after I saw Luka. He walked past me on the other side of the hallway. He started choosing the seat by the door in the lessons we had together instead of our traditional back-left-corner pair.

When I moved to sit beside him anyway, he stared furiously at his desk for the entirety of the forty-five minutes and was through the door before the bell had finished its first chime.

I didn't know what to do about it. I'm just not a confrontational person. I'm cautious. I don't pick fights because I've spent enough of my life trying to sidestep the fights that try to pick me. But I couldn't bear it. Every guilty feeling I'd been trying to fend off came back to sit on my chest, because now they all felt confirmed and justified. I was to blame. He blamed me.

ROISIN

And then, as if I didn't have enough to worry about, something was happening between the boys. If everything up to then had felt like things tumbling down around me, the trouble with Alec and Theo was like the steady foundations beginning to shake.

THEO

At home at least blame was stated quite explicitly. I'd had
to tell my parents about my mock results eventually. It was
that or lie, and I'm approximately as good at lying as a dead
donkey would be at driving a bus.

To say they weren't happy would be an understatement.
My dad, when angry, grows cold and distant. Mum gets
heated and cries. I couldn't say which was worse but dealing
with both at once was quite a sensory overload. Neither of
them were angry, of course. They were just disappointed.

ROISIN

Which is the worst.

THEO

It's the *worst*.

Ronit even called, with such suspiciously flawless timing
it was clear that Mum had issued her a strict edict: call Theo,
be sympathetic. I listened to her tell me that a few bad marks
were meaningless with the kind of detachment I usually
reserve for listening to teachers in assembly talk about
diversity and equality.

I mean, it's nice that they've made the effort, but I don't
really feel they understand it.

This would be my sister Ronit. Four years older. At

Cambridge naturally. Studying medicine naturally. Just like Dad, of course. I was fairly certain her only educational failing involved causing my parents to think the alphabet began and ended with 'A'.

Mum talked about my getting extra tuition from a bored local university student she'd seen posting on Facebook, looking for beer money.

Dad suggested I try revision schedules, until I showed him my notebooks full of them.

Finally they reached the destination I knew they'd been circling: *Darling, don't you think you should see a little less of Alec?*

I was so exhausted by it all that all I could do was laugh.

ROISIN

No one saw much of Alec for a while. He was around but checked out. A blur you'd catch a glimpse of sometimes, but who wouldn't acknowledge you.

Getting the silent treatment from one Booth is bad enough. Two starts to feel like a pattern.

ALEC

When I let myself think about it, I knew there was no one to blame but myself. Theo and Luka spent maybe five minutes together in the YHH – he didn't have time to tell me about it. And, as Roisin has delicately pointed out to me more than once since, if either of them had called me while they were with her –

ROISIN

She'd have fucked off so fast she'd have left a vapour trail, Alec. Don't pretend she wouldn't.

ALEC

So I didn't let myself think about it much. And when I did I pushed any blame as far away as I could. I let it reflect on to the nearest surface. And the nearest thing to me was always Theo. Even when I was ignoring him, I knew he was nearby. On the end of a phone, or two desks away in lessons, watching me when he thought I wasn't looking.

Maybe I'd have understood what I had more if I ever felt like I could lose it. You'd think I'd have learned that lesson by then.

Through my silence and my temper I was sure that there was an invisible elastic cord between us. If I pushed him away he'd always come back.

But even elastic wears thin after a while.

Way too long after I started being an asshole and long enough before the end of it, he found me at the school bus stop, mid-March.

THEO

We were the only two waiting, the world around us under assault by heavy, driving rain. Coming down in lances, it hammered over my head and drowned out my nervous pulse.

We'd usually take this bus together. We'd pile back into his house together and raid the kitchen before shutting his bedroom door on the world. He'd make quarters of cheese sandwiches and quarters of honey ones and I'd guess with each kiss if his lips would be salty or sweet. We'd hear William come home and he'd lock the door and spend an hour finding new places to press his mouth.

I couldn't just stand there, quiet and cold.

'Are you going my way?' I tried, giving him a smile as goofy as the line only to feel it falter on my lips when he didn't even bother to look up at me.

'Are you ever going to talk to me again?' I hadn't thought I'd be brave enough to ask, but given the chance there was nothing else I could say. The words pushed themselves into the air between us before I could think and hung there.

I worried I'd sounded more accusatory than I meant to, but it made him look up.

ALEC

I shrugged. It wasn't that I didn't care – it was that if I didn't numb myself to all the things I cared about *somehow* I

252

wouldn't have been able to breathe. It was exhausting. Just lifting and dropping my shoulders was an effort.

'What do you want me to say?'

The rain was playing the bus shelter like a snare drum but I heard a small painful sound catch in his throat and he turned away, looking down the street as if he was wondering if he could make a run for it without getting speared by those silver needles. Maybe being there with me hurt worse.

'We could start with hello, I suppose,' he said, after a moment, and tilted his head just enough to look at me.

His hair was hanging into his eyes the way it always does when it's wet and just for a moment my fingers twitched with the instinct to reach up and brush back a few of the curls. How long had it been since I touched him? Since I touched anyone? I was building walls around myself I didn't know how to break down.

He took a short, staccato breath and held it tightly before exhaling in a rush. 'It's been a while since we've even managed that. I missed you.'

THEO

He nodded. I thought he looked uncomfortable. Perhaps he wished I wasn't making ending things between us so hard on him. If I was supposed to be quiet and assume it was over then there was a memo I'd missed. I've never given up on things easily. I think there must be fingernail tracks in everything I've ever let go of.

So I waited for him to add something to his nod. Anything. If he was uncomfortable then I decided I'd watch him until it was too much for him to bear. Finally he hummed low in his throat and muttered, 'I've been here.'

It was such a terrible lie I felt a rare flare of anger rushing through me. 'Except you haven't, have you? *Technically* I suppose you might have been existing in a similar location to mine, but you haven't been *here*. I don't know where you are, Alec. Somewhere I can't seem to reach.'

ALEC

'Have you maybe considered you should stop trying? Like, God, maybe I just need a break from thinking about other people for a while.'

'Other people?' Theo's lips stayed parted for a minute, as if he was trying out other words, sorting through them and holding back some of the worst. 'What about all the other people thinking about *you*?'

THEO

He scoffed, a choking sound in the back of his throat that only made my hackles raise further. I couldn't bear him thinking I didn't care.

'Do you really think I'm not? Alec, so far as my parents

are concerned, I buggered up my mocks because the only thing I've been studying is you. I just want you to *talk* to me. Let me help.'

I'd moved in towards him, barely half a step away. Close enough that I might have reached out to him, but he rounded towards me, shoulders tight, hands rolled to fists at his sides. 'As if you've *ever* been able to help.'

ALEC

All I had in my head was Luka's voice telling me I was making it all about me. Again and again. And I thought maybe she was right.

It was hard to even look at Theo, but I made myself do it. He's always been as readable as the books he carries round with him. I made myself see what I'd shattered behind his eyes. Good. Whatever I'd broken between us at least he could get himself back. Get out of my orbit. Clearly I destroyed anything I drew in too close.

He stood there and it felt like he was getting smaller and smaller beside me, until finally he turned and walked out into the rain. I watched him get halfway down the street before he finally broke into a run, his feet kicking up showers of muddy water as he escaped me as fast as he could.

A small spark of instinct reached through from where I'd shut myself down to basic functions only and told me to run after him. Run and run and run and run. But the mechanical part of me just watched him go, and I thought, *Well, there's one thing I can't screw up any more.*

A sound choked its way out of my throat. This loud, painful hiccup so sudden I startled myself. Grateful I was alone I leaned back against the flimsy shelter wall and hiccuped again. Rubbed a hand over my mouth to try and push the sound back and found that my hand was shaking. The bus was coming and my whole body was suddenly shaking too much for me to move. I ducked my head low and watched the headlights swoop along the street beside me, slowing, slowing, and then – when no one hailed them – moving on.

Tucking my chin hard against my chest I whispered something I always saved for when it was silent and dark.

'*I want my mom.*'

Another hiccup rocked my shoulders.

'I want my mom. I want my mom. I want my mom. I want my mommy. I want my mom. I don't understand. I don't understand. I don't, I don't, I don't. I can't.'

I couldn't breathe, because every time I breathed I made that *sound* again, completely out of my own control, and then it was coming anyway, worse and worse. I stood there at the bus stop letting out deep, painful sobs as the rain came down, but at least I was alone.

At least I was alone.

THIRTY

ROISIN

It was a strange night for a concert.

Not because of the day. Mondays aren't known for being the wildest of nights, but Miles Riva was in enough demand that they were shoving extra shows in wherever they'd fit. Or the date. 16 March's not much different from any other day in the grand scheme of things. The weather was just edging toward something nice, and even by that late in the evening it hadn't quite turned bitter. Town was buzzing, people spilling out of shops on Brixton High Road all looking dressed up with somewhere to go.

Usually I love having tickets to something. A concert or club night, even the theatre. It's like being given a secret mission in one of those spy films. Something you hug close to your chest on the Tube as you work out how late you can get there and still have time to duck in to the nearest toilets and check your hair. And, like in the spy films, somehow everyone else in town feels like they're caught up in it too. You catch the eye of the girl across from you on the Tube before you notice the lyric tattoo running down her arm: *Darling, you're my daylight.*

You spot people in a shop wearing brand-new merch and know that they must have been on the same mission a day or two before. You exchange secret grins with people in the nearest chicken shop to the venue, trying to settle a layer of grease over your excitement.

That was all in place, that night. But as I stood under the Academy's dome and waited, it was all the more obvious it wasn't a mission to be completed alone.

Alone, the looks you get are different, more unsure. The bag-check lady rolls her eyes at you, waiting for you to make up your mind if you're coming in or not. There's no one to nudge and laugh with when you spot a super-fan and the excitement builds.

There's just no one. There's you, stood there like a stranger at a wedding.

And that was me that night. I had my invitation: two red-hot tickets folded neatly into my wallet. I had my outfit, that shirt I'd worn on my first day at a new school. But I didn't have Luka, nor any promise she'd be there.

There'd been nothing from her in all that time. Not a single word.

But I and my hopeful heart took ourselves along to wait for her anyway. And it was a strange old night because the virus was all anyone could talk about. All these horrible things on the news about China and Italy. Frightening stories about dying, gasping people that I had to turn off as soon as I came across them. But I couldn't turn off the news itself, even if I never watched it. It was everywhere. Creeping in.

A few of us had been kept home from school, and the local newspaper was saying there were people from the borough in hospital with it. Just a scattered few. Like everywhere. There were barely more people in hospital than you'd hear about being taken in after a particularly fierce rave. It just didn't seem as if it could be the big deal here it was turning into everywhere else.

But it was a nervy thing. Sitting on the Tube, stepping into a shop, picking up a takeaway, you thought about it. You could see other people thinking about it, especially if someone nearby let out a stray cough. Get a frog in your throat and you felt like you needed to convince people you didn't have the lurgy.

Or maybe you did. They were giving out the symptoms by then on TV. All the ways of telling if you'd a bad dose of the thing. And then you were supposed to lock yourself up for a couple of weeks while the folks in the village danced outside chanting *unclean, unclean*. Or, something like that. It all felt so strange and medieval.

Mam had tucked a pack of strawberry-scented hand sanitiser into my pocket on my way out the door, and I'd already used so much of it I smelled like one of those strings of red plasticky liquorice they sell at the cinema pick 'n' mix. You don't notice all the things you touch until any of them could be contaminated. On escalators I'd watched people reach absently for the moving handrails, then whip their hands away as if they'd been burned.

Meanwhile I was burning up from the inside out. I'm not the most angry person, not usually. I don't carry a flame of it with me ready to torch something at any second. It takes work to build me to the kind of temper where I can feel it simmering under my skin.

Heat licked up my throat and scorched over my cheeks as a couple of girls dashed past me and got held up by the mistress of the bag check. 'You can spare a minute,' she told them. 'You're only missing the support.'

I twisted on my heel and stalked up the road until I was far enough to turn and snap a picture of the venue, sending it off to Luka with the words *I'm here, where are you?*

As though she'd get back to tell me, oh, she'd just been waiting round the other side this whole time, getting as many looks and as worked up as I'd been. We could laugh about it then and go in, only missing the support.

I didn't wait long for a reply.

Did you even remember?

Do you even remember me at all? Do you? Jesus.

Ripping open my bag I fumbled around for those hard-earned two-am tickets, remembering how I'd barely talked Da out of a coronary when I told him the cost, but they were going to be so, so worth it.

I marched up to this long-haired lad who'd been

hanging around as long as I had, quietly approaching anyone who stopped outside to ask if they were buying or selling. I waved my tickets in his face. 'Are you still interested in these?'

He'd offered a decent amount for them earlier. Now he screwed up his face, running calculations. 'Hard to sell when it's already started.'

I tossed them his way. Watched him try to catch them before they fluttered to the floor and wondered if he spared a thought for how they'd been in my strawberry-scented but potentially germ-ridden hands just a moment before. 'Then take them. Keep them. Go and watch the bloody concert if you want to. I'm done. I am *so* done with this.'

Marching back towards the Tube it didn't feel like the world had changed, only that something inside me had shifted. The bars were open but half full, pubs had televisions on but there was no sport – I remember they'd called all that off a few days before. Still, I didn't pause to watch. Why would I, unless I'd a yen to humiliate myself just a tiny bit more: little lonely waif presses her nose to windows and sighs over all the happy people inside. Like an orphan in a Victorian novel. I just went home. Home and slammed the door and stamped up to my room with Mam suddenly following and me expecting her to give a lecture on how a herd of elephants would make less noise. But instead she just stopped in my doorway and said, 'Have you seen the news, Roisin? It's this virus.'

And so I went to look at it with her and there was the PM talking over a red running headline saying we weren't to go out any more. Not to pubs, or bars, or theatres, or concerts. Stay at home, he said.

And when Mam said, 'Are you all right, sweetheart?' and moved across to put her arms around me and fend off my attempts to stop her mopping up my face with her sleeve, I thought, *Well, at least I haven't anywhere else to be.*

THIRTY-ONE

LETTER FROM ALEC
24 MARCH 2020

Dear Luka,

Pretty fucking stupid writing you a letter when I don't know where you are, isn't it? Pretty Fucking Stupid: currently the future name of my band and title of my autobiography.

I guess I could shoot this over in an email but I know by now the chances of you reading that are as slim as they would be if I left this letter in the fireplace for the same postal service that delivers to Santa.

I could get it to you somehow, maybe. I could get it near you at least, but maybe these are things I don't really want you to see.

Where the hell were you on Sunday?

Remember last Mother's Day? Remember the nightmare that was the month before it? All the emails and banners everywhere saying *Don't Forget Your Mother!* like it was a cruel joke. I couldn't walk past all the racks of cards without getting caught in front of them, pinned to the ground with longing, until at last I cracked and bought one and when you found me sitting and staring at it in my room you took it gently from my hands and read the front: *I love you, Mum.*

And I said it was stupid, but you wrapped your arms round me until it felt like she was holding me again and you said 'No. No it's not. You still do.'

Remember how we said if we didn't have Mom then at least she hadn't left us alone?

I stood in that graveyard for hours after William and Allegra left. I refused to believe you wouldn't show.

I'm –

I'm terrified, Luka, and I don't know if it's for you or me but all I know is that with Mom gone and with you gone and Theo gone it feels like there's a fucking hole in the world. There's a hole and it's deep and dark and sucks all the light around into it. And the thing I worry about most is ~~Maybe it's me.~~

Maybe it's me. Maybe I'm the black hole here, drawing things close to me only to leave them crushed and ruined.

The prime minister was on the news a couple of weeks ago – he's on practically every night now, but a couple of weeks' ago was the one I watched. The one I can't get out of my head. He was giving this stupid blustering speech and he looked like someone had washed all the blood out of his veins and then he said something like, *Many of your loved ones will die before their time.*

And my blood's been ice ever since. Where were you on Sunday? Where are you??

Maybe there's something wrong with me. I've never told you – would never tell you – but I took photos of Mom after she died. When everyone left me alone for my last moment with her I didn't have any idea what to say so I got out my phone and I took a picture of her lying there under the white hospital sheets with flowers from the bouquets by her bed that William had pulled out and laid across her pillow. I took a photo of my dead mother. Is that sick? She'd just been in pain so long, Luka, and I didn't want a picture of her that was full of wires and tubes and the tightness at the corner of her eyes that she'd stopped being able to hide. When she was dead she finally looked peaceful again, and beautiful and so young and I took a picture because that's what I wanted to remember. It's still on my phone and sometimes I scroll past it accidentally and it kicks the breath from my lungs because maybe just sometimes a little part of me was starting to forget.

I have to keep it now, so I never can.

Am I sick? Am I wrong? I've felt wrong for so long now I don't know if it's just how I am.

You know how when someone dies everyone tells you they're sorry for your loss? Like you've just mislaid

the person. Like you've been careless. Well, maybe I have.
Maybe I screwed this up. Maybe I screwed up everything
with everyone. Maybe it's me, ruining everything I touch.
A black hole of a boy.

Where were you?
Where were you?
Where are you?
I can't do this alone.
I can't
Fuck.

THIRTY-TWO

EPISODE OUTRO

THEO

You're not here, Alec, and so you won't hear this until later, but I'm turning the recording back on.

Because this is the first time that I've heard that letter, and the first time I've really known everything you were putting on yourself when all this was going on and I really wanted to say something.

I wanted to say something about black holes.

You see, despite popular misconception, black holes don't suck. We may view them as vortexes in space, functioning like a vacuum cleaner that someone's accidentally left running while it gasps down everything that comes into reach.

It simply isn't true. Black holes absorb things, yes, but they function by attraction. A strong gravitational pull that draws objects towards them through the vastness of space. It's semantics, perhaps, but I thought after that it was an important point to make.

Black holes are highly attractive.

They don't suck.

And neither do you.

THIRTY-THREE

**MY NAME IS LUKA: EPISODE 8
'I CARRY YOUR HEART'**

THEO

When the schools closed down, it felt like a response to
a very specific prayer that involved me not having to sit
through lessons with my ex-boyfriend not speaking to me,
while fending off everyone who wanted to ask why.

Rather callous to have found the single sliver of a
bright side about the onset of a global pandemic, I suppose,
but in fairness none of us knew then what it would become.
It was a strange, sudden inconvenience to our teachers,
and a few unexpected weeks off school that not many of
us were initially inclined to complain about. I went home,
downloaded Houseparty to my phone like everyone else, and
scrolled through a Snapchat feed that whiplashed between
people talking about how freaked out they were, and a few
others planning 'lockdown lock-ins' already.

ROISIN

School became revision sheets and 'suggested' reading, with a couple of lessons a day that we were meant to turn up for 'in person' – meaning as a blank box on Microsoft Teams.

It was hard enough to concentrate as it was (although we all seemed to be paying attention somehow that day Mr Tang's husband accidentally mooned the camera, or Ms Thompson took in a massive delivery from Wines Direct to her apparently one-person household). But just sometimes she was there.

She always stayed muted. Just a black box on a mostly black screen with her name typed into the corner. But on those days I couldn't remember a single word the teacher said. I left those lessons with my head full of Luka Booth and nothing else besides a messy tangle of fury and regret.

THEO

And then, once we were banned from seeing each other, he started talking to me in class.

At first I took it for a mistake. A private message popping up in chat that just said *Hi* and made my heart clench like a tightened fist. I signed straight out of the meeting to keep the weaker part of myself from sending a reply and spent the remaining class time lying flat on the bed with my hands trapped under me, just in case they got any bad ideas.

Next lesson I had with him was blessedly silent.

And then English literature.

Hey, don't go.

I may have bitten straight through my lip.

ALEC

Now, there are plenty of things you hear people blaming the prime minister for when it comes to . . . pretty much anything, really, but especially things around the pandemic. I'm not intending to make a political podcast here, so we're not going to get into that.

But, in this case, you really could blame the prime minister for me messaging Theo that day.

I still had his words circling round and round in my head, filing my days with this constant, low-level terror. *Many of your loved ones will die before their time.*

Yeah well, I'd already done that. It sucked, and I didn't have many more people left to lose.

I just kept thinking how if anything happened, Theo might never know that's exactly what he was, to me. A loved one.

Even if he was done dealing with me and my shit. Even if we never got together again. If we never *talked* again. I just needed him to know that.

So I asked him not to go, and on the screen where Miss Preeti was going on about *The Great Gatsby* I watched his

eyes flick over to the chat box. He didn't leave. So I picked
up one of the books we'd been looking at in another lesson,
and I flicked through to a dog-eared page and typed in:

> *we are for each other: then*
> *laugh, leaning back in my arms*
> *for life's not a paragraph*
>
> *and death i think is no parenthesis.*

THEO

E. E. Cummings. I could remember being at Alec's house,
in his room, lying on our stomachs and paging through the
books we'd been given in class while I explained that he was
one of my favourite poets and Alec sighed and said –

ALEC

'I just don't think I understand all this.'

What can I say? They grew on me. Or, they stayed the
same while I grew and lived through a few of the things they
were talking about. So many of those poems had started
speaking to me by then.

I sat there feeling like all my nerves were pushing to the
surface of my skin, waiting to see what Theo would reply.

THEO

I didn't. I had no words of my own.

Next lesson, I signed in and seconds later –

ALEC

> love is less always than to win
> less never than alive
> less bigger than the least begin
> less littler than forgive.

I was typing in the next stanza, breath held, when I got a response.

THEO

Is that what you want from me? Forgiveness?

ALEC

Maybe. Partly. But you're focusing on the wrong word.

THEO

Perhaps I was. It had me in knots. These messages, the idea that – perhaps – some pretty words were supposed to make everything fine. The idea that I so very much wanted them to.

I dug my own book out from the pile. I know a lot of Cummings by heart, but I wanted to be sure of what I was quoting.

> You have played,
> (I think)
> And broke the toys you were fondest of,
> And are a little tired now;
> Tired of things that break, and –
> Just tired.
> So am I.

Stealing words from the middle of a poem stripped their original context and gave them mine. It felt satisfying to do – to find words that expressed things I could never feel comfortable with if they came directly from me. It's like listening to music – those particular songs where the singer spells out my secrets somehow.

I watched as Alec typed in his reply – still on camera while our teacher talked about structure and meaning.

I'm so tired. And broken, I think. But that's not an excuse to have tried to damage you too. You were only ever there for me.

I typed: *I wanted to fix things for you, but I wasn't enough.*

He typed: *I took that for granted. I shoved you away because I was scared to lose you. I've been losing so much –*

sometimes it feels like trying to hold on to anything makes
it worse. Like if I let it all go, I won't have anything left to
hurt me. But that didn't work either. I've just been making an
artform out of shooting myself in the foot this whole time.

And then a second later, he added: *You are enough.*
Theo, you're everything.

ALEC

You can't really meet someone's eyes when you're one of
a dozen faces on a screen, but it felt like he met mine. And
smiled. When the teacher ended the lesson I'd barely noticed
it had begun.

THEO

That night, he texted me:

> *And the coolness of your smile is*
> *stirringofbirds between my arms;but*
> *i should rather than anything*
> *have(almost when hugeness will shut*
> *quietly)almost,*
>   *your kiss.*

ALEC

I got a quick reply from him. *I see you get flirty outside of class.*

He replied: *I could be flirtier. There's one here about parting flesh.*

THEO

Filth. No wonder people burn books.

But they're beautiful, aren't they?

ALEC

Lots of them are. But there's one of these I've been thinking about kind of a lot. Like whenever I think about you.

I typed it before better sense could stop me. It was probably a mess of autocorrect and spelling errors but I got it out quick.

here is the deepest secret nobody knows.
(here is the root of the root and the bud of the bud
and the sky of the sky of a tree called life; which grows
higher than soul can hope or mind can hide)
and this is the wonder that's keeping the stars apart.
i carry your heart (i carry it in my heart).

He didn't reply for so long that I sent one more message. It just said:

Theo?

THEO

Sorry. I'm just wondering if it would be worth breaking the law to come and see you right now.

ALEC

It's not. I'm definitely not worth that. Just tell me if we're okay?

THEO

The big question. And I so wanted us to be. I typed out my reassurances, my yeses and of courses. And then I held my finger down and watched them all blink away.

No, I don't think that we are. I don't think that anything's okay just at the moment, Alec, and I don't know if it will be. You'll still be grieving. Your sister will still be coping in ways that rightly scare you. My parents will still want to lock me at the top of a tall tower until I emerge with straight As. People will think we shouldn't be together for a vast and absurd array of reasons, most of them too bigoted to argue with. And you may not have noticed but it feels like the world's on fire.

So I don't think that okay's the word.

But it doesn't have to be okay. You don't have to be okay to keep me.

I'm still yours.

ALEC

Theo will tell you that one of the things I love most about him is his verbosity (a word that he taught me). His vocabulary. His words and the way he uses them, the way an ordinary conversation can turn into the most fascinating TED Talk you ever accidentally clicked into. I love that.

But God, I wish he could have got to that last sentence first. I read the first part with a mouthful of my heart – ventricles caught between my teeth and coppery-salt panic running down my throat.

But I hadn't lost him, he said, and he never lies about anything. The world straightened up from a momentary jolt to its axis and kept turning.

I read what he'd said three times before I messaged back.

Maybe we don't have to be okay. Maybe we just have to be. And you're right I'm not okay. I won't be. And I'm not about to say what's happening with Luka isn't still going to be taking up all the brain space I have to spare. I can't seem to stop that. But I can't keep making everything about her.

Wait. I mean about me. I can't not worry but I can't let it completely take over my life.

THEO

I wanted to argue with the idea that he was making things about himself. If his world had pulled to a narrow focus, then

278

it was because he was making it about the way he needed to make it about her.

But then that wasn't entirely healthy either.

I don't want you to stop caring about her, Alec. I wouldn't recognise you if you tried.

ALEC

But I can care about more than one thing.

I do.

I don't know if you noticed but I was trying really hard to tell you I love you back there.

THEO

All this when I didn't even know if I'd be allowed to see him again, or when, by governmental decree. For a moment it felt like being in an old story. Destined lovers kept apart by fate. Star-crossed.

I love you too.

I closed my eyes and pressed my nose to the screen of my phone, pretending the brightness trying to push through my eyelids was him.

There was a long pause before another message came through, buzzing against my skin.

Do you want me to quote that filthy poem to you now?

Smiling, I typed back: *Go on.*

THIRTY-FOUR

LETTER FROM LUKA
2 APRIL 2020

Dear Mom.

One million cases, today. Last time I wrote to you there were a handful and now it feels like we're watching an avalanche, staring up helplessly as it builds speed coming down towards us. Standing in its shadow.

Last time I wrote to you and last time I left the flat are pretty much the same thing, by the way, so you don't need to worry about me getting into harm's way.

Between the lockdown and Cosmo there really isn't much chance.

But I guess he doesn't feel like I'm going to meet someone who could steal me away just visiting a graveyard. And that makes sense - the social scene here is dead.

That was gallows humour. With people dying on the daily in the kind of numbers that would make headlines for a week if they were caused by a train wreck or a terror attack, anyone who didn't understand what black humour was before is learning pretty quick. We're in a world where even the living are kept at home, interred in their own eternal dwelling places, baking tombstone slabs of banana bread.

I wish I knew who he thinks I'm going to meet. Who he's watching for, leaning over the screen when he lets me have my phone – I only use it for signing into classes now really, though he doesn't like that either. The computer's so full of password protection I might as well be typing on a brick. And he's home all the time. Who am I going to meet? How careful am I supposed to be? I can't figure out if it's other people he doesn't trust, or me.

And it's not like I do the same to him. I see him on social media all the time, because there's nothing else to do – although I'm supposed to manage without it. Sometimes I catch him smiling over a message, or a flash of a picture, a girl who's all tan skin and light hair, and I wonder if he just suspects me of doing whatever *he* would do if he had the chance. Blaming me for sins he'd like to engage in.

The strange thing is, when I think about that I don't even really feel jealous. I don't feel a lot of anything any more.

Sometimes I shut myself in the bedroom for hours and he doesn't notice until there's no food or no one to tell him where he left his vape. I lie on the floor beside the bed and stare up at the dark ceiling and imagine the world beyond it. Wide blue sky. Or stars. Infinite galaxies. I pretend I'm at the observatory using the telescope there and looking out into eternity the way I once promised Alec I would.

I think I'd call him now. Alec. If I had five minutes alone with my phone.

And then I pull that view back down from the outer edges of the universe and I look into myself. All the ropes and tubes of vein and ligament inside me. People are just puppets really. Held together by strings.

Sometimes, when there's been something about the virus on TV – images of what it looks like under a microscope, little prickly pestilent specks of cells – I imagine those particles coursing through me. Catching together into clusters, sticky and thick, and using those spikes to crawl along my veins on a quest to win my heart. They say it takes hold of you before the symptoms start. You don't even know you've got it until it's there, too late to shake yourself free.

And then Cosmo comes in and shakes me out of the reverie.

He's stopped saying sorry.

When he gets angry. When he does the things he does. He doesn't say sorry any more. He tells me it's my fault and that I drive him to it, and then suddenly I'm the one apologising for his hurt.

It's not like he hits me. Ever. He's not like that. Sometimes he just talks and talks about what use I am (none) and what I'm worth (nothing) and how loving me is ruining him but he can't stop. He loves me too much to save himself from me. He talks until I cover my head with my arms and then he pulls my arms away and holds them high above my head, wrists tight in his hands so that I'll listen to him.

But there was one night.

We hadn't fought. It had been a good day. A good few days. Things were quiet, and quiet is the same as good now. Quiet means I've done everything the way I should. I watered the plants before bed (I should do that less – Toothless is showing a little leaf burn) and he smiled at me warmly enough that I curled up against him without having to be pulled close and I fell asleep with his arm round my shoulder.

And I woke with his hand round my throat.

He wasn't squeezing hard. Just enough to wake me. Enough that when I woke I coughed and tried to swallow and that was harder work than it should have been.

I looked up into his eyes. The colour of warm honey. The colour of emptiness in the dark.

'I could kill you if I wanted.'

He said it strangely affectionately. He said it like the hold he had on me was a cuddle. He said it and then he let go of me and lay down to go back to sleep and I thought . . . maybe he will.

At least I'd see you again.

I've thought about leaving. You don't know how much it takes even writing that down. As if he'll see it and never let me out of the house again, even to come here and see you. I can't exist if I can't see you. I'm barely existing now.

When you died, I wrote a list of every memory I had of you. I added to it for weeks, because when someone dies they steal half your memories away with them. The confirming part. The part where I can say 'Remember?' and you'd say 'Yes' and tell me all the things I'd forgotten. So I wrote as much as I could, as fast as I could, while I was still sure of my memory. Before all the little stupid things I loved could slip away. So I'd always remember who you were.

I'm starting to think I should make a list for myself now. Of who I was.

Was I someone who would leave?

I called one of those helplines. Not on my phone, on Cosmo's when he left it one time he went out for food. One of those domestic . . . helplines. I just wanted some advice. I wanted to know if I how I feel is real or if I'm going crazy, like he says. I'm someone who lays on the floor in their bedroom and imagines being sick just for something to do. I must be crazy.

The woman on the phone freaked me out. She sounded so serious, as though this was a Very Important Call. I tried to explain I only wanted to ask a few questions. It wasn't a big deal. I wasn't an *abused woman*. I just tried to tell her how things were with Cosmo to see how normal it was.

You're very young. That's what she said. She said it three times – it's what she kept saying. *You're very young.* I don't know what that meant. If it meant she thought that what I was telling her was impossible or that I was a child, making up stories.

There was a noise from the door and I hung up, fumbling the phone in my hands as I deleted the call from its history, my heart a frightened bird.

He'd just brought back pizza. We got plates from the kitchen, he hugged me and smiled and stole my pepperoni and it was fine. He was sweet. Mostly it's fine, Mom. I just need to get better at keeping the days quiet.

I hope everyone's safe. I keep thinking about William's mom and the care-home coven.

I'd like to tell Alec that I'm fine too. But I'm not sure he'd care any more.

Love you, Mommy.
Luka

THIRTY-FIVE

ROISIN

London was an epicentre for the spread of the virus, as was understandable. Even the prime minister caught it, and went to the hospital, and no matter if it loves him or hates him, that shakes a city up. When half the place is layered up on top of each other like boxes of sweaty, coughing, commuting chocolates you can see how easily these things spread. People talked about R numbers and T-cells and other scary letters of the alphabet I didn't quite follow the meaning of.

We were told to stay home, so we stayed home, and we worried, and every time an ambulance pulled up outside my building or one of the blocks nearby we worried a little more.

Our flat doesn't have a garden so much as a communal concrete slab, and the walkways were lined with blank-eyed smokers twenty-four-seven during lockdown so I started taking a regime of daily walks out across the park just to remember how to breathe. It was glorious summer that April, and there are places out there that still feel close to nature, at least until a heavy-breather in athletic gear pounds past you through the grass.

I was out walking when mam called to tell me about Granny.

It just didn't make sense to me. *It still* doesn't. London might be a cauldron for contagion, fair enough, but how does a virus get out to a tiny, backwater town? Even the bus service can't make it out to where my granny lives if it's a Sunday.

But she was sick with it. It had come on sudden enough that she'd felt a bit wobbly one day and was in the hospital before the next.

I talked to Mam so long that by the time we were done I was ready to collapse under one of the trees on One Tree Hill, just to rest long enough to be able to run back home and hug her. All she wanted was to go to see Granny, but the travel rules were a confusing mess and no one was allowed in the hospital anyway. I closed my eyes, pressing my face into the palms of my hands, and I could picture my aunts, all seven of them, each of them fierce as a gorgon and desperate to get through that hospital doorway. I thought of the sheer force of will it took to tell any of the women in my family 'no'. This virus had somehow managed it without so much as a whisper.

I didn't want to think of my grandmother, that birdlike slip of a woman who would have faced down dragons for any of us, in a hospital bed all alone.

By the time I pulled my hands away from my face the sunlight had fallen into shadow around me, and it took a long minute to work out that evening hadn't come on suddenly to match my mood. The absence of the sun was due to the boy standing in front of me, blocking its path.

Tall, blond, face like a puppy with big dreams of being called a good boy.

Alfie bloody Newly.

WILLIAM

There are moments when you look back over the life you've lived and wonder how it has quite come to this. Some of these moments occur when your younger daughter loudly interrupts a final, frustrating attempt at recording a lecture none of your students are likely to ever bother with watching in order to demand a biscuit and a cuddle.

Some, when you abandon all efforts to retain professional distance for the day and turn on the news with her pulled on to your lap, biscuit in sticky hand.

Holding your youngest child close as you watch the sombre assembly of mobile morgues outside hospitals in New York City and hear of mass graves being dug was also quite the moment for asking myself that question. How had it come to this?

But then all of it was so very much a reminder of those terrible last days at the hospital. All of it a reminder to be grateful that, as my wife lay dying, I was at least able to sleep in a chair at her side, her hand in mine. A gift given to barely anyone in the pandemic's curious, touchless times.

What strange things this virus has given us all cause to be grateful for.

ROISIN

'And they don't know how long she'll have,' I was telling Alfie. He'd sat down at a safe, two-metre distance and I was already sure he'd be regretting making that choice.

Not that I could stop myself from talking at him. I can't hold things in. It's always been my way that if something makes me scared, or angry or upset I pour it all out as soon as possible. Can't help it. And it feels less toxic somehow than holding all that negativity inside. I was just glad not to be alone.

He had a knack for picking his moments when it came to that.

'It's touch and go. That's what they told Mam when she called, which is *ridiculous*. She only went in overnight. A person can't go downhill so fast in so little time.'

I start to *sound* like Granny when I'm upset. Thick accent, words so close together they're tripping each other up. Alfie frowned with concentration and my run-on-sentences skidded to a stop.

'Sorry, I'm putting this all on you and you barely even know me.'

'But I know the names of twelve of your cousins now.

That's more than I know about some people I've been friends with all my life.' He kept the teasing cautious, eyes on my face as he spoke. 'Please don't be sorry,' he said. 'I just –'

Alfie let out a strange frustrated sound and crossed his arms tight over his chest.

I looked at him. 'What's that you're doing?'

He squeezed his arms tighter, very determined about it, though I could see his earlobes turning cherry. 'It's a hug. I'd give you a real one – with your full and informed consent, of course. But while we're socially distancing, and given the circumstances, this is the best I can do.'

There was a long old pause until finally I nodded.

'You look like a vampire,' I said. 'Arms crossed over your chest. You look like you want to give me the cuddle of eternal life.'

'I do not,' he told me, indignant.

'Or like you're paying homage to Wakanda which, in all fairness, is a fine thing to do but I'm not sure they're your people.'

'*Roisin*.' He said my name on a tut, and I grinned.

'Alfie.'

WILLIAM

Later, with Allegra distracted elsewhere and the house quiet, I did something that I hadn't in some time. Since the funeral, if I'm not mistaken.

I took out my photographs of her.

Gabriella's bequeathal to me, along with three children to attempt to raise to adulthood relatively unscarred, one dog who had to be taken to the vets on a yearly basis for the crime of swallowing socks whole, and a well of sorrow I'd not yet found a ladder to escape from, were her photographs.

I had more of her young, from the days long before she met me, than I did from after our marriage. Such is the way of the digital world. I laid out the pictures from our wedding day: my favourites the ones that weren't posed. Unplanned, unguarded images capturing the blur of movement when we danced. The corner of her smile.

And beneath I traced her path backwards in time. Photos taken in the Arizona sunlight, every one of them a golden hour. Gabriella forever young and vital in paint-smudged T-shirts and cut-off shorts, a wary looking young girl at her side and a toddler peeking out from behind her calves.

Alec came to join me after a while, sitting silently at my side.

ALEC

'Isn't she beautiful,' he said eventually. It wasn't a question, just a truth staring up from every image. Some of them I didn't think I'd seen before, or not recently enough to remember.

I pressed my fingers to one taken in the kitchen I remembered growing up in, with my sister standing small but fierce at Mom's side and me in a romper suit behind them. She was beautiful, but if you looked too closely, you could see the last traces of a bruise on her cheek.

Touching her face, I smoothed my thumb over it as if I could wipe that stain away and looked up at Dad.

'She looks just like Luka.'

ROISIN

'There's something –'

Alfie hung those words in the air as we walked back across the park and just left them, like drying laundry, until I couldn't help but hurry him on.

'Something? Something in the bushes? Let's hope not, or it would have mugged us by now.'

He rubbed his hand across his face, with the pinched expression of someone who might be getting a headache. 'There's something I want to tell you, but I don't know if I should, or if this wouldn't be the right time.'

'Well, if that isn't the cryptic Facebook update of comments to make. You have to, now, or they'll find me dead with curiosity soon enough, like the proverbial cat. Is it something bad?'

He twisted his mouth up a minute, then shook his head. 'It might not help. Also, it might not be legal.'

'Well, there's an enticing combination.' I stopped and folded my arms in the middle of the path – the joggers could jog around us. 'Out with it then. I promise not to shop you.'

And it was like déjà vu, really. So much so that I couldn't believe I didn't see it coming somehow. He even had the same nervy way about him as when he told me over the lunch table. 'I know where Luka is.'

It turned out Alfie's dad had an interest in a company that scooped up as many reasonably priced flats as possible, whenever they came up for sale, and went on to rent them out for extortionate prices to people who couldn't afford to buy since the reasonably priced places had all gone.

It turned out that one of those places was being rented out to one Colin Allen – not a name Alfie would have known to look out for, but his da had him doing an internship while we were all on lockdown – working from home but playing messenger boy when he needed to, and he saw them while he was dropping paperwork off for the building manager. Saw Luka and Cosmo.

He said it was a while ago, and he didn't want to mention it in case he had the wrong idea, but when he saw Cosmo there a second time he decided to go through the files. And there was only one that could have been him, though it still didn't add up, not really.

So he called the building manager and asked why there were no references for Colin Allen's tenancy. Made out it was a question coming from higher up, and he picked up all the gossip that way – that Cosmo had claimed they were coming out of a bad situation. That his girlfriend's family were looking for her. Not untrue except he made out like they'd kidnap her to a cult or something if they caught her, the arsehole. And they were able to pay for the first few months with a cash lump sum, which meant the references just happened to be overlooked.

Anyway. Alfie had found him. He found him. And he was twenty-four. He wasn't *nineteen,* taking a year off from uni. He'd taken the whole of uni off from uni. So that was two lies he'd told her, among all the poison he seemed to give out about the rest of us.

'Are you mad?' Alfie asked.

And I was. I was fucking fuming to be honest with you, but I knew that wasn't what he was asking.

'Not at you. Why would I be mad at you?'

His shoulders danced through a shrug. 'For telling you. For not telling you sooner? I don't know.'

I tilted my head up to get the last of the afternoon sun under my skin, recharging before I got home and faced the dark things waiting there. 'You told me, that's enough. It's more than you had to.'

ALEC

William picked the picture up between two fingers and held it to the light, the way a doctor examines an X-ray, as if he could see into the room where it was taken. I remember everything about that kitchen. From when I was a little older but it was still the same. I remember the warm tiles under my feet and the way the smell of spices clung to the walls from years of Mom's never-mild cooking. Looking at it then, I could remember the way Mom's hand felt back when she could wrap mine completely in hers, and it made me ache inside.

'You both look like her. Allegra too, but she's still growing into herself. You two have so much of her soul that there are days she doesn't feel quite gone.'

Everyone always tells Luka she's like our mother. No one really thinks to say it to me – maybe because I'm a boy.

'Me too?'

'You're *so* like her,' he said, and I took those words and wrapped them tight within me, to keep them safe.

William put the photo down and sighed. 'I have to do right by her, Alec. I don't know yet whether that means making amends with Luka's boyfriend or some other course of action, but I have to resolve this somehow. And soon. We never quite know how much time we have.'

ROISIN

'You know how I *know* it wasn't an easy decision to tell me?' I asked Alfie, just before I left him at the edge of the park. He shook his head and I smiled at him, hopeful and hopeless.

'Because now I don't know whether to tell *them*, either.'

THIRTY-SIX

ROISIN

Days later, I still hadn't decided. To tell or not to tell. Hamlet had all the easy questions – this one was stumping me.

Points in favour of sharing my information:

Alec would want to know.

Points against:

Luka clearly didn't want to be found. She could have picked up the phone any old time and told everyone where to send her next birthday card, but she hadn't. She hadn't picked up the phone at all. And with everything *else* going on in the world, with the bone-deep exhaustion that living with stress every day will set into you, the rest of us had stopped trying to reach out too.

It's impossible to keep your arms outstretched forever, not without something tangible to hold on to. They start to ache.

But a point I couldn't fit to one side or the other: I had a bad feeling.

My granny always used to say she could feel things in

her waters, and I never understood what she meant by it. But it turns out to be a hereditary condition – we must be a whole family of prophets and diviners - because I know now. Deep inside me there's a river running, and when I thought of Luka and that man she was with the water turned treacherous and wild.

I made up my mind to go and see her myself.

ALEC

The rules at the time were these:

Stay at home, protect the NHS, save lives.

Still no school. Work from home unless it's essential.

Leave the house only for essential shopping or exercise.

You can walk with one other person.

But remain two metres apart from anyone not from your household.

Strictly under those guidelines Theo and I started going on dates.

THEO

We'd never exactly dated to begin with. Our relationship began as conversation one day and kissing the next –

ALEC

Kissing mid-sentence.

THEO

Kissing was easier than talking, I suspect. And then it moved to – everything else with no real distance in between. Distance was impossible then. I couldn't hold you close enough.

ALEC

I think if I could have got under your skin I would.

THEO

You do. In more ways than one. But lockdown – it was like a reset. A very long, formal purity dance at a 1950s American prom. The virus between us to keep us chaste. We went on dates.

ALEC

To the park.

THEO

And Aldi.

ALEC

And Tesco Express. All the grocery stores. The only places
still open.

ROISIN

And that's when I saw her. Out at the shops. At Boots.

I was coming down the escalator from the top section,
where everything non-essential was taped off like it was part
of a police crime scene, and she was at one of the pharmacy
tills. I was sure it was her. She'd dyed her hair. It looked like
she'd aimed for blonde and ended up with something the
colour of nothing – it was a mess, and God knew what she
was wearing, but I'd know her anywhere.
I'd know her in my sleep.

Jumping the last three steps of the escalator, I pushed
through a gauntlet of old ladies hovering around the
suppositories and made for the counter, calling her name.

'Luka? Luka!'

I knew she'd heard me. The people either side of her
turned to look and I could see her shoulders clench tight, but
she didn't look round. She stepped away from her spot at the
counter and the next minute she was on the other side of a

queue that didn't seem to know what social distancing was. I couldn't lose her.

THEO

There's something about not being able to touch. We entered shops separately. Stayed the requisite distance apart all the way round – not speaking, communicating via produce.

ALEC

What Theo means is that he held up an eggplant one time and tried to give me a smooth flirtatious look before laughing so hard the manager came over and told him to go back outside.

THEO

Well, we'd used up all our poetry. I had to find some way to be creative.

ALEC

There *is* something about not being able to touch. We sat on the low wall in the car park, or a bench in the park – not for too long, or someone would come by to tell us that parks were for exercise only. And we edged just our hands closer as we talked until our fingers could almost have brushed. Flirting with danger.

THEO

I don't think I've ever wanted something more. Someone more.

ROISIN

There was a spotty boy at the counter staring after her, and I made an enemy of the line of poorly people by inserting myself in front of him, breathless behind my mask. 'That girl just now. What did she want?'

He blinked at me, cow-like. I could have hauled him up by the lapels – there was no *time*.

'What did that girl ask you for? What did she *want*?'

'Um, she just asked about the consulting rooms,' the boy told me, then flashed a look that made clear he'd just remembered that he shouldn't have said.

I was already gone.

The consulting rooms. It took a second before the reason that shook me really clicked. There was a campaign I'd seen on social media where people trapped with abusive partners during lockdown could reach a safe space to access support. If they could just get out to Boots and ask to use the consulting rooms, they'd be helped.

Now I knew what that darkness was in the river at the heart of me and I knew I'd just fucked up with more fuckery than anyone had ever fucked up in the history of fuck ups. *Fuck*.

ALEC

That day we were in town and I was feeling dangerous. Like I might just let my little finger hook round his.

THEO

I'd brought hand sanitiser in my bag, but I hadn't wanted to be too forward.

Wouldn't want to be thought of as easy.

ALEC

We were doing it in public too. Leaning back against the wall behind M&S. So close. Just a centimetre more and we'd be touching for the first time in a month.

THEO

And then –

ALEC

And then my phone started to ring.

ROISIN

I'd searched the half-empty streets for almost half an hour. It wasn't a ghost town, even in lockdown, but it looked like the remnants of some apocalypse – the last survivors out foraging for food, eyeing each other suspiciously if anyone got too close. My panic was out of place amid the weary acceptance of their fate.

And then I found her, the door of an Uber held open in one hand. She saw me and ducked forward to get in.

'Let me help you.'

I called it as I ran, 'Please, please Luka. I'm sorry. I know why you were there. Let me help.'

Her grip on the door grew white-knuckle tight but she waited for me to catch up to her, stopping just past arm's length, the way you'd give distance to a frightened animal.

'I was buying aspirin,' she said, voice quiet and flat.

'You weren't. I asked the man what you were doing there. I know.'

Luka recoiled, starting to pull away, so I talked as though my life depended on it. Both our lives maybe.

'I've missed you so much – do you know that? And I know you've missed me. You say it every time I get close and then nothing ever changes – you're just as far away as ever.

And I know now. I *know* that isn't your fault. But don't you think if someone loved you they wouldn't want to take the other things you love away? He's a thief, Luka. You'll never be good enough for him because he's stealing the best of you.'

She shook her head sharply, drawing back and making to get into the car, bending one knee down on the seat.

'My granny died.'

I said it and it stopped her, and Lord forgive me for using my freshly dead grandmother as bait but it worked for just a moment, even if I had to talk round the lump clogging my throat. 'She died a week ago of this stupid virus. And I had no one to talk to.'

Luka exhaled a slow breath and took a step back towards me, because I was crying. Which is something I do all the time, but it's always over sad dog stories in films or someone's long-lost family reunion. It's never for me. Never just for me.

'I'm so sorry, Rosh. That's –'

'Terrible, I know. Grandma and Figgy Pudding going so close together, it's fair devastated the town.' I laughed and it came out like a sob so I had to shut that off quickly and rush on. 'And we . . . we couldn't go to the funeral. Because you can't now, can you? Someone you love dies far away and you just have to take everyone else's word for it. But I watched it, online. The church has its own video channel now, some sort of morbid Netflix full of dead people, and they just send you a link to watch yours. And then I worked out that the link's

URL was just a number, and if I changed the number I could watch other people's funerals too. Like reality-TV episodes. Every time it was the same setting but it had new characters there to cry in it over a different box. There were so many of them. Too many funerals for such a small place, but at least it made me feel somehow less alone. And I just wanted to talk to you so much.'

She looked at me like I'd just ripped out a part of her she'd forgotten existed. Then she nodded and went for the pocket of her jacket. 'I know I've let everyone down. I know I've done everything wrong. Believe me, I think about it all the time but I'm stuck now. I'm going to give you my number. It's a new one – I can't remember it yet.'

The phone in her hand was one of those cheap things you buy if all you want is to put a few pounds of credit on it once a month.

'What happened to the other –' I was asking, but I was getting my phone too. 'You can just call me on it, then I'll have the number.'

'I can't make calls on it right now, only accept them. I don't have credit. And you have to call in the mornings, after six, before eight. That should be okay.'

She was saying it all like it didn't sound entirely messed up.

'How are we defining okay? By what Colin allows?'

Her brown eyes flicked back up to meet mine. Then she was retreating. 'It's okay. Forget it. I'll find a way to call you.'

She went back to the car, to the back seat, back to pull on the door handle. Even a dead grandmother wasn't enough to keep her with me.

The door slammed but the window was open and I kept on shouting, like some crazed cult member trying to convert a sinner in the street. 'It's not okay, Luka. Nothing about him's okay. And I don't care if you never speak to me again after this, I'm going to say so. If I don't see you again until we're old ladies in the care home, I'll tell you now and I'll tell you then you'll *always* be enough for me. Please leave him. Please, please.'

'He loves me.' Her voice was a scratch of itself, an echo through the open window.

'*I LOVE YOU*.' Mine was desperate. Desperate. 'Why can't that be enough?'

I watched as she leaned forward and the car drove away. And then I checked I had the address from Alfie in my phone and made a call.

THIRTY-SEVEN

ALEC

'We're calling the police.'

William's voice was crisp and sharp, the relief I felt at having the decision taken out of my hands matched somewhat by a look in his eyes that said he was grateful for finally knowing what to do.

We had an address. We had evidence that Luka had been looking for help. And though I wanted to call straight away and report Colin for kidnapping my sister, I managed to keep the hyperbole under wraps and list what we did know. The lies he'd told her. What she'd told Roisin about helping pay for the place they were sharing, when her name wasn't even on the contract. That we thought she'd been trying to reach out to someone for help today. That had to be enough to get some sort of official assistance.

THEO

And yet, as it turns out, the criteria for that are very specific.

307

ALEC

I kept the phone cupped to my ear, blocking as much of the sound as possible as the operator asked questions that turned my stomach.

'No, there's nothing taking place right now . . . that I know of. I'm not there I – I don't think she's in any immediate danger.'

Coming up behind me, William smoothly took the phone from my hand and walked into the next room on it. 'Yes, I'd like to know who to speak to regarding a possible threat to my stepdaughter. It's not an emergency, which is why we've dialled the non-emergency number, but it is urgent. She's barely eighteen – I'm sure there must be *something* you can do.'

THEO

He stalked into the next room, the clipped edges of his words still carrying through. Alec paced to the window, fists balled at his sides and I . . . I said the last thing I hoped to have to say. 'I don't think we should do this.'

ALEC

I whipped my head round at that. 'What? Theo, we just found out she's being abused.'

THEO

'We just found out she *might* be in a controlling relationship. As far as I know she hasn't said that herself. She hasn't asked *us* for help.'

I expected the fury that lit his face, but I can't say I was ready for it.

'She hasn't asked us for help because *he's controlling her*. What about this do you need assistance to understand?'

I was well aware the anger in his voice was guilt turned outwards. Aware that we all shared the same wish that somehow we'd have been able to act sooner. But I like to think I have some understanding of what it is to be trapped in a life that's not your choice, but where the decision to leave it is no less intimidating than the one to stay.

Slowly I walked over to sit on the arm of the sofa, where the family dog had curled up, made anxious by the raised voices. I recognised the sentiment.

I didn't want an argument, just to explain.

'Isn't what we're doing now controlling? We're making her choices for her.'

ALEC

Listening to him talk was making my head spin. 'So you're saying trying to get her out of an abusive relationship is the same as getting her into one?'

THEO

'I'm saying consider what it might feel like for her. She already has one person telling her not to see people. That her choices and needs are the wrong ones. That *he* loves her and knows what's best. If she's hearing the same thing from us, I'm not sure where she has left to go.'

ALEC

Theo tugged his fingers through his curls and added, 'Sorry. It's just what I think.'

Theo, on my sofa, in my house, breaking every possible lockdown rule when barely an hour ago we'd been playing dare with each other over the risk of holding hands. Theo staunchly keeping two metres away from me in spite of that, but knowing that if I breathed deep we'd be breathing the same air.

I had to wonder sometimes how someone that brave and smart and kind had decided I was what he wanted to waste his time on.

'It's all we've done, isn't it?' I said at last. 'We've just been telling her we don't like her choice without asking her why she was making it, or what was wrong here that meant she couldn't stay? We never asked her how to help – just told her how we'd be helping.'

THEO

'I think it might feel something like that, yes.'

ALEC

His voice was very soft.

I nodded. 'Then maybe we shouldn't do that again. How do you always manage to see things in a way I can't even think of?'

THEO

I smiled, relief washing through me. 'I'm a little further back than you from all this. It's hard to appreciate the detail of anything when you're standing with your nose pressed to it.'

Alec went to the door of William's study just as it opened from the inside. His stepfather held out the phone to him, head bowed wearily but voice firm. 'Well, they've said they'll have someone stop by just to check up on her when they've the time. It's better than nothing, I suppose.'

I'd like to personally complain to every deity there may be for not being able to hug Alec for the way he looked at me then.

We said nothing. William's relief was so tangible that it made me think I'd been worrying too much. It helped that William was so impossible to doubt. The kind of person you think might have been born a teacher, given their natural inclination for always being right. He made me hope. I think he made Alec hope again too.

When I left, after as long as I could possibly justify loitering there for, Alec came to the door with me. Bluebell followed him, nudging her head up against his hand in a way I couldn't not be envious of.

'I'll call you as soon as we hear anything. *If* we hear anything. And thank you.'

I could have asked what he was thanking me for, but I'd been there when he took Roisin's call. I'd seen his face. I knew he was thanking me for not letting him spend that moment alone.

'*I carry your heart with me,*' I said, glancing past him to where William was making an exaggerated show of not-listening, rearranging a stack of magazines I'd never seen move in the year I'd been visiting.

Alec's little finger brushed the side of mine, and he closed his eyes, replying, '*I carry it in my heart.*'

WILLIAM

The call came some four hours later, when the two of us had given up our silent vigil, and Allegra had come downstairs for the fish and chip supper she'd been bribed with not to ask too many questions. She sat against my side on the sofa, her head lolling against my shoulder, feigning sleep so that I wouldn't feel the need to send her to bed.

For the moment her warm weight was a comfort. I allowed the deception until the ringing startled all of us. Then I didn't even think to shoo her away before I went to answer, and paused, and said, 'Alec, is this a video call?'

ALEC

It was more like a hostage video. One we were watching play out in real time. Luka stared blank-eyed into the screen, while I grabbed my phone to record William's. I can play what I have of it now.

LUKA

'– repeatedly that everything's fine. I now feel that I'm being harassed by my own family, simply because you disapprove of who I choose to love. I've told the officer here tonight that I want you to leave the both of us alone, and if you don't respect my wishes they're happy to tell me how to take out a restraining order. I don't know how much more clearly I can put this, but I don't want to see you. I don't want you involved in our lives. And I'm happy without you. I'm *fine*.'

THIRTY-EIGHT

MY NAME IS LUKA: EPISODE 9
'SOMEONE'S WORLD IS ALWAYS ENDING'

LETTER FROM LUKA
29 MAY 2020

Mom,

It's been a long time. Almost two months since I last got here to see you.

Though this isn't my first letter since then. I've written others and had to throw them out inside empty wrappers so they wouldn't be seen. It turns out visiting graveyards is now on the no-go list too.

But I think I'm going to get this one to you. I'm feeling like taking a few risks.

So. You want the important part of the catch-up first? The plants are *great*. Some of them are really beginning to grow now that summer's starting to creep back into the world. Sully the Monstera's really going for it – he sends out new leaves that are nervous at first, rolled up tight in on themselves before they hesitantly unfurl and spread into deep green paddles. I like to think I'm helping with his confidence. Every week when I water them all I tell him, 'Sully, you're beautiful.' He doesn't need to be perfect – he's just being the best little plant he can be.

They've become my whole world, that's why I sound like someone you hear talking to themselves on the bus. My friends, my verdant army, my safe space. A little green place to keep my heart.

I've learned how to do that now. How to take myself apart and put the pieces somewhere they'll be safe. I've done it with my heart. I do it with what's inside my head when Cosmo gets angry. I just take my thoughts and put them into a locked box at the bottom of the ocean where I can't hear what he's saying. The things he says can no longer penetrate. He opens his mouth and all I see are bubbles escaping to the surface. He thinks he's talking to me because my eyes are open and I'm looking his way, but he's talking to four steel walls and a padlock.

I'm still working on my soul. I'd like to extract that and send it out into the universe, up into the salt-sprinkled night sky. It's been stuck in one place for too long. I'm going to set it free. Become infinite.

Things got bad for a while. That's when I learned these tricks.

William called the police back at the end of April. After they came, things got bad. Not physically. I know I've told you before but I also know it's what everyone thinks – that if I let him take my phone and use my money, he must be beating me into it. I remember the face of the police officer they sent round to see me, and the way he kept scanning mine, every visible part of me, looking for marks. He asked if he could speak to me in another room and it was the first thing he questioned me about – low-voiced and serious. 'Do you feel you may be under any physical threat from this man? Has he ever physically harmed you?'

And he hasn't. He's never left a bruise. But they don't know how to take a look at your soul and see where it's been hacked away at with a chisel by someone trying to sculpt you into something you're not.

He's never hurt me, but quite often now when he's angry he wraps his hand round my throat and lets it rest there. My whole life in his one hand. It's something he says at night, when things have been quiet. 'I could kill you one day.'

And he could. There are days where I've wanted to ask him for it, days when I haven't seen any other way out.

There are days when he's still so heartbreakingly sorry for the way he acts that I think, *If I just try harder, I can fix him.* Because he does love me. It just comes out of him twisted. It's why the rest of me can't leave – the parts of me not put safely somewhere else. He tells me he might kill me. He tells me I'm the only one who can save him.

He tells me a lot of things. I never know which way to turn.

And then I got a letter. A letter promoting Miles Riva's latest album, *Darling, You're My Daylight*, with – according to the text on the envelope – unmissable information for true fans inside. I only found it because Cosmo had tossed it into the trash, and I usually sort through to pick out what can be recycled instead. And the thing was, *Darling, You're My Daylight*'s *not* his new album. It's old. The title song is the first of his I ever heard, and I remember that when I met Roisin and saw she had it on a shirt I knew immediately we were going to be friends.

I read her hidden letter to me in the dark by the orange security light outside our building, standing between the recycling bins so I wouldn't be seen.

It said she misses me. It said she goes for a walk at 2 p.m. every day across the park, and it let me know her route in case I ever had the chance to say hello. It said I was welcome at her house any time, lockdown rules be damned. It talked about Tiwa and a business she was starting delivering brownie boxes around Greenwich, always the most together of any of us. About school, and how the head's Zoom update to parents got bombed by an as yet unidentified backside. About small, stupid things in the world I'd left behind. It didn't mention Cosmo once. I can't tell you how much lighter that made me feel.

And it included a voucher for ten pounds' worth of phone credit taped to the bottom.

I kept that but I threw the letter away. Carefully. Wrapped back inside its double-agent envelope.

Cosmo's started going out more. He won't say where but everything's still closed, and I know it's not to work because the call centre let everyone go. There's no pattern to it. Sometimes he's gone for a couple of hours in the afternoon and sometimes most of the evening. Once he didn't get home until two in the morning and was angry I hadn't waited up and worried about him.

You'd think it would give me a break but it doesn't, because he can come home without any warning, and sometimes he's in a worse mood than when he left – prowling around, asking me what I've touched while he wasn't watching. Sometimes there's alcohol on his breath. I spend the whole time he's gone waiting for the click of the door.

But yesterday night he left in a hurry and when I walked past his laptop he hadn't shut it down and it hadn't set itself to sleep yet. His Facebook account was open, the message box at the bottom of the page flashing with a last response: *Can't wait to see you xxx*

She can't have been more than sixteen, the girl he was speaking to. Meeting. A lot of her information was locked down, like everyone's is, even to friends, but I could look through her photos via Cosmo's account. They were all just crossposts from her Insta – the most recent one a short video of her and her friends in school uniform put together against a song asking 'when will I see you, again?'.

The uniform was from a girls' school on the other side of town, and I know they don't wear it past Year 11. I started to scroll through their messages. It looked like there were weeks and weeks of them, but one comment pulled me out of it. Something he'd commented on a picture of hers: *Looking fine, Starshine.*

And I couldn't. I just couldn't. I logged out of his account so I couldn't look any more and, watching the door in case he came back – in case she cancelled or he'd forgotten something or he just *knew* and decided to come back – I logged in to mine.

I don't know why, really. I use Facebook to check a couple of groups and keep in touch with a scatter of distant family members in the States and that's it. But I logged in and my Messenger was showing notifications too. Dozens of them, along with a clutch of new friend requests. People from school I'd barely even spoken to. People who were kind of friends. A couple of teachers. Tiwa. Mark. Shauna. Alfie Newly, of all people. Roisin. Theo. Alec.

I didn't look at any of them. Just shut the messenger window and went to recklessly scroll through my feed. Almost all of it just crossposting from other social accounts.

Something Alec had put on Twitter pulled me up: *Hey, rule of six from June means we're allowed to meet up for Roisin's birthday in the park. 2 June, right? @roroagogo Are you sure you have enough friends?*

I couldn't stay on there. I couldn't peer at that little window into their lives and wonder what they were thinking of me. If they thought of me at all. If too many bridges had been burned.

My hand was sliding the mouse along the menu to log out when a new message came in as I watched – someone I didn't know at all adding two new comments to the total. I was going to log out. I clicked on those, instead.

And I did recognise her, after all.

She had a soft, round face and honey-coloured eyes and she looked older – maybe thirty. Her profile picture showed her clutching a toddler with chocolate smears across its face. But she had Cosmo's nose. She had a mouth like his. Unmistakable, with its sullen tilt and perfect, Cupid's bow.

He did have a sister.

I watched her messages come in, one after the other.

Hello? I think you might be seeing my brother Colin? And if that's true then I just want to say:

You're not imagining it.

You're not alone.

You're not crazy.

It's not you.

If you want to talk to someone, hun, I'll leave my number. I'll answer anytime.

I closed out of my account and started erasing any traces that I'd been there.

ALEC

Colin's sister, Leena Allen, agreed to let me play part of a short recorded conversation we had at this point in the episode. I'm incredibly grateful, as I know she didn't find this easy to talk about.

Honestly, none of us do.

LEENA ALLEN

Yeah, I found her through Facebook sometime in January. Mum had told me he'd moved in with another girl and I couldn't take it. I looked through the tags on his posts until I found her – she'd changed her relationship status. I notice he never changed his. Anyway, I got obsessed with her. I added her to Messenger so I could see if she was online but it never happened.

It was complete chance I saw her on when I did. I was signed on talking to one of the girls from my 'mummy's wine nights' Zoom group when the little lightning bolt by her name turned blue. Well, I just sent out as many messages as I could until it greyed out again.

Then at least I could feel like I'd done something.

ALEC

Because he's done this before?

LEENA

With other girls, yeah. And . . . I'm not going to say he's
always been like it – he wasn't born a manipulative little shit,
but he's always been a problem. Learned early on how to run
rings round Mum and she let him. He never stopped.

I mean, I got him to move out of hers when she finally
caught him in the act of lifting money from her purse. He
had to be caught doing it, you see, because otherwise he'd
tell her she'd forgotten how much she had, or that she must
have dropped it somewhere. I think he believed his own lies
– honestly he told them so well. Just somehow always made
her feel like the guilty one.

But she let him back in, still. Before lockdown it was
every week for Sunday dinner. Even during lockdown I knew
he'd been visiting, even though she was vulnerable. She's
always coddled him. Bought him everything he wanted, even
if he was never grateful. It was like she was waiting for it to
finally sink in, everything she did for him. But I don't think
he's the kind of person to ever realise what he's got.

ALEC

So what happened with the others? Was it the same as it was
with Luka?

LEENA

Not exactly the same, but she fit a pattern. He's never met someone he couldn't figure out how to take advantage of, that's his problem. He's too good at it, and it's the only thing he's ever *been* good at really. You might say you can't blame him for using his talents but I can. I do. I've met enough of the girlfriends, in the aftermath.

It's like he's a vampire really. He drinks these girls dry – of money, attention, everything of value in their lives – and then he goes out looking for the next drink, usually before he's finished the first.

One of them, the one before Luka, she tried to do something very silly – No, no. Something very sad. It was the day before Christmas last year. He never visited her in the hospital, but I did. That Christmas day he couldn't come home because he knew I wouldn't let him in the house.

So I just wanted to talk to Luka before it got that bad. Because I know how good he is at tying people in knots, and sometimes you need someone who knows his techniques to manage to unravel them.

That night, not long after seeing her active on Facebook, the phone did ring. But there was no sound from the other end and after a minute they rang off. I did think it might be her. She never called back.

I haven't said a word to him about it. I don't think he noticed I'd been on his laptop. By the time he got home it had shut and locked itself like usual.

It was a few hours after he went out. He threw himself on to the couch, TV on, and didn't look up until I brought him a drink over. Then he glared, eyes narrowed. I used to spend so much time trying to think how to best describe those eyes. Honey gold. Rich and deep. Never kind. I realise now I never thought they seemed kind.

He took his beer and looked back at the television. 'You're never happy to see me any more.'

And, no, I guess that happens when someone who was your escape becomes your jailer.

Roisin's birthday. In the park, 2 June.

I wonder if he'll go out then.

I'm going to do a test run first. Leave the house the next time he's gone and find out if he really can always tell, if he's always got someone watching, the way he says he does. It'll be a short trip – nothing he could blame me for. I'll be there and back without speaking to a living soul. I'll bring this letter with me.

So, see you soon, Mom.

Love,
Luka

THIRTY-NINE

ROISIN

'Go on then. Tell me how sad it is that the government changed the law specially to allow me to get six people together for my birthday, and I've only managed four?'

We were laying out a picnic blanket across the grass on the hill just down from the observatory – shaking off the dust from where it had been sat in storage for a year. I had a bag of Marks and Sparkles' finest picnic snacks slung over my arm and he'd wrestled a garden parasol up there for me. The sun was out to bake that day. I'd watched his blond hair turn tawny and damp with sweat on the walk over.

ALFIE BLOODY NEWLY

'Just tell everyone you were keeping the gathering exclusive. That's what my dad does when there's a disappointing turnout for one of his events. It's not about the quantity of guests but the quality of their company.'

The parasol I'd brought was a clear stroke of genius.

Not considering I might need something to stand it in had been slightly less so. Getting to my knees with it, I looked up at Roisin as I tried to work it down into the mud deep enough not to fall over if someone so much as looked at it the wrong way.

She looked down at me with her arms folded, quizzical. Fond?

'I'm still trying to work out how you made it on to the list.'

So was I, having thought I'd fucked every damn thing up at that party back at New Year's Eve. Fortunately Roisin seemed willing to consider the hideous mistake something more like an icebreaker, once I'd apologised. Now here we were at another party of sorts, and it was exactly what I'd hoped for back then – a party just the right size.

ROISIN

It was *not* exactly what he'd hoped for back then. I'd like to make that clear for the tape.

ALFIE

Well, if we're going to be technical.

I had asked after meeting her in the park before, if she might like to meet again and call it a date. She said no.

ROISIN

I said, specifically, 'I just don't want a boyfriend right now, Alfie. I might not want one ever. But I could really use a friend.'

And he said, 'You've got one.'

And that was that.

ALEC

'We've got ice cream!' Theo called out when we were still halfway up the hill, catching the attention of the sprinkle of sunbathers draped over the grass.

'You sound like you're selling it,' I hissed, when really we were just trying to get back to Roisin at a speed that wasn't fast enough to set a puddle of vanilla slipping off its cone and slapping me in the face, or slow enough to have the whole thing melting down my arm.

We were carrying two overfilled cones each, and I dropped to my knees as soon as I got to the blanket and held both mine out to Roisin and Alfie. 'Both unlicked, I promise.'

ROISIN

I made a grab for the biggest one, of course. Birthday girl's perks.

'You got flakes! I like to think of them as nature's birthday candles.'

THEO

'I think they're Cadbury's birthday candles, Ro. In the sense that they're not exactly natural.'

'They're also not exactly candles,' Alfie pointed out.

She hushed us both. 'Shh, will you let me have my moment?'

ALEC

And Theo smiled, slipping down beside me to pass over his spare ice cream, before he quietly started to sing 'Happy Birthday.'

ROISIN

Everyone joined in. I must have gone beetroot over it.

And, sure, it wasn't the way I'd have expected to spend my eighteenth birthday. But it wasn't the worst either. I felt hopeful and anticipatory in a way I hadn't for what seemed like a very long time. There was the sense things were on the cusp of change.

ALEC

When we finished singing, I leaned across and kissed Theo – warm and vanilla-scented, soft curls full of sunlight.

ROISIN

And I threw a Haribo at their heads. 'That's *illegal* still. No kissing between different households. You'll get the lot of us thrown in jail for your crimes of passion.'

THEO

Drawing back from Alec reluctantly, I glanced over to where she was trying to stifle a laugh and grinned. 'Worth it.'

ALEC

But we just let our hands rest together after that, little fingers touching. Alfie offered round some crisps – he was quiet when we were around, but not a bad addition to our circle. I had to mentally retract some of the things I'd said about him before.

After a minute, Roisin leaned forward on an elbow. 'Not to be creepy about it, but that's the first time I've seen you two kiss without looking all around you first, as though something might be about to launch an attack from the long grass.'

ROISIN

Theo twirled the bottom of his ice-cream cone thoughtfully. 'It does feel like that, sometimes. Perhaps not an actual attack – although that really happens to people far too often. But the looks people give us for just holding hands in public sometimes make me feel like they want to tear us apart.'

Alec lifted his little finger from where it rested over Theo's, looking at him questioningly before Theo turned his own finger into a hook and pinned it down again.

'But I think, after this year – after everything, I'm really quite *done* with trying to live my life not doing what *I* like in order to accommodate what someone else *doesn't*.'

ALFIE

I popped a crisp into my mouth, wincing through a sharp mouthful of salt and vinegar. 'Are the people feeling grievously injured over strangers touching palms with each other the same ones who go on about snowflakes when people want safe spaces? Because it sounds like they might be the overly fragile ones in this situation.'

'*Exactly.*' Theo pointed a finger in my direction, as though I'd just given the prize-winning answer on his pop quiz. He does have that air of a teacher about him – it felt rather good, actually. 'They just want the whole world to be their safe space. Well, I *love* Alec and I want people to know, and I honestly don't care any more who likes it or not.'

THEO

Alec slid his palm carefully under mine, letting our fingers tangle. It felt a little bit illicit. A little bit electric. Lockdown really did do incredible things for the simple act of touch.

When I turned my head, his expression was impossibly tender. 'Big talk while barely anyone's been around to see us.'

He knows me well enough to know it's a resolution I'll make and go back on a thousand times. That there will always be rooms, restaurants, crowds and classrooms where touching each other will feel like too big a risk. But I think there will be less of them after this. I won't say I'm unafraid of standing out. Beyond being with Alec, I don't pass perfectly yet and maybe I never will. And even if I do, there may always be some reason for people to look at me and I may always worry sometimes about who's looking. But I'm not afraid to be who I am and love who I love. I won't be made to feel unsafe in my own skin – I want to feel joyfully, hopefully proud of it. I'm going to be me, more and more, and damn whoever doesn't like it . . .

All of which would have been a bit too big of a speech for a picnic. In reality I blushed and said, 'I mean it.'

'I know,' he said. 'I love you feisty. And I love *you*. This whole pandemic keeps making me rethink things too. I guess it's the whole sense of "You could die tomorrow".'

ALEC

'Let's hope you don't,' my sister said, kneeling down on the blanket beside me. 'Some people might miss you.'

ROISIN

Luka had on this long beige cardigan over grey sweatpants and a top. Her hair and skin seemed to have washed out to a sort of beige too, and if it weren't for the fact it all stood out so palely against the green of the hill I wouldn't have given her a second look. Her outfit looked like it was drowning her. But as she sat down with us she might as well have been surrounded by a choir of attendant angels for the way we all turned our awed faces her way.

'You made it!' *Jesus,* but the urge to hug her was overwhelming. It was as if I might have been able to squeeze a little life back under her skin. I held a plastic tub of cupcakes out instead. 'Now it's a birthday.'

ALEC

Luka had started texting Roisin a couple of days before. Of course Ro told me, though I never quite believed we'd really see her in person. It had almost started feeling like I was missing the concept of my sister. Like she didn't really exist any more in a touchable, tangible form.

But there she was, eating a cupcake. Not quite two

metres away. A mirage, when I'd been in the desert for a really long time.

She was apologising to Roisin.

'I'm so sorry not to have got you anything, I didn't have much of a chance . . .' She bit her lip and trailed off.

It's because that bastard has your wallet, isn't it?

I didn't say it. Ro gave me very strict rules to abide by if Luka showed up today, number one among them being not mentioning *him*. But, Jesus, she looked like something that had washed up on the beach after being slammed around by the tide. I could feel myself checking for bruises, though she was covered wrist to ankle. Which was suspicious all by itself.

Theo was suddenly by my ear. 'It's rude to stare.' His voice was quiet and almost teasing, but his hand rested flat in the small of my back and it felt like the only thing holding me up.

ALFIE

So. That was awkward.

We all knew there was a chance she might turn up, but the probability wasn't high. Roisin said that starting to get messages from her was a miracle in itself and she didn't want to mess with that. We'd all been pretending it wouldn't happen, just so there wouldn't be too big a mood crash when that turned out to be true.

333

Except now she was sitting with us, and everyone was trying to be as normal as possible despite knowing that at least two of the group would have liked to have dropped a net over her head and dragged her home.

It was very important, Roisin had said, not to try to push things. She'd been researching online – she texted me links to pages from Women's Aid and the National Domestic Abuse Helpline on coercive control and how to help someone trapped in that situation.

And the main thing, apparently, is when someone's being controlled you can't help them by trying to control things back the other way. But you can be there if they need to talk. Or hopefully, when they decide to walk away.

THEO

We were exercising the 'being there' principle. Sharing stories that had nothing to do with her. It was a curious reminder that, although it felt like we'd been auxiliary planets revolving around her sun for the past several months, life had in fact gone on.

Roisin was on her knees in the centre of the blanket, showing us some patterned cloth masks she'd bought online. One was leopard print, one scattered with actual tiny leopards.

'Well, I've worn a mask more often than I've worn a bra the last month, so I decided to get some I actually like.

And then I thought, why not combine the two? What do you think?' She held up a mask on either side of her chest, waggling her eyebrows like an old-fashioned stand-up.

ALEC

Alfie looked like he might faint.

ALFIE

And then Luka's phone started to ring.

ROISIN

She went ashen. The colour that had seemed like it was just starting to return to her face bleached to grey in a moment.

'I'm going to have to go.'

Scrambling to her feet, she ran a few steps away from us before she answered. I could hear her voice carrying back to us, its forced lightness making a stark contrast to the fear on her face.

Fear. It made me want to forget every last thing the ladies at the domestic abuse helpline had told me. Surely you're allowed to force someone to leave a person they're afraid of?

'No, I'm not at the flat but I'm just on the way back. I noticed we were out of painkillers so I just went –

'I thought you wouldn't –

'I used five pounds from the take-away jar, but I'll put it back, Cosmo. I'm sorry.'

ALEC

Standing up, I shook off Theo's hand when he tried to catch mine. No. I wasn't going to fuck things up, but I couldn't just sit there and listen to her plead with him over five pounds either. I just walked over and wrapped an arm round her shoulder.

I pulled her in against my side and stood silently there with her. *For* her.

It was all I'd wanted to do for months.

And she let me. I could hear Cosmo's voice, low and deceptively calm, asking if she was sure she was just at the shops.

'I promise. I'm just walking to the bus now. You can meet me at the stop. I'll be home soon.'

The call disconnected at his end. I could feel her shoulders heave under my arm as she turned to look up at me and the worst part –

The worst part was that she looked afraid of what *I'd* do too.

'Alec, I really have to –'

I held up a hand. 'I know. I'll walk you down to the gates.'

She was so grateful that I didn't make a fuss. I hated every second of it.

ROISIN

The three of us went through the park together in the end. Alec, Luka and myself, each of us holding one of her arms, like we were walking her to a place of execution.

At the park gates I pulled her up short and went through my bag.

'Wait just a second. I've got you. These are half finished but they're still in the box.'

I passed over a pack of painkillers. I've been well trained by my mother's constant headaches to carry some with me at all times. I had a fiver from a birthday card with me too, and I'd brought another phone credit voucher, a tiny notebook, and a pen. Part of me thought if she ever wanted help she could drop a note through someone's door.

She hugged me as though I'd handed over the Crown Jewels. The first person beyond my family I'd so much as touched since March – it was hard to let go.

'I *will* keep in touch this time.' She held my hands and looked between me and Alec. 'Really. I think I'm going to –'

ALEC

'Like you're *really* just out to buy some pills?' A car door had opened on the street. I hadn't even noticed until Colin was walking up to us. Luka still had the packet from Roisin clutched tight in her hands.

'I'm meeting you at the stop,' Colin said, and his smile was bitter. 'Oh wait, did you mean the one at home?'

He stopped in front of us, hands in his pockets. 'You really shouldn't believe the things she says,' he said, 'I mean, you should hear what she's told me about both of you.'

FORTY

ROISIN

'Cosmo, don't, *please*.'

I tried to put a hand on Luka's shoulder but she shook me off, going to *him*. He had the kind of smile that twisted his whole face off centre, and he stepped back and wouldn't let her touch him. I could remember thinking he was handsome once, but I couldn't see that now.

'The words she uses, talking about you, you wouldn't believe it,' he said. 'Deviant. Obsessed. Disgusting. Needy. Selfish. Weird. Lonely.'

And of course for a second we did believe it.

There were words in there I pinned to myself without even thinking about it. Looking across at Alec I knew he was doing the same. Colin read out his little list of our fears and some deep parts of ourselves couldn't help but believe that the worst of what we felt about ourselves had been seen.

That's how people like him work, I think. They know just where to dig the needle in, and they worry it deep.

Luka didn't seem to know which way to turn, staying

339

close to him but looking at us. 'I didn't – I –'

ALEC

'I *didn't.*' Colin pitched his voice high and whiny to mock
her, then dropped it low and cold. '*Your Facebook account
has been logged into from a new device.* Those notifications
come up on the screen of your old phone. Did you know
that? Just a standard security check.'

ROISIN

She took a quick breath in. 'I looked at my account for a
minute the other day.'

ALEC

'On *my* computer. That was sneaky of you. And then I
looked at your new phone last night. I hadn't *seen* you
texting, but there they all were. Long, long conversations,
planning this. Why didn't you just tell me, Luka? What have
I done to deserve being treated like this?'

It was enough. I stepped forward, ready to finish what
I'd started on New Year's, if it came to it. I didn't think I'd
flattened enough of his nose. 'What have you *done*? Can't
you see she's afraid of you?'

'Alec, *no*,' Roisin said from behind me.

'Please don't.' Luka put herself between us. In front of him. And over her shoulder, Colin smiled that smile.

'Yeah, looks like it's you she's afraid of, Alec. We're going home.'

ROISIN

Alec moved again. 'You don't have to.'

'Don't!' She screamed it at him, her hands up, backing closer to Colin. 'Please just let me make my own decisions. I want to go with him.'

And all the time Colin was there behind her, not even touching her, just letting her be drawn towards him like some kind of malevolent magnetic force. The bastard hadn't once lost his smile.

Dropping the hand reaching out to her, Alec stopped where he was. He stood like a statue and watched as the pair of them walked back to the car. Colin opened the passenger door for her, like a gentleman, then slammed it a little too hard.

He walked round. Got in.

Alec was carved marble.

The engine started up. Signals went on that he was about to pull out into the road and steal her away with him. Neither of us moved.

Then the window opened on the passenger side. I could see Colin leaning across her, wrenching her arm out into the

341

air with a grip like a vice around her wrist. The things she was holding tumbled into the gutter beside the car. A phone-credit voucher. Some pills. Five pounds.

We heard her saying 'no' as he shook everything out of her grip, then pulled her arm back in. And it was as if the string holding Alec back had snapped. He burst forward, hammering on the back of the car, trying to pull open the back door, then the front, even as the car was pulling away. He was screaming and swearing in at them.

I screamed at him. 'Alec, don't – you'll get hurt!'

The car backed up, millimetres from reversing over his foot, then sped off down the road.

ALFIE

'Hey, hey, what's going on? What can we do?'

Theo and I showed up with the blankets and leftover food brought down from the hill just in time to drop it all and run at the sound of Alec yelling a blue streak out on the street. He was standing in the road with his fists balled at his sides when we reached him. Theo didn't stop where I did – he ran and wrapped his arms around Alec from behind.

I looked at Roisin. 'What's happening?

ALEC

And I turned and said, 'We're going after them.'

THEO

There was nothing for it but to call William and convince him to come.

ALEC

I got him on the end of the line and was thrown by how he sounded. Before I'd even started to explain, his voice was more shaken than mine was.

'Yes. I'll come, yes,' he said. And then: 'I've just been at the graveyard.'

THEO

When the car pulled up outside the park, William handed Alec a small bundle of papers as he got in. A collection of envelopes, each one labelled with 'Mommy' written in purple pen.

ALEC

He'd finally caught Allegra spiriting the most recent one off Mom's grave that afternoon, and then she'd given up her entire stash. He'd been reading when I called. *I* was reading them on the drive to Luka's apartment building, the whole of her side of the story unspooling in my hands. I was ready to march in there and break down a door.

ROISIN

Which we wouldn't let him do. It was Alfie who slipped out of the car once we finally made it to Luka's building and went in to the one next door only to return triumphantly with a key.

ALFIE

I told the building manager that William had received a distressing phone call from his daughter. He needed to check the flat or he'd call the police.

I rolled my eyes with the guy and listened to him joke about 'girls like that' being trouble just long enough to take the key from him and leave, saving the recording on my phone to play back to my father.

ALEC

And we were in the building. Looking at the fire escape map on the wall and trying to figure out which side of the staircase she'd be, and how many floors up.

Theo nudged my shoulder and said in a low voice, 'So do we have any idea what we'll do when we get up there?'

The only plan I had was the insistence banging at the back of my brain that we had to do something. Do *something*.

ROISIN

Alec looked like he was ready to storm upstairs with fists raised, so I started up the stairs ahead of them all to try to see that off. We were making a mistake. This would only make things worse. I knew that because I'd read all about it.

Yet still I had to agree with Alec. I couldn't do anything but this.

At least if I could get a head start I could try to mediate. William would be calm about it, even after seeing those letters. I've never met a man on such an even keel. And if Alec just wanted to watch the world burn, at least we had Theo with us to douse the flames.

I got to the third floor ahead of the rest of them. I knocked.

There was nothing.

Not the slightest sound from behind the door, only the echo of my own fist.

ALFIE

Of course I followed her. When I spotted her sneaking off I made my own way up the stairs close behind. Just as I made it to Luka's floor a neighbour poked her head out of the next door along, her hair up in a messy tie.

'You're not here to make more noise, are you?'

'Noise?' Roisin asked.

'They've left, but before they did it got mad over there.

Crashing and banging. Sounded like they had a demolition team in. All I'm saying is, it's woken the baby once. Can you keep it down now?' Then she shut the door.

I hurried towards Roisin. 'They've left?'

She hadn't backed up an inch from the door. 'We still have to go in there. We have to know.'

So I gave her the key.

ROISIN

And it was . . . devastation. In the main room there was a chair on the floor, its legs lying against the wall where black tracks in the white paint suggested they'd been smashed off. A laptop open and broken, its hinges snapped. Everything that used to be on a surface was now on the floor.

I went through to the bedroom.

A trail of broken plant pots paved my way. Green leaves snapped and scattered and stamped on.

'What's this?' Alfie asked, bending to pick something bright out of the dirt and hold it to the light.

ALEC

'It's my mom's pendant.' I could see it from the doorway. I'd know it anywhere. I'd lain with my head on Mom's shoulder and stared at that heart around her neck for hours when she was sick. When she was dying. 'Luka never takes it off.'

Neither had my mom.

Alfie tumbled it into my outstretched palm and I curled my fist round it and brought it close to my heart.

ALFIE

'So what do we do?' I asked.

Theo walked Alec to sit on the only clear part of the couch, then looked up at me. 'Find her.'

ALEC

William had come in after us and he walked a quick circle around the room, stopping in the heart of it. When I looked up at him, hoping he'd know what to do, hoping maybe he'd have some answers, some kind of hope, his face was pulled tight with an expression I'd seen before.

That's how he looks when he mourns.

'We *find* her,' Theo said, standing. 'If there's nothing here, then we'll have to go out and look. Anywhere they could be – anywhere they could have gone.'

It sounded hopeless to me. Or like hope without justification.

ALFIE

'There might be something here,' Roisin said, coming back

from the bedroom.

She had a little scrap of card with her, and there was something scrawled on it. It said: *5:23 BLKHTH*.

THEO

'That's a train time.' William was suddenly alert again, getting out his phone. 'I'd know their little quirks of scheduling anywhere. And the letters – Blackheath? The five twenty-three must be one of the skeleton of commuter trains still running, and it's . . . thirty minutes away.'

FORTY-ONE

ROISIN

The five twenty-three leaves from Blackheath and goes to Dartford.

ALFIE

'Should we call the police? Someone should call the police.'

ALEC

'And tell them what?'

WILLIAM

'Someone should call. But then someone will have to stay here.'

ROISIN

There was less than half an hour. It was a twenty-minute drive.

'We'll stay.'

THEO

That meant we left. William, Alec and me, running down three flights of stairs. Running to the car.

ALEC

'What if we miss her?'

THEO

'We won't miss her.'

ALEC

'But what if we –'

THEO

'We can't.'

ALEC

The five twenty-three leaves from Blackheath and goes to Dartford and we were fifteen minutes away when we drove into a road closure.

THEO

'What? What's happened?'

WILLIAM

'An accident.'

ALEC

'What? Who has accidents in lockdown? Who's fucking driving? How long do we have?'

ROISIN

The five twenty-three leaves from Blackheath and goes to Dartford and while we waited to find out if she was on it I fought the urge to clean the flat.

ALFIE

'You shouldn't.'

ROISIN

'I know.'

ALFIE

'Not before the police get here.'

ROISIN

'I know.'

ALFIE

'Just in case they need –'

ROISIN

'They won't. They won't need that.'

THEO

The five twenty-three leaves from Blackheath.

    We were at Blackheath.

    It was five twenty-five.

ALEC

We were only just outside.

THEO

William dropped us and went to park.

ALEC

We ran for the doors.

THEO

We ran for the doors and met a cluster of people coming out of the station. I hadn't realised there would be so many people there.

ALEC

'What's happening?'

THEO

A woman turned her face towards us – she was pale. 'The station's closing.'

ALEC

And in the background I could hear an announcement confirming it. 'Ladies and gentlemen, your attention please. Will all passengers leave the station immediately.'

THEO

'There's been an accident,' she said.

ALEC

The five twenty-three train leaves from Blackheath and goes to Dartford.

THEO

But it didn't. It didn't go.

FORTY-TWO

EPISODE OUTRO

ANITA REDMAN, ASSISTANT STATION MANAGER

I know it sounds blunt, I know it sounds harsh. The thing is, even when someone's world is ending right in front of you, you've got other passengers who need theirs to keep turning. And that means the trains running on time.

Someone's world is always ending.

But it doesn't happen much here. Thank God. I mean, I don't think I'd be able to stay in the job for long if I had to see what I saw that day happen over and over again. The mess on the tracks. That poor girl.

JAMES TABBETH, STATION MANAGER

We have to consider our drivers. On the very rare occasion of accident or suicide by train they become the unwilling victims in a disaster, but they often feel like they're at fault.

There is no way to stop a train in an instant. Even at the speed they enter our stations, if someone goes under there's very little chance of survival. Our drivers will live with that their whole lives.

ANITA

And the staff who deal with it all. There's trauma to that, no matter how necessary the job. They won't forget that sight the rest of their lives.

That's why we keep the public out.

But those two boys got through.

I thought they were just messing around. I yelled at them to get back out. I had no idea they were family until they were racing up the platform and grabbed that girl like they'd thought she was the one under the train. Hugged her and hugged her while she cried.

JAMES

We took them to the back offices in the end to await the emergency services. We couldn't just have them standing there.

The young man's body would have to be recovered before the trains could start running again.

FORTY-THREE

MY NAME IS LUKA: EPISODE 10
JULY 2020
'BECOMING INFINITE'

ALEC

Are you ready?

LUKA

As I'll ever be.

ALEC

Okay. Then the tape is on.

LUKA

Everything I put in those letters is true, by some definition of the truth. At some point my reality got shrunken down and redefined by the situation I was in, but there are truths that still hold.

357

Colin Allen never hit me. He pushed me against walls and he held me by the throat without ever pressing down hard enough to bruise. He gripped my wrist sometimes when we were out in public, as a reminder that I couldn't walk away even if I wanted to.

But he never hit me. There were days he made that sound like something I should be grateful for. There were days I was.

But he didn't need to hit me when his words knew all the right places to strike.

In the beginning he used that gift to make me believe he loved me. He picked apart the mess I was tangled into and found the raw endings of every thread. The need for somebody to look at me and understand the way I hurt. The need to try to fill the chasm in my life left in my mom's absence. The need in me, in general. And he stepped in to fill every space.

He was so insistent and so passionate that eventually I started to believe all the good things he said about me, and to me. And from there it was an easy card to flip – why wouldn't I believe all the bad things too?

I felt crazy for questioning him. Defensive when other people did.

I felt like I'd done something wrong to make him this way, and if I could just get back to who I'd been at the start I'd have that early version of him back too.

I felt like I'd burned bridges with everyone else.

And I loved him. I really did. I loved the person he'd pretended to be.

That last day of what I believed was our love, he was frantic in the car as we drove away from the park. Banging the steering wheel and yelling at me. I kept thinking he was going to drive right into a brick wall.

He kept saying we needed to get away. London was toxic. It was full of people who wanted bad things for me. We needed to leave. He'd got train tickets. He had a bag packed for me in the back.

I didn't understand where we were supposed to be going. We weren't supposed to travel during the lockdown. There weren't any hotels open. But he said he knew a place and he said I was going to go with him.

And I was. I agreed. I just said I needed to go back to the flat first. Only for a minute. I said I had my period, that there were things I'd need on the train.

A minute.

That was all I was allowed, and he went with me. He followed me into the bathroom and stood there while I bent to look in the cupboard where I kept boxes of pads. He'd shaken almost everything Roisin gave me out of my hands but somehow I still had the pen tucked up into my sleeve. It was from the merch stand at Miles Riva: Darling, you're my daylight.

All I had time to write was the train time he'd told me on a scrap of cardboard from a tampon box, and then I let that fall to the floor.

When I stood, he pulled Mom's pendant straight off my neck.

No ties, he said. No reminders. Everything was toxic.

We left the flat in tatters.

I was still going with him. And some part of me still thought he was doing all this to save me – to save us. Which meant there had to be some part of him still able to be saved.

I reassured him the whole way. I walked by his side, but he wouldn't let go of my arm. It was like I was an animal, something he was certain would run at the first hint of freedom. He kept pulling me along the platform. It was quiet. Just a few people waiting on our platform, a few more on others. No staff I could see. The announcements went off for the train and he pulled me out to the edge of the platform. Right to the very edge.

I said, 'We have to step back.

'We have to step back. It's coming.

'Cosmo, *please*, we have to step back.'

He was pulling me with him as the train pulled alongside us. Until his grip twisted as he yanked me forward, and the handful of sleeve he was left with slipped through his fingers.

He was reaching for me as he fell.

ALEC

I won't repeat the description we were given about how they found him, after he'd died. All I'll do is repeat what the station managers told me when I went to interview them. It was a mess.

We all were.

LUKA

I still wonder if I'm like him. If that dark obsession I saw in him has a mirror in my heart. I've been spending some time at the observatory lately, with Alec and Theo and Roisin. I've listened to some of the talks they give there and I've finally looked through the telescope into infinity.

And I've learned that we're all created from the same matter that formed the universe. We're made from the dust of ages and the dark that's between the stars. The same stuff that's in me is in Alec, and my mom, and Roisin, and the man I sat next to on the bus this morning, and Colin. So maybe we do have a darkness in common, but that's not important. What's important is what you do with it.

I've been trying to do better. I've started painting, like Mom used to.

I think everything I try is a mess, but William disagrees.

ALEC

William's got us both into grief counselling. He goes too, but separately so that we don't have to hold anything back. But he talks to us more now too. Before, we each kept our losses in separate bubbles, never wanting to let the hurt out for fear of it popping someone else's.

I don't think any of us understood how much we needed each other.

William told me Mom shared once why she named me Alec.

LUKA

It's because A's the last letter of my name. She wanted us to overlap, so we would always be there for each other. We wouldn't be alone.

ALEC

Neither of us is alone. I have Theo, who holds my hand everywhere we go now, fiercely, like he's making his own personal statement. I love it. And him. And Luka has Roisin. But what we needed most was each other.

LUKA

And we needed William.

When I tried painting the first time, and then threw down the brushes, he came in to find me screwing the paper up, and he said, 'Looking for perfection undoes the miracle of what you've started.'

He's full of fancy lines like that.

Alec, because he's a smartass, got up and came to look at what I'd been working on. 'It's nice, Lu, but I'm not sure it's a miracle. And I can't tell which way up it's supposed to be.'

ALEC

Listen, I like making him roll his eyes. He looks so fond when he does it. But he put a hand on my shoulder and he said, 'The both of you have been through a war. Hear me out – loving someone who is dying of cancer is like living in a small, personal war zone. You see things that people shouldn't see. Deal with things your minds are barely capable of comprehending, and you watch, helpless, as everything stable, everything that you relied on . . . that you *loved,* is blown up around you. You've been through a war and only very recently escaped, and I think this is a miracle.'

He gestured at the crumpled art. 'As are both of you. Do you know how hard it is to create something in a time of destruction?'

LUKA

I've thought about that a lot. In some ways it gives me hope that we'll rebuild something from the ashes, even if it will never be the same world we used to live in. But mostly it was the acknowledgement that it's been okay to be broken. Okay not to be strong.

ALEC

When Mom was ill, people sent her endless cards saying how strong she was, and how she'd get through it. She didn't. And when she died, they kept telling me how strong I was being too. Strong, just because somehow I was still standing up and not lying face down on a rectangular patch of dirt in the graveyard's long grass. No matter how much I wanted to. I know it was all well meant, but it made me feel so much worse knowing that all I really wanted to do was fall apart. Like I'd have been letting everyone down.

LUKA

If people tell you how strong you are, it can feel like they're saying they don't want to help hold you up. Well, strong people die. And strong people need support too. And maybe they take it from places they know they shouldn't, just because it feels so exhausting trying to stand on their own.

Or maybe they just find it hard to see that they're not standing at all.

ALEC

You've got it now, though, right?

If not, I've got nine more episodes of something you really need to hear.

LUKA

Yeah, Alec. I think I'm back on my feet.

And, Alec?

ALEC

Yeah?

LUKA

Thank you. For all of it.

FORTY-FOUR

LETTER FROM LUKA
7 JULY 2020

Dear Mom,

I used to feel ashamed that it had been a whole year and I still wasn't over losing you. Now it's nearly two and things have changed a little.

I'm still not over it.

I'm just not ashamed any more.

After all, people think babies are still pretty new when they're only a year old, right? Why should death be so different from its opposite? You're still learning to live with something new. Babies grow and they get harder to handle for a while, and I think something similar happens with grief. After a year of loss, some people might find that the small, often docile sadness of the first year has become an unruly grief toddler, throwing tantrums in unexpected places.

And loss is just not something you get over. It's

something that moves into your life and never leaves. Like a hole in the floor that you get better at edging round over time.

No matter what happens, it's never not going to be shitty not having a mom. While there might be days when I'll wake up and not *think* about how much it sucks you're not here with me, it will still suck somewhere in the background. I'll never celebrate an achievement or take a major life step without being sad you're missing it. It's shitty. It will stay that way forever. I'll be at the end of my own life one day and it'll be shitty you're not holding my hand.

But my grief counsellor said something the other day: 'Grief is just love with nowhere to go.'

I think maybe everything that's happened in the last year has been my love trying to figure out where it lives now. And getting lost, and lonely. Wandering into the bad parts of town.

And maybe I finally figured it out. It lives in Alec, and Theo, and Allegra. In our sweet Bluebell. Even in William.

It lives in Roisin, and maybe eventually a little of it might live in Alfie bloody Newly, to whom I owe an unexpected amount.

Roisin rescued Toothless and Sully and George from the floor of my old flat so I guess I can say it's growing in them too.

Love lives in every one of these letters I've written you, even the angry ones. I'm still writing them, but not to leave on your grave any more. I'll keep them with the ones that Allegra saved, and one day if not having you leaves her feeling lost too, I'll give them back to her so she knows she's not alone.

So I think things might be okay. And just in case you're still worried about school – exams were cancelled. Without mocks and with almost a year of absences my predicted grades wouldn't have been enough to get me into Bristol, so I'm retaking the year. I'll be in Alec's class. When I told him I was happy about that he looked at me like I'd just moved back from the moon. Maybe I did. Maybe that's where I've been.

Last night the five of us went up the hill in Greenwich Park to watch a comet.

Comet c/2020 F3 NEOWISE.

New wisdom.

I'd take that.

Theo was talking as we watched for light in the sky. He was saying that half the stars we can see aren't single stars at all. They're binary – two stars circling a common gravitational core. And there are other systems with three or four or even more stars, held together by the same force.

I think all of us, even the stars, can falter when we feel alone. But sometimes maybe we just miss that there are other people caught up in the same gravity. Because there are. There always will be.

I looked over at Roisin, one part of my gravitationally linked constellation, and she lifted her hand with her little finger hooked over. She linked it with mine. On the other side I could see her hand brushed against Alfie's, and when I turned to link hands with Alec his other was already clasping Theo's.

'There,' Theo said.

One point of brightness lit up infinity above our heads, and I remembered how, when things were at their worst, I'd imagined my soul detaching and floating away to become part of it.

It is beautiful out there.

But not as much as here. Mom, there's so much down here that I love. I'm going to stay.

I'll tell you all about it.

Love,
Luka.

Author's Note

My mum died from a mix of ovarian cancer and complications following surgery to treat that cancer, at 12:30 a.m. on January 10th, 2018. My dad and I were at her side, and had been throughout the three months that she'd spent in that same hospital room, and the four months of chemo that preceded it. It was a long rollercoaster of hope and despair.

I don't use the war zone analogy in this book flippantly. Compared to those living in war-torn areas I am spectacularly lucky to have my home still standing, a roof over my head, places to buy food safely and water I can drink. Cancer is so often described as a battle, which feels unfair on the patient, considering they're not equipped to pick up a sword and go out swinging.

Though for those of us left behind once someone's gone, it can feel like living in the eerie quiet after an explosion. You may have been fighting for your loved one's care, fighting to stay positive while in a very sad place, fighting for just a little more time. You fight even knowing you'll lose in the end.

During the Covid-19 pandemic described in this book, with frightening statistics regularly announced on the nightly news, grief and loss became part of everyone's daily landscape.

The next stage is learning to live with that loss. If you lost someone to Covid-19 or during the strange time of our world being turned upside down by it, I'm so sorry. While writing this book I've thought about you every day.

Remember you're a part of them too – whether it's their memories that you'll carry on through the world, or a biological link you share, or just that the same stardust and fragments of infinity that filled up their bones fill yours too.

And, most importantly, there is one thing you can do for the whole of someone else's life, no matter how long:

Tell them you love them.

Tell them you love them.

Tell them you love them.

There's a finite number of times we get to say that to any other person. It will never be enough.

But it's enough.

Love,

Sera

On topics covered in this book

Abuse is not just physical. Often it's not physical at all. Abuse can take the form of someone controlling your money, or where you go, or what you do. It can be someone regularly saying things that make you feel stupid, ugly or worthless. It can be someone suggesting you're not good enough just as you are. They might even make you think they say those things out of love, and that you're crazy to suggest they're not trying to help you.

All these things and more are a form of abuse called coercive control. In writing this book I took advice from professionals who help people in relationships like these, but not all the characters in this book make the right decisions all the time. Sometimes there really isn't a 'right decision' to make.

If you or someone you love is in a controlling or abusive relationship, please talk to someone qualified to help you. It can happen to people of any gender and any sexuality. You're not alone – you will be believed.

You could try the National Domestic Abuse Helpline

(www.nationaldahelpline.org.uk) or Women's Aid (www.womensaid.org.uk – they have a section on their website to help you hide what you've accessed online) or call the National LGBT+ Domestic Abuse Helpline on 0800 999 5428.

The Men's Advice Line – a helpline for male victims of domestic abuse – can be contacted on 0808 8010327, www.mensadviceline.org.uk.

Love Respect is aimed at 16–25-year-olds, exploring what is and isn't a healthy relationship – from physical violence to coercive control: www.loverespect.co.uk.

If you have been bereaved, and need someone to talk to, you can find support and information on the website of www.ataloss.org or contact Cruse Bereavement Support at www.cruse.org.uk.

Finally, if you're transgender, nonbinary, or gender-diverse, or a friend of someone who is, and you're looking for some support, advice or resources, you could talk to the lovely people at www.mermaidsuk.org.uk, www.genderedintelligence.co.uk or www.stonewall.org.uk – and please know you matter, you belong and you deserve the world.

Acknowledgements

I began *Vile Stars* in the summer of 2019, when the first chapter popped fully formed into my head in the middle of the night, in a hotel room in Exeter. By the time I read it to a friend the next day I knew who my characters would be, and I knew what had happened in the train station, but so many of the strands that would become this book's plot were so far in the distance I couldn't even have imagined them.

Still, that first chapter appears here almost word for word as it did in my late-night iPhone notes, so I'd better thank Gee Mumford for listening to me ramble about my very earliest ideas.

I also need to thank Camila Tessler for being my Arizona correspondent, personal archivist, a good friend since forever, and for letting me steal assorted family names (thanks, Grandma Mici).

Thank you to my sensitivity and early readers who helped shape the story and nudge characters into being better versions of themselves: Kathryn Clarke, Eris Young, Amy-Jane Lehan, Fox L, Lukas, Anna.

This was a wildly personal book for me. So many people helped me in ways small and great after losing my mum.

Sharing experiences, sending tiny felt robins in the post, bringing cake to the doorstep, traipsing round Christmas fairs with me or just giving me a hug. I'm pretty sure you all know who you are by now, but I'm going to keep thanking you.

Thanks always to my editor, Sarah Levison, who I not just couldn't but wouldn't have written this book without, and to Lucy Courtenay, Lindsey Heaven, Pippa Poole, Jasveen Bansal and the whole glorious team at Farshore for your constant support and general excellence. Thank you too to my brilliant agent, Molly Ker Hawn for being such an amazing constant.

And, as ever a huge (big, huge!) thank you to the book community, be it Bookstagram, Booktok, Book-other-platform-of-choice. To the people who took the time to talk about, photograph, review and just read my last book *This Can Never Not Be Real* and are coming with me on this journey – you're the best.

And, of course, this book is for my mum – i carry your heart with me(i carry it in my heart).